ABOUT THE TRANSLATOR

ŽANETE VĒVERE PASQUALINI was born in Riga, Latvia. She graduated from the Faculty of Foreign Languages, University of Latvia, in 1995, at the same time completing a course at the University of Perugia, Italy. She worked for the Latvian Embassy in Rome, which has led to her now dividing her time between Latvia and Italy. Presently she works as an agent promoting Latvian literature. Her translations into English include: the children's poetry collection *The Noisy Classroom* by Ieva Flamingo (Emma Press); a children's book, *Dog Town* by Luīze Pastore (Firefly); two short stories, 'The Birds of Ķīpsala Island' by Dace Rukšāne and 'The Shakes' by Svens Kuzmins, in *The Book of Riga* (Comma Press); and the short story 'The Quarry' by Jana Egle (Words Without Borders).

OTHER TITLES IN
THE WORLD SERIES
BALTIC SEASON

Kai Aareleid, *Burning Cities* (translated by Adam Cullen)
Sigitas Parulskis, *Darkness and Company* (translated by Karla
 Gruodis)

PETER OWEN WORLD SERIES
'*The world is a book, and those who do not travel read only one page,*'
wrote St Augustine. Journey with us to explore outstanding contemporary
literature translated into English for the first time. Read a single book
in each season – which will focus on a different country or region every
time – or try all three and experience the range and diversity to be found
in contemporary literature from across the globe.

Read the world – three books at a time

3 works of literature in
2 seasons each year from
1 country or region each season

For information on forthcoming seasons go to
peterowen.com

THE
GREEN CROW

Kristīne Ulberga

THE
GREEN CROW

Translated from the Latvian by
Žanete Vēvere Pasqualini

PETER OWEN
WORLD SERIES

WORLD SERIES SEASON 4 : BALTICS

Peter Owen Publishers
Conway Hall, 25 Red Lion Square, London WC1R 4RL, UK

Peter Owen books are distributed in the USA and Canada by
Independent Publishers Group/Trafalgar Square
814 North Franklin Street, Chicago, IL 60610, USA

Translated from the Latvian *Zaļā Vārna*
Copyright © Kristīne Ulberga and Dienas Grāmata Ltd 2012
English translation copyright © Žanete Vēvere Pasqualini 2018

Paperback ISBN   978-0-7206-2025-2
Epub ISBN   978-0-7206-2026-9
Mobipocket ISBN   978-0-7206-2027-6
PDF ISBN   978-0-7206-2028-3

A catalogue record for this book is available from the British Library.

Cover design: Davor Pukljak, frontispis.hr
Typeset by Octavo Smith Publishing Services

Printed by Printfinder, Riga, Latvia

The publisher gratefully acknowledges the support of the Ministry of Culture
of the Republic of Latvia and the Latvian Writers' Union in the production of
this book.

Ministry of Culture of the Republic of Latvia

I want to throw a stone, hit my husband on the head – you never know what a crazy person will do next, and, anyway, they can't be held accountable and you can't take offence at their actions. But I don't have a stone to hand. They have all already been thrown. Over the past fifteen years stones have rained down like hail. And anyone who tells you that stones never run out on earth, since they were created first, is a liar. First, God created light – so we would do better to throw light at one another, as light is never-ending.

LOVE THE ONE WHO EATS YOUR PORRIDGE

We are walking very slowly, as if afraid I might break down or suddenly come to a halt in the way that clockwork dolls do. The slower your pace, the further you have to go.

The sun shines in through the windows, the bars splitting its rays, cutting slices of light and shadow like knives. There are no windows at the end of the corridor, just a wall and a shadow and a big plastic tree. In the mornings, when the sun is shining, I step only on the sun-filled patches on the floorboards and, if there happens to be a strip of wall between the windows, I jump over the shadow. Nobody reproaches me or wonders why.

'We will be late for the soup. You know, you look totally mad doing that.'

'You go ahead. Get a place in the queue.'

'OK, fine . . .'

F22 runs ahead. She is always hungry. It's amazing how two servings of soup, three main courses and a helping of fruit compote, so watery it could be boiled in a kettle for coffee, can fit into such a tiny woman. She also gobbles down my morning porridge, along with that of Snow White and Fright.

I walk up to the plastic tree and then return, keeping to the squares of sliced sunlight.

Years are just numbers; the prison a room; the hospital a

corridor with sun-filled squares. Numbers. A room. Squares. And life.

The doctor's room is down another corridor. There are no windows, just doors like tall men pressed against the walls. I shouldn't go there. The floor is all cold shadow with nothing for me to step on.

'Sit down, please.' The doctor pokes at his plate with a fork. 'Tell me why you are here.'

'Well, you see, my life has been terribly hard . . .' I say and bury my face in my hands. No tears come, however.

The doctor lets out a sigh and pushes his half-finished plate aside.

'Your clinical records state that you experience hallucinations.'

'Yes, such is life . . .'

Suddenly a blank sheet of paper and a pen appear on the desk.

'Write.'

I stare at the doctor, at a complete loss.

'Write down your life story, from the very start.'

I grab the pen and begin.

I'm six years old. My mum is forty-one, my dad is thirty-five, our house is sixty-nine, but our neighbour, with whom we share the toilet on the stairwell, is seventy-five. The clock, the glass front of which my dad has removed so I can touch its hands – move them backwards and forwards to learn to tell the time – is ticking in the kitchen.

'Why do you need a clock?' I asked my dad.

'To get to work on time,' he answered.

'Why do you have to get to work on time?' I couldn't work it out.

'To earn money,' he explained.

'Why do you need money?' I wouldn't leave him alone.

'Now you're just being irritating.' My dad left the room, like a bird that steals away only to return after surviving an epic migratory round-trip.

I sit in front of the blank television screen and watch a film about the forest. I do this every morning after my parents have gone to work, and our neighbour has left a clump of sticky mint bonbons for me on the table. My film always starts with butterflies in my stomach, as if it were forbidden to watch a film about the forest. There is no forester in my forest, no foul-tempered witch; there are only trees and animals, blueberries and mushrooms. There are no red ants, no rabid beasts, no trails on which to get lost. My film starts with me standing on the edge of the forest, looking back at the houses far away in the grey huddle that is the city. I'm wearing my polka-dot wellingtons and a blue raincoat. My mum says the coat's far too small for me now, but in my forest I could even wear my dad's checked shirt or my mum's black bra if I wanted to. They'll never find me there. They are at work.

I'm building a house in my forest. It's a secret. I started a week ago. My dad said a house requires a lot of building supplies and utilities – boards, bricks, cement, electricity, water. My dad takes things far too seriously. He would never believe that I'm putting up my house using branches, making the roof from pine fronds, and that I have no need for windows, as there's no point to windows unless they look down from the fifth floor. When the house is ready I will strip bark from a birch tree and make a basket in which I will put the blueberries I pick for supper. A host of different creatures will come to my house. I will treat them to the blueberries, and then we will fall asleep together and keep each other warm.

The door chain jangles, and I'm running home, tripping over molehills, humped toads, rocks and deep puddles.

'Why are you sitting in front of the TV when it's turned off?' My mum races into the room, smelling like a perfumed city flower, her white hair arranged in a neat crest. Out of breath.

'Mum, how can I make a ceramic mug?' I ask this, as I need a cup for scooping up freshly drawn forest spring water at my house.

'What are you talking about? We've got plenty of china, haven't we?' She sits down next to me on the bed and puts her hand on my shoulder. 'I want to introduce you to someone. Just don't tell your dad, will you?' Now her voice is like a soft song, just like other mothers' voices, and the forest house recedes to the back of my mind.

I have no time to reply before a man comes through the door. He brings with him the sweet aroma of biscuits, a warm southerly wind.

'This is Zigis. We work together.' My mum glances at Zigis, and her voice is again tender and gentle, how a real mother's voice should be.

'Is he a man?' I ask. I want to laugh at Zigis – small and grey and not resembling my dad in the slightest. The palm of his hand is like a teaspoon; my dad's hands are like two soup ladles. Zigis's hair is thick and curly, while my dad has a shiny bald pate. Zigis smells of biscuits and a southerly wind, while my dad's smell comes from the north. Zigis hovers in the doorway, while my dad would already have walked through the whole house, still wearing his muddy boots and cursing the muggy weather. No, Zigis is no man. I calm down.

'Yes, Zigis is a man. He has his own car!' Mum pushes me into my room and quickly makes me get changed.

We are driving. My mum is silent almost the whole way. Zigis's hand has found its way on to my mum's lap. Every so often they glance at each other and smile. For the first time ever my mum is wearing the blue dress that her beloved foreign relatives gave her. Today my mum is not screaming. Maybe this evening I'll reveal my secret to her – I know exactly what will happen. She will hug me, kiss me on the forehead and say that she would very much like to visit me in my forest home. She will ask if I need any household items; she will help me carry the heavy branches I'm unable to heave up on to the roof alone; she will teach me how to make a fire, and we will sit around it, drinking hot juniper tea.

With every breath of the southerly breeze I like Zigis more and more. We walk along a foreign-looking seafront – there are enormous stones that look like spellbound men punished for their evil deeds, and the pine trees along the ridge of sand dunes kneel humbly, pleading with the sea not to ask for necklaces of amber. I jump from stone to stone, stumbling once in a while, yet Zigis's small hands are there to hold me up. My mum is not cross. She is smiling.

On our way home we stop off at a café. Zigis buys us everything we wish for, and, for the first time in my life, I taste candyfloss. It smells of a southerly breeze and biscuits.

'Just don't tell your dad!' My mum is getting changed in her room, turning around to face me, bare-breasted and wagging her finger. She is also putting away her black frilly panties, carefully folding them up and placing them in the cupboard. Normally she wears grey knickers with moth holes in them. Zigis is certainly no man.

My mum switches on the television, the signal for me to vanish into my room. I close the door and crawl up on to the window-sill. My pockets are full of tiny bewitched people who have committed evil deeds. Some have a hole in their chests, some have a seashell growing into their heads. I line them up from tallest to shortest, so when they become human again they will find themselves standing in a neat row, listening to me telling them what I think about the world.

'Terrible heat. Will you open that window!' My dad bursts into the room, as cold as the north wind. He smudges the floor with his muddy feet and gives me a lemon ice-cream.

'Dad, look at the people I brought back with me from the seaside!' I shrink into the corner of the window-sill so my dad can have a proper look at my stones.

'Have you been to the seaside?'

'Yes. Me, Mum and Zigis . . .'

Dad, frozen to the spot, stares at my array of evil little men.

'That's great that you went to the seaside with Zigis . . .' he mutters. Then with great north-wind-like steps, he disappears from the room. There is a loud thud, as if our gypsy neighbour had fallen straight through the ceiling from the floor above to land in my parents' bedroom. I tear into their room to enjoy the scene, as I've never much liked the gypsy, but no gypsy is there – just my mum sprawled on the floor crying. My dad is looking at her without helping her to her feet. He seems to be shaking, and his massive hands are balled into fists.

'Whore!' He spits on my mum's tummy and leaves the room.

'Go away!' My mum looks at me; it's as if she is a creature made of stone, transformed back into human form but with her eyes still under the spell – cold, stony eyes. The man who had said nothing for seven years, despite being mistreated in various ways while loving my mother most tenderly, must have lifted the spell and changed her back into a human being. It's just that a single teardrop or a casual word was not enough to bring any warmth to my mother's eyes.

'Mum, I'm going to tell you a secret. Do you want to hear it?' I step back, as if my forest hut were just behind me.

'I told you to get lost, didn't I?' Mum looks tired. We have had a long and exciting day.

Dad is lying full-length on my bedroom floor. He has a bottle in his hand, and every now and then he takes a good pull from it and grimaces.

'Did you like Zigis?'

'Yes, we had a nice walk along the seafront and some candyfloss.'

'Fuck . . .' My dad collapses on to a cushion and falls asleep.

Although the golden rays of the setting sun are rubbing their stony backs, warming them, inviting them to awake, my evil little men still haven't come to life.

I will not look at my dad in his drunken stupor or my mum lying on the floor weeping. I shall prepare her favourite dish, and then we will both set off for my forest hut, where we will sleep warmed by the beasts and drink juniper tea. I set about my preparations – I pour some milk into a pan, add a pinch of salt and a teaspoon-tip of sugar and wait for it to come to the boil, like a cat suddenly arching its back or someone launching a carrier pigeon into the sky. Slowly, as if sifting gold sand, I gently pour porridge oats into the milk until it thickens like a clot of blood. My mum's absolute favourite.

I place the pan on the window-sill, close my eyes and run off to my forest hut. I have to arrange everything, fix things so my mum won't refuse to sleep in a place where the wind blows in and the rain pours through the roof. I gather twigs for the fire, make pine-needle cushions to sit on and pluck a single night violet to fill the house with its sweet fragrance. Then I run back, hurrying to return while the porridge is still warm. I grab the pan, plates and spoons and rush to my mum's room. She is no longer sprawled across the floor with dried tears on her dimpled cheeks – she is sitting, looking at herself in the small mirror. Mirror, mirror, on the wall, where is the best place of them all? I want to shout that it's my forest hut, but as my mum turns to me I see her eyes are those of a cold stone creature.

'What do you want now?'

'I've brought you supper. Porridge.'

Mum gets up and comes towards me. Now she is she going to hug me, kiss me, like any other mother would. We will eat the porridge, I will pull out the blueberry jam I'm hiding under my jumper . . .

'What's this?' She takes the pan from my hands.

'Porridge. Your favourite.'

She cracks a cruel smile and turns the pan upside down. The porridge sticks to the bottom like glue.

'Get a knife so I can cut it – or, better still, just chuck it in the bin!'

All my bodily fluids surge upwards, bursting out of my eyes, while my feet are glued, like the porridge at the bottom of the pot, to the brown linoleum.

'What are you standing there for? Go!'

I run to the kitchen, all dried out. Now my evil stone men have more life in them. My dad is snoring in the other room. The clock – without its glass – is ticking. I poke my index finger at the black clock face and move its little hand. The big one won't shift. So this is how a king, with the power of life and death in his hands, must feel! I draw a circle until both hands meet and then continue their homeward path together. Then I take the clock and throw it out of the window. There is a subdued smashing sound, a sort of tinkling like a bell, and it's over – time doesn't exist any more.

'Ahem, ahem,' someone coughs in the pantry. I open my eyes, believing only in my hut set deep within the forest – no well-trodden path leads to it and no mother has ever set foot there, despite everything being arranged and a night violet filling the air with its scent. It's cold outside, and I'm waiting for the beasts to warm me, allowing me to curl up in their warm paws.

'Ahem, ahem, ahem,' someone is coughing again. Maybe my dad has come to get some water or my mum to eat her porridge. Once again, I run out of my forest back to the city along the invisible path – paved with iron to prevent it from wearing out, keeping it serviceable for as long as possible.

'Who's there?' I press my ear to the pantry door.

'Who do you think it is?' I hear an unfamiliar voice.

'I don't know.'

'Let me out then, and we can introduce ourselves to one another.'

Dad repeats endlessly that all strangers are evil and suspect, all black cars take children far away for ever and all sweets offered by strangers are poisoned.

'Don't try giving me sweets. I won't take them!' I hiss through the keyhole.

'I wouldn't dream of such a thing.'

'All right then. Have you got a black car?'

'What nonsense! What kind of idiot would use a black car if they have wings?'

Although shifty-sounding and a little hoarse, there was something familiar about the voice.

'Please, let me out. I need a smoke! I'm all cooped up, and it's very cold in here . . .'

It must be an adult then. Could it be the south wind hiding in there?

'Is that you, Zigis?'

'Silly child, does your Zigis have wings?'

'No . . .'

'So what are these then?'

I cry out and jump backwards. Across my foot, covering it entirely, is a green-blue film, light as the Devil himself, soft and warm.

'That's my right wing.' I hear the voice, but I just carry on staring at the warm film. A feeling washes over me that I could stay like this for ever. I only wish somebody would warm my other foot, too.

'Feels nice, doesn't it?'

'Very nice.'

Warmth is rising through my head. A grey swirl is slowly escaping through the crack in the door; it smells like cigarette smoke. My fingers reach out to the handle on the pantry door.

'My mum could come in at any minute.' My hand freezes.

'Your mum, my girl, is sleeping soundly and dreaming of Zigis. Right now, they are at the seaside without you. Later, they will go to the café without you. Then they will go to the cinema, again without you and, at the end of the dream, they will kill you – also without you, by the way.'

'How do you know all this?'

'And don't bother running off to the forest.'

'What? How do you know about my forest?'

A red-hot bullet surges through my insides and passes painfully upwards through my tummy. My forest! It's mine! Mine! Hell!

'Fine. Go and have a look . . .'

I draw backwards into the corner and close my eyes. Tightly, tightly. The air grows cold, and I am weightless. The earth under my feet is the palm of my left hand, complete with the lines of destiny, life, marriage, false death and crossroads. All paths lead to my forest hut. All marathon runners and children go home at some point, back to the place where moss never grows over their footprints, not even after a hundred years.

Tonight the air around my forest is not as sweetly fragrant as usual. There is heavy grey cloud. It's getting dark. Brushwood crackles under my feet – a gentle crumbling sound, not unlike the noise the biscuits from the bakery on Lenin Street make when you break them. The earth has a memory, and it's saying to me, I shall never burn down, for I am the earth. And you . . . you, too, my girl, can choose who you are going to be . . .

But this time I don't want to see my hut. It's better simply to listen then forget it, as I know it has burned down along with the forest honeysuckle and red clover. I turn back.

'My forest has burned down.'

'I told you . . .'

'How did you know? Who are you?'

Silence reigns in the pantry, and I wait.

'I'm the Green Crow. I escaped from your forest. The rest is all burned down . . .'

Sobs interfere with words, they snatch up my hand and open the pantry door. Stale foul-smelling cigarette smoke rolls into the kitchen along with a sea-green bird, almost as tall as my dad. Her beak is as yellow as the bread in a painting by Cézanne, her eyes a beautiful blue.

'Hello!' The Crow extends her wing to me; it's incredibly soft. I take hold of it and find I don't want to let go.

'Hello . . . er . . . I don't feel much like talking because my forest has burned down . . .' I don't look the Crow in the eye.

'Never mind. Perhaps you have something I can eat? Some porridge, maybe?'

'I do. Here.' I push the pan of porridge I made for my mum towards the Crow.

The Crow thrusts her beak into the pan and eats noisily.

'I've never eaten better porridge in my whole life. Crow's honour!'

My hand is tired, so I slide the sheet of paper across the desk back to the doctor.

'That's enough for today.'

SHE'S NOT THAT BAD

There are four of us: F22, Fright, Snow White and me – Green Crow.
Peace and quiet reigns over our room. And maybe even love. Certainly,
none of us here lounging around on our beds can hurt our families
any longer. Nor do we worry about the state of the nation, as there
is no television or newspaper in our room or on the rest of the ward.
The only reminders we have of the times in which we live are
our iron bedframes, the acrylic paint on the walls and the Snickers
bars on F22's bedside table. All we can see out of our window is two
real trees with real leaves and a brick wall. It was because of this
ridiculous scene that on my first day Fright had an argument with
F22, who claimed it was just a projected image, an illusion. Fright
stood her ground – the linden trees and brick walls were real. In an
attempt to settle the dispute, they both wandered all around the
hospital grounds on a quest to find that exact scene. They couldn't.

'I was right!' F22 was jubilant.

'Yes...' Fright admitted quietly, but later that evening she came
up with the following theory: 'We might assume that the world
is nothing more than one big illusion, simply because everything
seems different depending on your perspective. People and things.
However, the moment in which we look out the window is real.
We are both right!'

I'd heard that Fright graduated from the Faculty of Philosophy
because, as she said herself, her ugliness was 'of secondary relevance'
there. When pondering the constructs of the world's most meaningful

ideas, no one has time to reflect upon the ugly person sitting next to them picking her nose. That's our Fright. So ugly that the world should be ashamed and God should beg forgiveness. She is short and fat with a hooked nose, hunched shoulders, eyes as squinty as a Second World War sniper and barely a tooth in her head. On top of that, she hasn't a penny to her name. How is someone like her supposed to find her place in the world?

'I had hoped that here, in this nuthouse, I'd be given some medicine that stopped me caring, and it would stop mattering to me that I'm so misshapen. I wouldn't wish for a family; I would walk around proudly, my head held high.' Fright was justifying herself. 'So I pretended that I had tried to commit suicide. They bundled me up and brought me here.'

So we named her Fright and told her she was the ugliest woman we had ever seen. Fright wasn't in the least put out; she already knew it. She is waiting for her medicine.

It is said that ugly people's souls are egg-shaped diamonds, but it would appear that Fright hasn't had much luck in that department either. Her only hope is the medicine.

F22 is a much more severe case. She is not alone. She has a voice dictating her every move. So, for example, F22 goes to a shop to buy a currant bun. If the voice is asleep just then, all is well; F22 eats her bun and leaves the shop. But if the voice speaks up while she's deciding what to get, F22 then wanders around the shop for several hours looking for a kosher meat pie for her voice. If F22 can't find the right thing, the voice starts screaming and swearing, deriding F22 in every way possible. All this, of course, does little for her self-esteem.

And there's more. Some of F22's capriciousness is punishable by law. Like, for instance, when the voice suggests snapping the wing mirror off her neighbour's Mercedes Benz or telling her child's teacher that he looks like an old paedophile.

'My voice tells nothing but the truth,' F22 assures us. 'It's just that some people have no love for that.'

Snow White is our third roommate. A pensioner of about seventy. Very calm and quiet, since she spends the whole time sleeping while tied to her bed. When the princes are coming, the nurses wake her up and untie her, shaking a fist at us lest we breathe a single word. Fright is of the opinion that the old lady had been living locked up in the attic of some rich mansion.

'Like in *Jane Eyre*. Have you ever read it? Now she is kept sedated – and tied to the bed, too, just to be on the safe side. And her good-hearted, wealthy son, who comes nearly every day to see her, is told that his mother is slowly getting better.'

F22's voice is convinced that Snow White is, in fact, our psychiatrist's mother. A mother he can't stand because she, in turn, can't stand any of his women. Thus he has committed her to his clinic so his women can make pancakes any way they please, raise their children any way they please and pretty much live any way they please.

'And what about you? What's the matter with you?' F22 and Fright asked me when I first set foot in this room.

'I'm friends with the Green Crow.'

They exchanged looks and began backing away towards the window beyond which was the illusion.

'I can tell you . . .'

'Better still, call her!'

'No. The Crow has vanished.'

'OK, tell us instead then – we need to know how to behave around you.'

I sat down on the edge of my bed, next to the illusion, and went back to the very beginning, with the porridge, the same as I told the doctor.

'You're completely normal,' F22 concluded after listening to my story. 'There is nothing unhealthy about that, don't you see? All children have playmates.'

'Yes, exactly,' Fright said. 'I had a friend, too, when I was little. My parents didn't believe in him, though. "A child as ugly as her can't have friends," my mother once said to my father when she thought I was in my room. My friend was really cunning, you know, he never showed himself to my parents. I invited him for birthdays, Christmas and New Year's Eve, but he would never come, and my parents concluded that, rather than just being invisible, he simply didn't exist. Around the time I was offered a place to study philosophy at university, my friend suddenly died. And so, to this day, my parents don't believe I once had a friend. Can you imagine how much that hurts?' Fright buried her face in her pillow and sobbed at length.

'My voice is saying, isn't it funny how childhood mistakes have led to us ending up in a loony bin.'

'The Green Crow isn't dead, and it's not a childhood fantasy . . .' I made this statement so loudly that even Fright would hear through all her sobbing.

Fright and F22 sat closer together and said, almost in unison, 'Tell us!'

It is just another morning. The house is as silent as the grave, or else my house is just a dream, a neatly packaged and sanitized dream, and I, the bloody princess, am asleep. My mum calls me a princess when she's cross. But my dad is no king, that I know for sure. Kings don't work long days and nights on the mail vans; kings don't cheat on their country; kings don't steal postage stamps from envelopes to please their children. No, my dad is no king, and I'm not a princess. However, my mum is a servant and often says as much, as if we couldn't see that for ourselves. Her clothes are so old there's no point washing them any more – her clothes are impregnated with servant sweat for ever more. I don't remember my mum ever smelling like a real mother because she smokes. She smokes sitting on the little kitchen stool, her eyes half closed, her legs spread apart, abandoning all claims to femininity. She is no queen, and my dad is not a king, and I am not a princess. Today is my birthday, and on such a day every last mongrel will usually be the happiest creature in the world, as this is the day it came into the world. But mongrels learn, among other things, to bark, to piss on the vast expanse around them and, if only once, to bite the person who, as their master, imposes their will upon them. I probably bit my mum and pissed on her as the vast expanse surrounded me. While giving birth, no mother is thinking about how she will later be pissed on and even bitten.

Today is my birthday. I'm going to be eight.

'Mum, what time was I born?'

'I don't know. In the evening some time.'

My mum is tired. She is always tired. She says that she gets tired of me and my dad and the grubby rooms. Would it be better if no one ever walked through those rooms again?

'What a silly thought!' Mum thinks we will live for ever and all our one-day-we-won't-be-here-any-more talk is mere fantasy. But I know that one day it will happen. We won't be here any more.

'Where's Dad?'

'At work. Where else would he be?'

'He could be anywhere.'

'He couldn't. He has to work.'

It's useless arguing with my mum – she is dyeing her hair blue with carbon paper; she has made a copy of herself. Besides, she doesn't believe my dad could be anywhere other than at work. It must be love.

'Go on outside and play with the other children. Get out from under my feet – I need to get your birthday lunch ready. Go on!'

'Exactly what time was I born?'

'Have a look at your birth certificate. It will be on that.'

In my parents' brown wardrobe there are some special compartments where Mum and Dad keep their underwear. My dad's suit, for weddings or funerals, hangs there along with the blouse brought by foreign relatives from abroad, which she never wears to stop it from wearing out. There is a Rubik's Cube I'm forbidden from touching until I come of age. There is some money, set aside for rainy days. There is a red life-and-death shoebox, split down the middle by a divider my mum made herself. At first our passports, birth certificates, vaccination records and sundry documents were to be kept on one side, while credit notes and death certificates were to be filed on the other. But, seeing as none of us had died, my mum mixed up the life and death compartments – she put her documents in the life one but buried my dad and me on the death side. I suppose the death compartment was more spacious, two people could fit in it easily, although, as far as my mum was concerned, my dad and I were one and the same person.

At birth, as in a duel, one has a second. The birthing second notes the time just as the head of the new, single-use body crowns, when the clavicle breaks because its mother has tensed, fearing death. Despite being splashed from head to toe in blood, just like in a real duel, the second keeps counting to ensure we will be able to find out the exact time of our births, since we all ask our mothers at some point.

I was born at midnight. Or I wasn't born at all.

'Midnight means on no particular day,' I tell my mum, and I want to cry. I do cry.

'That's what they said, too. Then they made me choose the day of your birth so they could keep their records straight. Today is your birthday.'

I thought that the dear Lord decided everything. I hadn't known that mothers could be so omnipotent – it turns out that a child can quite simply be tossed from Pisces into Aries.

'Why are you crying?'

'It sounds like childbirth can make you mad.' I can't stop crying.

'Yes. I almost lost my mind because of you.'

'The whole giving-birth thing must be pretty painful?'

'There was a Russian woman giving birth in a cubicle next to mine. When the baby's head crowned, she started cursing life itself.'

I don't really know how babies are born, but it doesn't sound as if there's anything very nice about it. Nothing nice at all. I feel sorry for my mum and what she went through giving birth to me. I will never be able to repay her, as I can hardly give birth to my own mother and curse life itself when her head, with its dyed carbon-blue hair, crowns.

'Where do those babies come from?'

Mum lights a cigarette. She has started peeling carrots, still sitting on her kitchen stool, feet apart, knees open.

'The head comes out down here.' She points between her legs.

I feel sick. I'm out in the street. I throw up on the tram tracks while my mum is peeling carrots for my birthday lunch. A baby crawls out from between its mother's legs? Sticks its head out and blinks? I can't believe that after all this my dad still touches my mum and kisses me on the cheek. I feel ashamed for the whole human race. But I don't curse life. Today is my birthday.

There's no one in the playground. Not even the four-eyed Paedo – he's a year younger than me – is out there digging tunnels in the sandpit. They have all disappeared. Maybe they are playing war games and most of them have been shot in the nearby bushes. When you get shot in our war game you aren't allowed to move for three minutes so you know what it feels like to be dead. On my own I won't go after the four-eyed Paedo with a bit of cat shit impaled on the tip of a stick. All alone, I'm no warrior. I can't believe we were all born the same way as Paedo – through our mothers' crotches – or that we have anything else in common. You've only got to look at him!

I race to the new brick house that was finished just last month and shout at the top of my lungs, 'Croooow! Croooow! Crooow!'

She lives on the roof of the newly built house, but I'm afraid of heights so never go to visit her. She tells me that the world seems much lighter from up there, that looking down from on high the city is like a toy town and it all seems totally insignificant. That in all the houses, back gardens and streets, the people who live there change all the time. To the Crow, the world is just one big haystack that people sleep in, one after another, without knowing anything much about the person who was there before, since we're interested only in ourselves. And if we do think about the previous sleeper, it's only to make sure there are no harmful germs, nasty diseases, lice or cockroaches left in our haystack.

Up there you're on your own, the Crow says.

'Croooooooow! Crooooow! Today is my birthday! I was born on this day!'

'Have you got any pies?' The Crow finally flies down from the rooftop on to the third-floor balcony.

'No, I . . .'

'Then come back with pies!' The Crow flies off again. The four-eyed Paedo, who is *always* in the playground, stares at me, his mouth hanging open. He is expecting a pie. My friends are still dead. And I haven't been born yet. The Crow is expecting pies. My mum is smoking. My dad is working. The world seems small from above, but I've never seen it as I'm afraid of heights.

I go to my mum. She really dislikes the Green Crow. My mum says she is ruining me, distancing me from humankind. Besides, the Crow has all sorts of bird-like outbursts – like suddenly upping and flying away. 'What will I do when you suddenly fly away?' my mum once asked.

'You will not follow me,' I answered.

My mum is sitting in the same place, on her small throne, looking at the flesh of minced animals to which an egg, white breadcrumbs and black pepper have been added. That delicious dish made of animal flesh called meatballs. I hate meatballs, but there's nothing to be done – today is my birthday, and several guests will be arriving, all of whom love my mum's meatballs.

While my mum has her back to me, I steal a couple.

The animals' flesh comes into contact with my own flesh. On my birthday we meet here, by the saucepan, instead of in the sty where I could scratch the pig's flank until it slides to the ground in ecstasy or feel the rasping, warm tongue of a cow on my palm and wonder at its long eyelashes, wishing my children might have similar ones. No. Our meeting is entirely different. I hide the meatballs in my pocket.

The first guest rings the doorbell. It's my godfather. I rather like him as a man. I sometimes dream about him kidnapping me and never letting me go, binding my hands and feet to abduct me. I like the smell of his furry moustache. On one occasion he and I went for a two-hour drive in his car without once speaking to each other; it was as if I weren't by his side. When we got to our destination my godfather said he wanted a wife just like me, one who didn't talk at all. My godfather is the only man I feel embarrassed in front of. I would like a husband like him, but he is my godfather and nothing can be done about that.

The next guests to arrive are Grandpa and Grandma. Very grumpy people. I'm scared of them, especially when Grandma falls silent and stares at the floor. If I were Grandpa I would never live with such a person. Would you choose to live with someone who first looks at the floor and then shouts? I don't want them to kiss me. Their mouths stink because they are old and tired of all the same words. I offer them my cheek all the same, as today is my birthday. I even offer the other one, too. For my birthday present they give me a book with a dedication saying they have given it to me on this day and date. People need to leave something behind on this earth. A dedication in a book is a good bet, as no one throws books away. After death they travel from one bookcase to another, maybe even with the whole bookcase in tow. Grandpa and Grandma are old. They have already started thinking of their own deaths, how life on earth will continue without them and about all of us on the day after their deaths. The Crow believes that after death people's lives don't change at all. The living mourn for a month or so, then all that's left is the graveyard, tended as if it were a beautiful small garden where nothing expensive can be planted, as small-time cemetery thieves would only pinch it. My book is about distinguishing good from evil – a collection of folk fairy tales. A good read.

The last to arrive is my elderly great-aunt. She is much talked about in the family. My mum is very, very fond of this aunt. Once, when my parents had a fight, I heard Mum saying that she was the only sane person in my dad's family. She had been there when my dad first took my mum home to meet his family. My aunt is said to have given her a sock to mend, which my mum darned so carefully that she declared her nephew could do far worse for a wife. It was after that that my grandma had allowed my dad to marry. Then I was born. So it turns out I might not be here if it hadn't been for my great-aunt. Today she is wearing her green dress with orange, blue and white flowers. It seems to me that she was born in that dress, as I've never seen her wearing any other. Just like clouds and the scent of the earth in spring, my great-aunt's dress will one day be part of the film I'll watch shortly before I die.

My mum confiscates all my presents and puts them away in her wardrobe, leaving me with just the book with the dedication, the gift from my grandparents. And so, for the first time in my life, I steal from my parents' wardrobe – the beautiful necklace given to me by the man I shall never be able to marry. I steal my godfather's gift so I can show it off to the Crow. I really want to go to the cinema with the Crow to see *Robin Hood: Prince of Thieves*, starring Kevin Costner (who, after my godfather, is the next husband in line and someone I should be delighted to marry if he didn't live in America and wasn't already happily married).

While my mum is otherwise occupied discussing life, I steal

the money-filled envelope generously given to me by my aunt and the necklace with a real piece of aventurine, the stone of fortune, on a gold-plated chain. I sneak past the kitchen, where my birthday gathering is in full swing. I'm a thief, and the most important thing for thieves is to make a quick getaway. On my way to the door I hear the adults sounding off about *them*. I'm not sure who *they* are or what they have done, but it's plain that they are just about the most despicable people on earth. Every misfortune, war, all poverty and even death is their fault. God is powerless, as they don't believe in Him, and God has no power over non-believers. Although it would appear that God had once had a laugh at their expense. It had happened this very winter. In every apartment, tunnel, hospital and school, people enjoyed God's laughter for quite some time, it was that mighty. God laughed at one of them, and His laughter was broadcast on the radio. They would never have permitted such a transmission, but nobody knew that God was going to attend the funeral and burial of one of them. We all heard how the coffin fell with a loud thud into the grave, and we all laughed, relishing the scene. Following this incident, they arrested anyone who had laughed and began to fear God. My grandma thinks things are improving and someday soon people will come to their senses and they will get what they deserve. And God will help. Real chocolate and bananas have started to appear in the shops. This can only be the hand of God at work.

I run down the stairs with the two meatballs in my pocket and the envelope stuffed with money and the stone of fortune on its almost-gold chain, all stuck together in a greasy clump. I run across the street, which is alive and tired of the heavy trams, tired of continually saving small children and cats, of rubbish thrown out of open windows because there is no more space in the apartments – all the cupboards full, the shelves stuffed, the rubbish bins stinking, the minds wise and the hearts overflowing. Every seventy years or so there's a changeover of people doing all this, unwillingly giving up their warmed seats to others. And so the world never cools down. The pavement never loses its warmth. I'm wearing red sandals and white socks with pompons. They're the fashion. Every period has its own fashion, and clearly we can do nothing to change it, as time has already been invented and can't just be put out of sight; we've all got used to it. Time will die along with the last person alive. Then only the Crow will be left, flying around an empty world while everyone else is in line for Last Judgement, endorsing the theory of time. She really could do it. Out of sheer boredom, naturally. Superfluous things are generally borne of boredom.

The tram trundles away along the rails. One of them almost ran me over. Trams have difficulty braking; instead, they have a loud bell, which is far more useful than church or school bells. If I were a tram driver I would ring it whenever I saw someone beauti-ful on the street; I would ring it to scold naughty children on the pavements, to say hello to big dogs, to smile. I would ring it the whole time. The Crow says that in that case I should under no circumstances become a tram driver, as no one needs tram drivers who smile sincerely all the time.

What's more, even Jesus with all his sermonizing love came to a sticky end, as there's something suspect about anyone who loves everybody and everything without question. The Crow says that Jews are the most intelligent race on earth, so quick were they to size Jesus up and finish him off.

The entrance to the courtyard of the block of the block of flats is like a vaulted stone gateway to another world. There is no access for cars, unless you have a magic key. All my friends – the four-eyed Paedo, bald Berta, the Green Crow and all the cats that escaped being drowned at birth – live in that other world. Today is my birthday. The cats know this and rub up against my legs; the four-eyed Paedo digs holes for his plastic Russian soldiers. He wants to hide them from us, but we will look for them, and, if we find them, we will hide them from him. My friends have all been called for lunch; their mums busily fry and stew and call their children up to eat at two o'clock sharp so no one feels hungry or left out. My friends' mothers love their children very much. They call each other up to discuss menus. None of them would ever, ever, ever fry pork cutlets for *karbonāde* without using fresh meat or use meat that might be on the turn. They cook grey peas so their children can take part in farting competitions; they prepare beetroot salad and blueberry dumplings so their children can mock each other with their red and blue tongues. Once, the mums competed for the title of the stinkiest kid – they prepared a dish that turned their children's mouths into fetid wounds that could speak. I don't remember who won. I really don't know who stunk the most. The winner got a slice of homemade cake and his mum's congratulations. Yes, my friends are all having their meals now.

I call the Crow because I have meatballs, money and a fortune necklace in my pocket.

'Crooooooooooow!'

She comes at the first call. She has probably been waiting for some such treat all along. But, oh, this is terrible! Oh, madness! She has flown straight over me and has landed next to the sandpit, right next to the four-eyed Paedo. He lifts his head and looks at the Crow through his thick glasses. I don't know exactly what

Paedo sees there, but he smiles, flashes his yellow teeth and extends one of his plastic Russian soldiers to the Crow. Oh, for shame! And the Crow actually takes it and wraps it tenderly, as if it were precious, in her green wing. They don't talk because Paedo is Russian. The Crow doesn't speak Russian. But I dislike this even more than if they had been talking. Companionable silence can signal the start of a true friendship. I rush over to join them.

'What are you doing? Can't you tell that he stinks, the four-eyed Paedo! We beat him up because he smells, because his mum looks like a Jew – that's what all our friends' mums say anyway – we make him eat hard cat shit rolled in sand. We don't love him at all! Please, you mustn't love him either!'

'Now why is that? Paedo offered me a Russian soldier! He gave me his corporal and left himself just with privates. How can I fail to love someone who does that?'

'He is a paedophile, don't you understand?'

'What's a paedophile?'

'A very, very bad person.'

'Can there be words so very bad?'

'There are, there are! Just try making friends with him, and you'll see. Crow, please, today is my birthday . . .'

The Crow's eyes glow with great tenderness.

'All right. Here you go, little Russian, play with your corporal.' She gives the plastic Russian soldier back to Paedo, and the four-eyed boy stops smiling, then snatches up handfuls of sand and throws it, trying to hit us.

'He really is a right paedo, isn't he?' The Crow laughs. She is a bit slow on the uptake – well, she is a bird after all.

So while Paedo is throwing sand around I press my cheek

against the Crow's bony beak and pull two meatballs out of my pocket.

'My birthday treat. Here you are.'

Now the Crow is looking at me the same way Paedo had looked at her earlier. She isn't smiling.

'Don't you have any cabbage pies?' she asks.

'No, I'm sorry.'

'Then I'm not eating!' The Crow folds her wings over her chest and points her beak skywards.

'What's wrong with the meatballs?' I ask, although I was aware that the Crow ate meat differently, not like us humans. I knew that, I did know, but I had brought the meatballs anyway, as, quite simply, I had nothing else. People often do that – they bring something inappropriate because there is nothing else. Once my dad bought me a pen that had four different-coloured inks in it for my birthday, even though I had asked for a doll. I still couldn't write at that time, and my dad had known that. He bought me a pen simply because all the dolls – the ones whose heads moved because they had magnets in their mouths – had sold out. I cried, thanked him but wouldn't so much as touch the pen. Then my dad got angry and roared that I was an ungrateful, spoiled child. 'What am I supposed to do with a pen if I can't write?' I asked him. 'You must learn always to look to the future!' he hollered, his words seeping into the walls of our flat. Yes, I could see them making their way through the cavities to the neighbours above, below and beside us, like some slow-acting poison. Today I turned eight, but there's no guarantee I'll ever get to nine. There's only any certainty about future events the second before they take place. The rest of time, going towards the future, is very, very distant.

'I never eat meat unless I can apologize to the animal before swallowing it.' The Crow is looking up to the sky, her wings still crossed.

The Crow enjoys eating May bugs and June bugs and their offspring, so May and June are her favourite months. These insects' babies are the most delicious of all – pale-yellow maggots with a swollen semi-transparent underside. Beetle babies are juicier and there's much more to eat than in bigger grown-up beetles. The Crow swallows them still wriggling. What could she possibly have against meatballs? Does an apology change the maggots' fate? What can be changed by an apology anyway?

'Is there any point in apologizing?' I ask tentatively. The Crow can be very touchy, either taking offence or loving the whole world at the drop of a hat.

'I thank the maggot for feeding my hungry tummy and ask forgiveness for robbing it of its life. That's all.'

'But what difference does it make?' I don't get it.

The Crow flaps her wings and lands on the concrete slab by the sandpit. It's the roof of an air-raid shelter, about a metre and a half above the ground. Well-intentioned people installed it during the war so that residents of the rich people's houses could hide from the bombs that the plastic soldiers were dropping on them so they would die. They were Russian and German plastic soldiers, corporals included. The roof of the shelter hides deep stone tunnels along which testimonials to wartime love and fear are strewn. We found two old dolls down there, spoons, plates and a letter in Russian. Most likely it was people scared of being killed who wrote to the Russian corporal to ask him to stop dropping bombs, pleading with him, begging for mercy, weeping, smudging the ink between the lines. We went looking for human bones down there but found only some ribs, probably veal. My dad said it may well have been a goat. How could they have got a goat down there? It must have been taken down as a kid then allowed to grow into an adult while the war was on. Then, on the last day of the war, it had been grilled and eaten to celebrate the end of the conflict. It was said that during the war everything had grown and come to fruition much faster than nowadays – especially faith, hope and love. Now the tunnel to the shelter is full of rubbish – anyone not wanting to be given a piece of the caretaker's mind chucks bottles and sweet wrappers down there. The caretaker can't be bothered to clean it, seeing as the war is long over!

The Crow, standing on the air-raid shelter roof and flapping her wings energetically, says, 'Before they die people should be reminded of all their good deeds in life, their friends and relatives should apologize to them and the dying should come clean about anything they might need to own up to. That way they can pass away peacefully. I do the same thing with maggots, May bugs, June bugs, gorgeous rose chafers that I gulp down to survive. There's no point saying anything to your meatballs, not now. Can't you see that?'

'What language do you speak to them?'

'The same I do with you, my dear.'

'And what sort of language is that?'

'A comprehensible one. That should suffice, don't you think?'

'Yes, but . . .'

'It's not a language to be found in dictionaries. Maybe only the Bible could be of any use.'

'Do you believe in God?'

The Crow hesitated over her answer as if pondering the matter, as if in a matter of seconds one might find a god to believe in.

'Who doesn't?' She spreads her tail feathers. 'You'd better give your meatballs to the four-eyed Paedo, and then let's fly away from here, where everything is so dull and predictable.'

The Crow can be a little harsh. She shrieks at me more fiercely than my mum, my teacher or even an army officer in a war film. The Crow gets in a huff quite easily, but I don't want to lose my one and only true friend, even if she is just a bird who likes eating insect babies, but I don't want to give my birthday meatballs to the four-eyed Paedo either. I would feel disgraced, far more disgraced than the time I licked a broken tube of mayonnaise I found lying on the pavement – I desperately wanted to find out what it tasted like, as my parents had never bought any. I only wanted to know what it was, but I got called shit-licker by the courtyard kids because of it. The tube had 'mayonnaise' written on it, not 'shit'. The worst thing that could happen now was that they would call me Paedo's mummy. I see that the Crow is running out of patience. I go over to Paedo.

'Here you go,' I say, and the meatballs drop in the sand. They jump out of my hands; they don't want to go to Paedo.

'Happy birthday,' he says in Russian, squinting somewhere in my general direction, as if his vision really was almost zero. Then he feels about in the sand for the fallen meatballs and shoves them in his mouth. Sand grates between his teeth; there might even be a seashell or two in there, as a couple of days ago new sand was put in the pit we share with the cats. I can only imagine that Paedo is tasting meatballs for the first time in his life, in pretty much the same way as that mayonnaise I had tried. Paedo's mother doesn't eat meat. She is a hypochondriac, workaholic, stigmatic, lunatic, stoic, scopophiliac, diabetic. One of those people who doesn't eat meat, anyhow. She doesn't feed Paedo any proteins or fats, which explains his appalling eyesight. Paedo will die before any of the rest of us.

'You're such a scumbag!' I respond in Russian.

'Bless the Lord Almighty,' the Crow caws. Swift as a missile, she whizzes through the air from the air-raid shelter straight on to me, and I somehow find myself astride her back. Now, green crows are pint-size birds, smaller than grey crows and certainly smaller than almost all eight-year-old girls. I'm not sure if I have shrunk or the Crow has got bigger; all I know is that we are flying. Once upon a time there was a man named Milarepa who took shelter from the rain in a horn on the ground, yet Milarepa had not grown smaller nor had the horn grown bigger. I think I might know how it happened – you simply have to want it to. You need to be afraid of rain, and you should want to fly.

The Crow knows that I'm afraid of flying. She knows that my eyes are shut tight.

'Open your eyes!' she croaks.

'No!'

'Open your eyes!'

'No!'

'When you leave the ground everything is different, especially if you are sitting on the back of a bird. The earth cannot harm birds the way it can people – it can't simply drag them down. The wind is different up here, unlike the one gusting along the ground. Up here it caresses you.' The Crow gains height and, just like a mother gently nudging her small child who has just learned to crawl, the hands of the wind gently propel us upwards. We fly along serenely, the Crow suddenly losing height or executing an occasional wild sideways lurch.

'Seagulls', she croaks, 'are such brazen birds. So what if they are bigger than me and can swim, too? So what?'

'Jonathan,' I cry out, although I'm not sure the Crow can hear me. 'Does Jonathan live here?'

'Oh, yes. Do you know Jonathan?'

'I read about him in a book. I liked it, but my dad said it was stupid. I want to meet Jonathan.'

'Then let's fly to the sea. Open your eyes now, please,' the Crow caws as we speed up.

I clutch on to the Crow's feathers like a horse's mane. Once I went horse-riding with my class somewhere in the countryside by the river. The following day my teacher gave me a letter to take home to my parents that stated I had failed to 'observe commonly acceptable rules of behaviour – instead of holding the horse's reins, she clutches on to its mane. You are requested to discuss the norms of conduct on horseback with your daughter at home.' Mum and Dad shrugged, consulted encyclopaedias, called our neighbours – they had never even seen a real live horse let alone have any idea about rules of conduct on its back. My parents were angry with me all the same for not holding on to the horse's reins. A horse's neck is strong and warm, and his mane smells of hay and life. At one point I even took to wishing that the horse was my father. Maybe my mum would have liked that, too?

Holding on to the Crow's feathers, I open my eyes. I feel stunned, overawed.

It would appear that up here you no longer have any understanding of who and why you are and why you should be. You question whether the place where you were born and live is your true home; you allow the possibility that there might have been some terrible mix-up. Once you have been there, you never want to go back to a stairwell that stinks of basements and soldiers' piss; you don't want to get up every morning and go to work until you reach retirement; you don't want to be a cog in the great Soviet machine; you don't want to queue up at the order desk for foodstuffs; you don't want medals for your work; you don't want to put money aside for your coffin; and you don't want to be buried deep in the ground. You want to fly and be born anew each and every day.

'We're getting close to the airport. Pull your feet up for landing!' the Crow roars, and I bend my head, putting my hand to my ear to make sure that none of the passing aeroplanes had ripped it off. You can't actually feel pain in this vast expanse – it just falls to the ground where someone else picks it up and takes it home, incapable of living without it and maybe unwilling to do so, too.

A massive jet overtakes us – it's a little too close, but the aeroplane is not as powerful as seagulls, who can also swim. 'Aeroflot' is written in red letters down the side. A chubby-cheeked boy looks at me through one of the windows. He is eating a bun and waving. Probably to me and the Crow or possibly to the sun, which is already hunkering down behind the pine trees.

'How are you doing back there?' The Crow turns her head back, touching my forehead with her beak.

'Great.' I've opened my eyes.

The Crow gives a loud cry, and then something happens I shall dream about until I take my final breath. The Crow gains height and turns upside down in the air; she does a loop-the-loop, which for birds is known as the loop of joy and for aeroplanes the loop of death. As if predicting the Crow's movements, I grip on to her feathers, wrap my legs around her warm body and scream. Seagulls, who can also swim, and aeroplanes, with 'Aeroflot' written on their sides, would both take fright at a scream like mine. They would be alarmed, but they wouldn't look back as they would if it had been a cry of pain. Loud happiness makes people look away.

'That felt good, didn't it?' the Crow caws and abruptly drops in altitude. We are approaching Jūrmala.

We land on a patch of newly sown grass between two roads, along which brightly coloured cars race past us.

On the other side of the bridge lies Jūrmala.

I came to Jūrmala once with my dad for a walk along the front. He sent me off to the playground while he met a woman. They laughed, but at times it sounded as if they were crying. My dad took a swing and threw a stone into the sea. I didn't know he could throw a stone so far; he had never shown me anything like that before. Then he snatched the woman up and carried her. The woman fought back and shrieked. She probably frightened my dad, and he decided against throwing her in the water, but I wanted him to do it so that she would crawl out of the water dripping wet and go home to dry off.

Members of the Militsiya stand on the bridge. Just like the other time.

'I don't like the Militsiya,' the Crow says.

'No,' I say, 'my dad doesn't like them either.'

'I wonder why the world doesn't stop creating professions no one likes?' The Crow lowers her voice.

'My dad says that that all professions are necessary.'

'Really? I truly didn't know that . . .'

'What are we going to do if the Militsiya stop us? They might clip your wings!'

I put my hand in my pocket. I feel grease from the meatballs, the stone of fortune and the money given to me by my cool great-aunt. Ten roubles, more than enough for a film starring Kevin Costner, maybe even enough for three. I don't want them to clip the Crow's wings. We would never be able to fly again.

'All right.' I pull the envelope out of my pocket. 'Let's go! Let's fly!' I shout and sit on the Crow's back.

We are on the wing. When we are directly above the Militsiya car I let the creased envelope drop from my hand.

'My dad says that every profession likes money. He says that professions are meant for making money.'

I turn my head and see a Militsiya officer picking up the envelope, opening it and looking up to the sky. He knows well enough that God doesn't exist, but we are already a fair distance away. Below us are toy cars, wind-up trains, matchstick bridges and slow-moving plastic people. The only real thing is the sea air, awakening our senses and urging us on. The roads criss-crossing the dense pine forest look like worm tracks; lightly scorched, dirty, rough paths. Thank God the worms haven't eaten their way as far as the sea, thank God that would be against the law, thank God that worms are scared of deep water. The worms had parked their toy cars reverently behind the sand dunes. If a really big storm blew up, everyone would realize immediately that the man-made world was no more than a doll's house tossed about on a real ocean, and all the fussing of people the world over was no more than a great gift of mercy granted to them. Some unknown benefactor allowed them to play until they could take no more.

We flew in a circle above the grey-blue waves of the sea. Exactly the colour of my eyes – maybe these are my eyes that always look up, scared of heights, scared of falling. My eyes are cool when they are unwilling but warm when they are encouraging. They are wet with high and low tides, the treasure of sunken trips to the sea's depths, bloated drowned bodies and cachalots, blood-encrusted fishermen's nets.

'You are the Green Crow, and I am you. We are everything.'

The Crow shakes me off her back on to the warm sand at the water's edge.

'My dad said that everybody is different, separate and unique.'

'Your dad, my girl, is a fool!'

I beg to disagree with the Crow on this matter, despite wishing her always to tell me nothing but the truth. I can't be a grain of sand or the sea. I have circulating blood and a brain, unique fingerprints, a birth certificate, a mum and a dad.

'You should fly more often.' The Crow pulls a handful of chocolates out of her pocket and flicks sand over them. 'When you do, you stop thinking about ID papers and fingerprints.'

'I'm quite an in-di-vid-u-al.' I pronounce the world slowly so as not to embarrass myself. My grandma believes that anyone who uses words they don't understand is a fool.

The Crow doesn't answer. My birthday shrinks, becoming insignificant, as tiny as a grain of sand. I feel all alone, again like a grain of sand, one that has accidentally fallen into the boot of a car and will never find its way back to the sea because a man – a rushing, not-knowing, not-understanding man – will take it far away.

'Do we have to talk?' The Crow turns her tear-covered beak to me.

'Why are you crying?' My throat tightens.

'Why do you think?'

'I really don't know.'

The Crow digs the sweets out of the sand. 'One day you will be forty years old and you will have two children' – she looks me straight in the eye – 'and you will not want me any longer because you will be an in-di-vid-u-al.'

I have a feeling that the Crow is somehow right. Adults sometimes get carried away talking about their childhoods, their faces contorted into expressions filled with longing. Yet adults have never been children. Their stories are lies. Who are these people, rushing around the whole time and then, in the evening, irritably rolling up newspapers and swatting flies? Who are they?

'I will always want you, Crow. You are my sanctuary, do you hear me?' I put my hand on her shoulder and snuggle up close. Even as I speak I am aware of how cruelly I am lying to her. But I cannot do otherwise.

'Let's go and visit Jonathan. There!' The Crow shrugs off my hand like a grain of sand and looks into the distance, where I can just about make out a lone figure.

I get to my feet and walk over, not really believing what I can see. The Crow's words seem to possess some kind of magic power. One day she might ask me to kill someone. At first I wouldn't want to, but within five minutes I would be standing, axe in hand, fully aware of what I was going to do and why.

'Don't interrupt when Jonathan is speaking. Your parents have taught you how to behave with elderly people, haven't they?'

'Yes, but Jonathan is just a seagull.'

'What have you been doing in your nature-study classes at school? Haven't you learned that seagulls generally only live for fifteen years, and yet there are a few rare cases of seagulls living to forty!'

'Crow, I'm only in Year 2.'

'Oh yes. I had forgotten that life is measured in school years.'

I don't know why the Crow doesn't like school. Maybe because she didn't go herself, crows never having been given the opportunity. My dad once told me that everyone experiences envy. For example, if you were to find yourself holding a chocolate bar and not wanting to share it, you would soon be told that it was smuggled counterfeit chocolate and that the factory workers had spat into the vats during its manufacture just to mock you. My dad says that nothing in this world is for certain. That means that the Crow is not for certain either. But I love her very much just the same.

'When we get there, bow as low as you can and look Jonathan in the eye at all times. Promise?'

'Yes.'

I'm terrified but keep quiet. I think the Jonathan in my book is quite different, not the sort of bird you would have to look in the eye and bow to. You can open the book and then close it again straight away.

We are approaching, but the outline of the seagull hasn't moved at all. As if he were real and we a mere flight of fancy.

'Greetings,' the Crow says, and bows deeply, grazing the sand with the top of her greenish pate.

'Hello.' I bow, too, then burst out laughing. It's all too funny.

Jonathan turns his head towards us. His eyes are sea-blue, his beak yellow with a red bulge as if he had dirtied it treating himself to some leftover pizza from one of the Jūrmala rubbish bins. His head looks so clever and strong that it makes me think anyone with a head like that could never die. The world needs things with such power: Jonathan's head, an autumn pumpkin, a lioness, a wooden spoon, fairy tales and someone to watch over us – God perhaps.

Jonathan is smaller than me and so serious that I let out a giggle

– the Crow steps on my foot. Never mind that she weighs less than a couple of hundred grams. Her claws are as sharp as a cat's and cut into my foot painfully. And yet I can't stop laughing.

'She will be forty years old and will have two children. She will forget about you.' Jonathan turns to the Crow, and for the first time ever I detect a look of fear in her eyes. She lowers her head and says nothing. I no longer feel the slightest urge to laugh. I feel guilty about the future, even if I don't think I will ever have any children because I might have one like the four-eyed Paedo and then I would become a Jew who doesn't eat meat. I don't think we should necessarily believe everything Jonathan says.

'But we don't chose who to love.' He gives out one of those sharp seagull shrieks.

And I change my mind again. 'Well said, Jonathan,' I say quietly to myself, but the Crow and Jonathan both turn their heads sharply towards me, and Jonathan lets out a laugh. He opens his beak as wide as he can and laughs. The Crow, too, realizing that this time the laughing is serious, lets herself go and laughs like mad. I laugh as well, and, as if touched by magic, find myself enveloped in a darkness like blackberry jam, I spin as if I were in a tumble-dryer and hear distant laughter. Well said, Jonathan, well said. We can't choose who to love, we just love them . . . Yes. Well said.

The tumble-dryer slows down. The programme is about to come to the end of its cycle, and there will be a click. My head knocks against something hard, as if someone had put bits of paving stone or dried-out cheese rinds in the machine. I hear voices. A click. The programme has finished. Someone is pulling me out of the dryer, yanking me out by the shoulders past the octopus-sucker rubber flange. Someone is slapping my cheek. I turn the other one.

'Are you all right, little one?'

I open my eyes, but they snap shut again. A dust cart buzzes along somewhere near by, so it must be nine o'clock in the evening. All my friends, including the four-eyed Paedo, are standing on one side of the street with bags overflowing with rubbish in their hands, ready to meet and clap each other on the shoulder.

'Nine o'clock!' I exclaim, and my eyes suddenly flick open like a cheap doll that never actually closes them.

Quite a crowd has gathered around me, three of them bending down over me, their eyes bulging like fish. I jerk backwards but maybe shouldn't have done so – right behind me is the rough wall of my building.

'I just fell,' I lie, jumping up and running around the corner and right into the building. I slow down as I reach the third floor, dragging myself along like an old, guilt-ridden horse that has run away into the wilderness of the savannah for seven hours on its birthday. My only hope lies in my dad and the football championship being on.

'Where did you get to? I looked for you everywhere in the yard! Where were you, you imbecilic child? You'll turn my hair grey!'

The sound of cheering and the commentator's nasal voice emerge from the back room. The football is on! My mum won't clout me, and her hair was already grey before I was even born.

I disappear to my room and lie down perfectly still so I can hear the sigh of every bedbug and woodworm.

'We need to take that child to see a doctor, you hear?'

'Wait, it's going to a penalty shoot-out,' Dad is muttering indistinctly, and the tiny creatures' noises are drowned out by my mother's tripping footsteps and the spring of the door handle to my room.

'Where have you been? Answer me!' Mum shouts, and I imagine

how loud her hollering must seem to the bedbugs, woodworms, mice and my dad who is watching the football.

I curl up into a ball, covering my head with my hands.

'With the Crow,' I say.

'And the money?'

'I spent it. We went to Jūrmala . . .'

My mum raises her hands like a football fan, sighs heavily and runs from the room. Her footsteps cross the corridor to her room.

I sneak out into the corridor and take up a position just outside the door.

'She needs help. That Crow . . . ! This time she says they've been to Jūrmala. Can you believe that? It's your daft family's genes . . . She comes up with all these things that have never happened. The Crow, Jūrmala. Last week she said she had eaten an earthworm because they're full of protein and the Crow eats them . . .'

'Yes! We've done it!' my dad roars.

I creep back to my room, get undressed and crawl into bed. The sand from the beach grinds between my toes, my eyelids like doors to another world. Only my ears are still awake as I hear my dad comforting my mum. 'She's not that bad. You always make too big a deal of it.'

F22 and Fright are both weeping. Snow White's cheeks seem to be streaked with tears, too.

'Do you still want a family, Fright?'

LAUGH AT *TITANIC*!

'Listen, F22, is the sun shining through our window an illusion, too?' It's the first question that springs to mind every morning when I open my eyes. But F22 is still asleep. She carries on snoring until Fright yanks her cover away and drags her off to breakfast. Failure to eat well makes the doctors think you've taken a turn for the worse, and that would mean F22 and her voice being moved to the second floor or pumped full of much stronger drugs. And veins can't hide or conceal drugs to be spat out later.

Someone flushes the toilet. One, two, three, four times. I want to scream 'Have some respect for the sun', then I wake up properly and realize there is something very odd about flushing the toilet so many times. I glance at the beds. F22 is snoring rhythmically under two blankets. Snow White, as ever, lies on her back – her position reminds me of a corpse in a coffin. Fright's bed is empty and messy. A sweet smell wafts out of the bathroom.

Fright comes back into the room with a towel wrapped around her head. She doesn't know that I'm watching her from under my covers.

Fright is singing quietly – I wanna be loved by you . . . boop-boop-a-doop – her checked slippers dance happily, gliding across the floor as if their owner weren't the ugliest woman in the world.

Fright sits down on the edge of her bed, takes an invisible mirror from her bedside table and looks into it, gently tracing the oval contours of her face with her fingertips. Then she opens the drawer and takes out an invisible make-up bag, extracting from it an invisible lipstick, mascara, eyeshadow . . .

Fright continues making a fool of herself like this for quite some time. Then she carefully puts everything back in its place and sets about doing her hair.

I close my eyes and try to go back to sleep – I can't let Fright know I've seen her performance. Even a sane person could be driven to depression knowing that someone else had seen them wash their hair down the toilet and put on invisible make-up. Let her do as she likes. After all, this is the only place where you could get away with that.

I pretend to be asleep for a whole hour. I don't move a muscle and, to make it more believable, every so often give a little snore. Fright hates snoring and claps her hands at each noise. I stop immediately, as if she has touched a magic button. Peeping out from under the covers, I see Fright smiling happily, delighted as she can be.

It's terrible having to lie perfectly still, as I desperately want to cry. I keep thinking of things and body parts I would willingly give away if only that big bird with her familiar beak and blue eyes would appear at the window, which is only an illusion even though the sun is real. I would pledge to give away my children, my favourite books, my school diplomas, my left hand, an ear maybe, an eye, all my teeth if only I could see my Green Crow. Yet something tells me that things and body parts would be of no use – I would have to surrender my soul – but children, the children I would only be able to exchange for a small butterfly. White, yellow or multi-coloured – whatever I wanted.

I have no idea how to surrender my soul. Outside the window is nothing but an illusion.

Meanwhile Fright has made herself comfortable in bed, book in hand. If I pretend to sleep, why shouldn't Fright pretend to read Proust? No one can pretend for ever, act for ever, but there is something odd about a morning such as this, making the pretence necessary. Can F22 pretend? Probably not. The voice would give her away immediately and shame her for her falseness.

All the same, F22 takes part, too, pulling herself up to a sitting position and saying, 'I had the weirdest dream.'

'What?' Fright puts Proust to one side, and I pretend to have just woken up.

'It went like this. I was on a bus and was reading a book that the voice had recommended borrowing from the library. It was a detective story of some kind. I had to go somewhere far away for as long as the dream lasted. All of a sudden, a father and a son sat down next to me. I can tell immediately that they are from the countryside – their hands are rough, there is a lost look in their eyes. The boy is tiny; his head shaved, his eyes large. About ten years old. But, girls, can you imagine? He has a fluffy white toy kitten in his hands. He cuddles it and presses it to him like a girl, but he is actually quite manly, like his dad. So there he is, squeezing his cat and looking out of the window. Such a big boy to have a cuddly toy. At first I thought he was probably soft in the head, a simpleton . . . And then my voice spoke up. "Rejoice, you fool, that there are boys such as he in the world!" she said, which totally blew me away.'

F22 falls silent and looks from me to Fright.

We drag ourselves to breakfast in silence, I give my porridge to F22, and everything is just the same as usual, only F22 is unusually pensive.

'Do you have children?' Fright nudges F22 with her elbow.

'Hush!' F22 puts her finger to her lips and looks around warily. 'Keep your voice down so the voice doesn't hear! She can't have children, so I don't like to talk about it. It's painful for her. Yes, I have a son. He's nineteen.'

'Aha,' Fright and I both nod.

'And what about you?' F22 looks at me.

'So, we can speak about children then?'

'Yes, yes, of course. The voice doesn't care about other people's children.'

'I have twins. A boy and a girl.'

'Oh my God, you've got twins! How exciting!' Fright exclaims loudly, her voice carrying right across the dining hall. 'Tell us about them. Isn't that lovely?'

'What do you want to know, Fright?'

'I don't know, tell us everything!'

'Every Saturday we drive to our house in the countryside. We chat the whole time in the car. The twins hate silence.'

'Mum, where did you put those pies?'

'Sweet or savoury?'

'Either. We're hungry.'

Our children save everything for later. Even at the cinema they save their popcorn until the film actually starts. 'Is this our film starting? Do you think it's getting darker?' One of our little traditions. Driving to the country, they quietly wait for us to pass the sign with the name of the city crossed through with a red line so they can start eating the buns we bought and pop open their Cokes.

Incredibly patient.

'Pass me a meat pie,' my husband says, quietly salivating.

From rustling paper I unwrap a pie resembling a layered tricorn hat, like those worn by French artillery. I don't eat meat myself. The inside of the car smells of boiled mince. I picture the brains of an artillery soldier inside the triangle, grey and stupid.

'Do you know what meat is in that pie?' I turn to the twins who are sitting squeezed together on the back seat.

'We don't care. We are eating poppy-seed buns.'

'They mince up hearts, boil brains, chop up spleens, mix in some pancreas, but they leave out liver as that tastes odd . . .'

Silence fills the car, then the air cracks with a retching sound. Silence, then another retch. They are twins, after all! My husband hits the brakes sharply. A couple more silences and a couple more retches.

Fifteen minutes later we are back on the road, leaving by the roadside a heap of tissues and a scrunched-up vomit-filled copy of the 'true-life' gossip magazine *Patiesā Dzīve*.

'What did you do that for?' my husband asks.

'Because she doesn't eat meat.' The twins answer for me.

The world outside the windscreen changes, exposing me like photographic film, wiping out all that is superfluous. That is everything. Nature takes a photograph of our car and stores the image in her memory; she has known us all along, from the very beginning, but has got to know us better over the last twelve years since we've been going to our country cottage – observing as we go every felled tree, every haystack, every fox squashed by the roadside, every pothole caused by the sharp frost. We will never be able to caress every centimetre of this love-and-bun-filled road because we are not ready to devote our whole lives to it. We must educate each other and then die.

'Hey, what's that?' My husband is slowing down. In the distance there is a dark patch on the road. 'There must be roadworks.'

The car draws up to it slowly. Everyone leans forward. What a great game – who will be the first to identify it.

'It's a pile of sand,' my boy twin says.

'No way. It's an enormous tree.' I feel my daughter's breath on my neck.

The twins have poor eyesight; the doctors say it's a common defect in children nowadays. Many can't see further than their own aura. Ours are lucky that they can distinguish a pile of sand from a tree and one another.

'It's a dead animal.' My husband stops the car.

'What kind of animal?' the twins exclaim, almost in unison, and jump out of the car.

A brown, warm mound swells between the two streams of traffic, right on the white line down the middle. The children and my husband have already circled the giant to see his face and how he died. I just see a huge back and a flow of blood that, in a thick stream, is running from one side of the road to the other. A tear wells up. I wipe it away so the others don't see, like when I ran to the bathroom to cry at the end of *Titanic* while the others wondered out loud if freezing to death was painful or not. It's my nerves; they make me cry.

'Mum, come here. Look. He's so beautiful!' my girl twin calls out to me.

'Has he been hit on the head?'

'No, Dad. He must have been knocked quite a distance, been killed on impact; all his organs have been crushed.'

'Yes, but why is blood leaking out of his mouth?'

The moment you feel like killing someone or calling them names, count backwards from twenty. It helps. I bury my face in the fur of the dead animal and count. At seventeen I reflect on the difference in smell between a dead animal and a live one, at ten I admit that I've never actually smelled a living forest animal, at three I hear a heartbeat.

'Get away from it! It could be full of corpse poison.' My husband is standing next to me but does not touch me.

'Do they poison corpses with corpse poison?' My daughter steps back from the animal.

'Idiot, a corpse can't be poisoned.' My son hugs his sister. Then he crosses his hands behind his back and slowly circles the dead animal. 'Corpse poison is a mixture of substances appearing when amino acids break down. Lysine develops into cadaverine . . .'

'How do you know all that?'

'A friend of a friend of mine has joined a group of cemetery desecrators. They have their own webpage, so now I know quite a bit about corpses.'

'Gross.' My daughter shrugs the hand off her shoulder that her twin brother has placed there.

'What do these cemetery desecrators do?' My husband joins the conversation.

'Take an interest in corpses.' My son shrugs his shoulders.

'Just like a computer virus?'

'In some ways the two are comparable. The Troy virus might be compared with the flesh of a cadaver that the cemetery desecrators fry and then add to their parents' and teachers' stews. The virus, like the cadaver flesh, mocks and humiliates its consumer.'

For the fifth time now I'm trying to tell my family that the beast's heart is beating, but they are too engrossed in their heated debate about corpses. My husband has crossed the road to the other side where he squats down and throws up.

'Cut it out, Dad! It's not easy to dig the corpses up, not to mention secretly frying them and adding them to food.'

'He is alive. His heart is beating . . .' I gather my strength and shout as loud as I can.

'Mum is having a flash of one of her visions.' My daughter bends towards her brother's ear while their dad is wiping his mouth with dandelion leaves.

'Don't use words if you don't understand what they mean.'

'Everyone knows what *vision* means.' My daughter stands her ground.

'Well, speaking of flashes, Mum doesn't look flashy at all. She hasn't for years.'

'Meaning that people having visions are not flashy . . .' my daughter mumbles to herself while her brother puts two fingers to the enormous animal's neck.

'And what do you think you'll do if the thing is still alive?' My husband, his arms crossed in front of his chest, is leaning against our car.

The animal's body is silent. There is a moment when it seems to me that the giant moves his ear, but, no, it's a vision caused by the wind. I would like to think that my family is a vision as well, created by me. Having visions and being flashy is a form of happiness.

'I wonder if he's edible?' My son circles the beast thoughtfully.

Nobody answers him.

'He is alive,' I say and sit down on the rough sun-warmed asphalt.

My husband gets into the car. 'Let's get going.'

We follow. We have always followed each other.

Through the rear window I look the beast in the face. My lips say sorry, sorry, sorry, sorry until the beast turns into a heap of sand or a fallen tree, an outline of a dark figure in the distance, a puzzle for other passengers in passing cars.

The twins babble away in the back seat.

'Too bad, we should have taken him. We could have made shashlik out of him.'

'Well, I'm not sure. Maybe Mum was right and he was alive.'

'Shall we turn back?' My husband is stepping on the brake.

'No!' the twins roar. '*Finding Prince Charming* starts in half an hour . . .'

A care assistant enters the room and leads me away. It's time for me to go to see the doctor. In any place other than a hospital Fright and F22 would have attacked anyone taking me by the hand and leading me away at the most interesting point of my story. But they do no more than follow me pitifully with their eyes. While I'm putting on my dressing-gown Fright scribbles something on a piece of paper and presses it into my hand as I pass her bed. 'I hope they don't put you in the "electric chair" and turn you into a vegetable. I want to hear more.'

'Where are we going?' I ask the care assistant.

'To the electric chair!' She smiles, and I can't work out why.

We go to an unfamiliar corridor on the floor below us. Rumour has it that all the incognito patients are brought from the second floor where there is a room where they attach electrodes to your head and give you a good bolt of electricity. They say it's a cleansing machine, shovelling up all the snow covering the paths in your brain to help keep you from going off-road. When necessary, electrodes can clog the pathways for ever. Afterwards, it takes you years to head off down another path.

'I don't want to go in there,' slips from my lips.

The fat woman stops and stares at me, questioningly. Her hands clench into fists. Her chest clenches into a fist. Her eyes are drawn into fists.

I have no choice but to turn around and run.

Now I'm stretched out on the floor of the corridor. Fatty has pinned my hands behind my back, and I feel an immense force flowing through her body. I remember the four-eyed Paedo. And I remember that there is always someone more powerful than us out there, radiating their force as they kick us, take us from behind, don't give back our hard-earned cash, always ahead of us in the present. Power is like that.

My whole life flashes before my eyes, but not because I'm about to die; it's just that my whole life there has always been someone over me: my husband, because he has so much money; my children, because they are younger, cleverer and more beautiful; friends, because they have more freedom; teachers, policeman, salespeople, airline pilots, priests, ticket controllers, photographers, judges, presidents, doctors . . .

Fatty pulls me to my feet as if I weigh nothing, shoves me to the door, mocks me and pushes me into the room.

'She flew into a rage,' she explains apologetically, looking at the doctor sitting behind the desk. I don't see an electric chair anywhere. The only wires in the room run to a mobile-phone charger.

The doctor, a man in his fifties, nods, and the fat care assistant leaves the room.

'So, madam, can you tell me what set you off?' He smiles and makes his blue eyes bulge, as if he thought he appeared kindlier that way.

'I wanted to run away . . .'

'Aha, and where were you planning on running to then?' The doctor speaks like a man who has never had and will never have children. In this case, I am clearly the child. Or maybe he thinks I have poor vision and hearing.

I give an honest reply. 'The fat care assistant told me she was taking me to the electric chair.'

The doctor smiles, and his smile bears a great resemblance to the care assistant's.

'Do you always believe what everyone says?' He comes closer and gently pushes me towards the free chair. Gently, gently.

'But she . . .'

'Well, the woman made a mistake. A mistake, you understand? The problem with patients suffering with their nerves is that they always believe everything they are told. You see, if you lived all alone – like Robinson Crusoe, for example – on a lonely island somewhere, you wouldn't have any problem with your nerves.'

'Robinson Crusoe was made up by a writer, and, anyway, he had Friday . . .'

'Of course, of course, but don't you think the author was trying to say something to all of us when he wrote that novel?'

'Yes. He wanted to say that you should never trust anybody and that sooner or later you'll be dragged home by your hair.'

The doctor pulls a file with my name on it from the shelf. He goes through the pages in silence.

'So you don't like to trust anyone and think that anyone who wants to help you is actually against you?' The doctor puts on his glasses and squints at me over the top of them.

'Not really, no . . . I just . . . it seems to me that Robinson Crusoe didn't want to go back to his old home, just as many people leave and don't want to return, but they are coaxed, tempted, tied down –'

'But at your age you should realize that a family is the very centre of everything, a core value.' The doctor, licking his index finger every so often, is still going through my clinical records. 'And if someone wishes to leave the ones who love her there is something seriously wrong with her. Maybe a childhood trauma? In your file, madam, it states that a green crow appears to you, and your family is not happy about that. A colleague passed your file on to me. I am not a psychiatrist but a psychologist, and I would like to help you by talking things over and giving advice. Do you understand?'

'Could you call the Crow back then?'

'What? What do you mean by *back*?'

'You must understand . . . the Crow has gone, and I'm miserable and I'm depressed . . .'

'I see . . .' The doctor hastily jots something down. 'My colleague has told me how your crow appeared, but please tell me now how she disappeared from your life!'

'The first time?'

'Oh, so the creature has left and come back more than once?'

'Yes.'

'All right, tell me.'

I recount how both my grandparents had died, together at the same time. I lie.

'How? Do you have grandparents?' the twins ask after my announcement.

'Not any more,' I answer. I don't want to hurt them. If I told them that Biku-Bē had died they would fight to come with me and weep for a week at least; Biku-Bē was very dear to them. Biku-Bē is a creature comprising both my grandpa and grandma. Biku is my grandma and Bē is my grandpa. But our children don't know the word *grandparents*; they live in another era.

My husband is not surprised that two old people died at the same time.

'It happens,' he says and clutches his half-empty beer can even tighter. 'Go tomorrow, though. It's all over now, and you'll change nothing.' He stands at a safe distance, as if the death of my relatives is infectious or as if mourning them is something dirty. He doesn't hug or embrace me, maybe because I'm not actually crying – because I have made up my grandparents' death. 'I've had four beers and can't get behind the wheel, otherwise I'd have driven you . . .' he says, and a feeling of joy pours into me like a hot, sticky, bluish contrast liquid.

I feel slightly ashamed of lying to my family like this. My husband will never check the facts, he will not call my surviving relatives, he will not offer his condolences; he doesn't even know the names of my mum and dad, grandma and grandpa. He has only ever met my dad three times and my mum about eight times – at her insistence. To my family, the only important thing is my presence; all other events – deaths included – don't matter.

'What were your grandparents like, and why don't we know them?' the twins ask. My husband wants to add something, but I step on his foot.

'I'm allowed not to answer that because I'm so sad,' I say and adjust the strap of my backpack. My husband pulls out his wallet and opens it, spreading the banknote compartment wide for me to choose the most pleasantly coloured one for my bus ticket. I choose the light-brown one so I'll have enough for two bottles of wine.

I look back at my family and leave. 'Muuum! Muuuum . . .' I hear my children roaring. I stop. The twins' voices come to me on the wind. 'What did they die of?'

'Your great-granddad died of boredom, and your great-grandma died because your great-granddad did. Boredom is infectious!' The twins exchange glances and don't ask any more questions. I continue walking away.

The road is dusty and fragrant, the house shrinks in size in the distance, and soon it becomes a red spider, then a red grain of sand and, finally, all that's left is the fact that I know that the house exists, and my sand-children and sand-husband with his sand-money and sand-watch on his left wrist all live there.

A dog with a bloody nose and joyful eyes tangles around my legs. A neighbour is skinning a pig in front of his house. I want to stop and watch, see where the butchers hang up their blood-stained aprons when they finish, see how they pinch their grand-children's cheeks, how they will be wading through pig entrails left uneaten by the dogs for days to come. How? How do they live and how do they die? When he sees me, my neighbour stops scraping out the pig's belly. He, too, wants to watch – to see where the mother of a family is off to without her children, without her husband, to see how the mothers of families live and how they die. This is the second time in fifteen years that I have gone past my neighbour's house on my own with a backpack.

I get a lift to Riga from a free-spirited bassist in a country band.

'Where are we off to then? Aren't you afraid of hitching by yourself?' he asks.

'I've run away from my family,' I tell him.

'What?' His eyes bulge.

'Just for the day.' I smile at him.

'It's not that serious then.' He smiles, too.

So I'm taken home by a free-spirited man, a bassist in a country band.

It's dark outside. On the velvety asphalt of the narrow street my steps make a quiet scraping sound; the corner of our house emerges in the yellow warmth of the outside light. I feel that such serene beauty will cause my third eye to open in the back of my head. In the supermarket carrier bag the wine bottles have tipped over each other the wrong way – a 2006 Tokay over a bottle of Kagor, a Bulgarian dessert wine. The bottles clinking together have an effect – my third eye drops, and I find myself standing in the porch. I prop the bag up against the wall and go in search of the big stone three steps away – beneath the stone is a box, holding a wrapped-up key. As I put the key in the lock I remember that our house has an alarm system, but it's too late, the fanfares of horror roar full blast over fifty thousand square kilometres, levelling all disagreements, service ranks, heights and genders. The light goes on in the neighbouring building, and naked male and female chests, pretty and drooping, are pressed against the windows.

'We're not under atomic attack, sorry,' I say and push the bag of wine deeper into the hallway. Anxiety sweeps over me, followed shortly afterwards by the arrival of four giants in black uniform, as tall as skyscrapers, with guns in their holsters and sunflower seeds in their moustaches.

'Who are you? Why are you here? Where are your papers and your accomplices? What calibre of gun do you have in your pocket? What time is it? Has anyone got a cigarette?'

'It's my husband's house. I ran away from my family. I have no documents. My accomplices are in the countryside. I have a weapon in my plus-size bra. I will not give you a cigarette.' The truth isn't enough for them, they need something more – taking me to the police station, for instance – but I want my wine. The door is wide open. I want the skyscrapers to get lost.

'Can you prove that you live here?' the heaviest of them asks me, distrust in his voice.

'Yes,' I tell him and extend my hand that holds the shiny key.

'You found that under the big stone, didn't you?' the smallest skyscraper interrogates me.

'Yes.'

The skyscrapers get cross and then burst out laughing; again the light goes on in the neighbouring houses and chests are glued to the windows once more.

'That's no proof; the only proof is the code to turn off the alarm,' the middle skyscraper says. 'Thieves don't know codes so they have crowbars and skeleton keys.'

'My husband knows all the codes in the world. All codes off by heart,' I say.

'So why the fuck don't you know them? You, your husband's wife?' thunders the fourth, the quietest skyscraper.

I give an honest answer. 'Because I never go anywhere, and we are not officially married.' The skyscrapers back off, adjust their holsters, light up cigarettes. 'You should have said straight away that you were a housewife.'

I feel confused, which translates into my looking down at my shoes – scuffing a hole in the soft mud.

'I'm not a housewife, I'm a woman,' I finally manage to utter, but they have already gone.

The bedroom lights in the neighbouring houses go out, the kitchen lights in the neighbouring houses go on. The hall light in my house goes out, the kitchen light in my house goes on.

'Aaaaaaaaaaaaaaaaaaaaaaaaaaaaaaaaaaaah!' I scream, and anyone else seeing what I saw would do the same.

'So, what did you see?'

'The Green Crow.'

'Why did you scream then?'

'She hadn't appeared for fifteen years. I thought she'd died. It's like a warrior coming back from war, turning up years after the war is over ... You, too, doctor, would scream – but for entirely different reasons.'

'All right, I do understand. My son also left home and showed up married with five kids ten years later. I screamed that time, too. However, it wasn't clear from your story why you lied about your grandparents' death. One shouldn't lie about death.'

'Yes, of course, I agree with you about that, but you'll find out later ... My husband was terribly jealous. He wouldn't let me out of the house alone not even for a couple of hours. When our children were little, while they were at nursery, I used to ride my bicycle a lot. My husband didn't like it, and he wouldn't speak to me for days, weeks even, if he didn't like something. I begged him, I cried for him to talk to me, but he just turned his back on me and pretended I wasn't there. The reason I never went anywhere was because I wanted peace and quiet at home, to be loved and have someone who would talk to me. But that time I lied about my grandparents' death I just had to get away, do you understand? No other excuse for my absence from home would suffice – only a death. My husband disliked my parents and grandparents intensely, and my friends, and everything I did, so I knew for sure that he wasn't going to call anyone and check whether they were dead or alive. He wouldn't go to the funeral either, because he doesn't like to look at the dead. And, you know, doctor, I didn't have that many friends or relatives who might have conveniently died so I could get away from my family. It was a bit of a one-off.'

'So, how did it all end up?'

'At the beginning it was all fine, but then . . .'

'Tell me!'

That evening the Crow and I talk at great length about life, and I tell her about my awful lies. I am not the sort of person who tells lies as a matter of course. The Crow listens to my story and gives me some advice.

The following morning I go to the secondhand shop and buy a black dress. I cry. The Crow says I should cry so I look like a person returning from a funeral. Should I run out of tears, she advises me to imagine that my grandparents really have died. Whatever happens, it won't make me a total fraudster.

I pick up the phone and call. My grandma answers.

'Get over here immediately,' she says. 'Your grandpa has gone completely nuts. He's going on about the meaning of life . . . I can't listen to any more of it, on and on about the meaning of life – as if it matters. I think I'll take some pills and do myself in . . .'

'Can you die from taking pills?' I ask.

'A lot of pills are like a lot of weeds. They finish off the potatoes.'

'When are you going to take them?' I ask.

'There's some leftover roast beef in the fridge, absolutely

delicious . . . Let's eat that, and then I'll take those pills and top myself. That way the old baboon can carry on searching for the meaning of life.'

'You're not thinking of giving him some pills, too, are you?' I ask.

'Have you been drinking again?' my grandma whispers into the receiver.

'No', I say, 'it's sorrow – I buried two people today.'

'Is that so? Who?' My grandma's voice is brimming with interest.

'They lived together for many years and died together on the same day by poisoning each other. Bye.'

I finish the conversation and, to prevent myself from telling any more lies, I turn my phone off. All you have to do to stop yourself lying is to stop talking. It's probably one of the finest art forms there is – stopping talking when you still have something to say.

It wouldn't be so bad if Grandma went ahead and poisoned Grandpa and then herself. They are very old and yell at each other the whole time. What kind of existence is that – being old and yelling all the time? I love them very much; no one else would wish them dead. Once my grandma cried and asked me what she could do to help. Back then I didn't realize that she would have saved me from lying today if she had, in fact, poisoned herself and Grandpa. But that really would have been too big an ask, even when life is utterly senseless and death inevitable. No good deed comes without added conditions.

There is a school and a children's playground close to our home. I'll wait there. Yes, I'll sit right here for an hour exactly and wait, watching the dirty, cheerful, happy, beautiful children. I'll entice them over with fluorescent lollipops and tell them the truth about life.

'Hey, little guy, come over here!'

'What's up?' The boy spits some pretty stones into his hand; he'd found them on the ground.

'Did you know that one day you will die and be laid out in a coffin and will never come here again? You will leave all the love you have gathered in this world and all your money and everything else to others . . .'

'It's my turn on the swing,' the boy cries and runs off. I see how he takes hold of the seat on the swing with its brightly coloured ropes, how he smiles, completely forgetting all about death and, even if he hasn't forgotten, laughing in its face. Now it's another child's turn, and the boy jumps off the swing and rolls in the sand. I sit down by his side.

'Sweetheart, is there nothing you are afraid of?'

'I'm afraid of the dark.' The boy stops kicking the sand.

I lean towards his ear. 'Then let me tell you this: death is darkness.'

The little boy jumps up and, wailing, lurches away from me. His mother is sitting behind the trees. I see the boy pointing his finger at me and wailing even louder. His mum, a beautiful woman in her thirties, drops her magazine on the bench and walks over to me.

'I'm going to call the police.' She stops a safe distance from me – I might well be mad and could possibly infect her with rabies, which is incurable and would result in death. 'Why did you tell my son that he is going to die?'

'But he is going to die. I didn't tell a lie.'

'He's too young . . .'

Meanwhile, the boy has quietly snuck up to his mother and is clutching at her jumper.

'Little boy, do you know how you were born?' I take advantage of the momentary silence.

'The stork brought me.' He takes a step forward, sure of himself.

'There is no death,' I lied. 'The stork brought you and the stork will take you away.' I shake the sand off my dress. The boy smiles. There is no death. And as for storks – there are no storks in this part of the countryside. And, if there were, his mother would have shot them all out of the sky.

My phone is silent. My grandparents live. People do their shopping. Dogs are put down. Aeroplanes are filled with fuel. Someone is born. The homeless are fed. Prisoners rape new inmates. Nothing changes in life. My family is waiting for me.

My husband's car is parked next to the house. They are at home. Shame.

'Where have you been?' they exclaim almost in unison as soon as I come through the door. My husband, my son.

'You are wearing a black dress,' my daughter says.

'I buried my grandparents, which explains the dress,' I say without looking anyone in the eye.

'Dad, she is lying! I know it! On Wednesdays after *House* we watch *The Theory of Lies*, and they showed exactly what someone looks like when they're lying.'

I have already mentioned that my son was very clever.

'You were at the funeral, weren't you?' My husband has picked up some of my son's sagacity.

'I borrowed the dress from a friend . . .'

'It suits you.'

'Thank you.'

'Very well.'

'Well.'

'What are we going to have for dinner? The children have been living off sandwiches for two days.'

'I'm not hungry.'

'But we are,' they scream.

Without taking off my dress, I start cooking. Everybody is hungry; they are sitting around the big kitchen table, watching in silence as I peel the potatoes. I'm silent, too. I take a large chunk of meat out of the freezer, throw it in the sink and run hot water over it. My son looks at the slab.

'Dad, do you have a lot of money?'

'What do you need it for?' My husband fumbles in his inside jacket pocket.

'I have a business idea!'

You only start living when you know you are going to die. At least one person in the world has come to understand that today. The little boy in the playground will have a hard time living in fear of storks and darkness, but nothing can be done about that. He has begun to live.

I would like my family to start living, too, to fear God and retribution, death. But they have no time. All three of them are leaning in around the table, eagerly discussing the new business plan proposed by my clever son.

'You simply have to buy a freezer and post stuff online!' My son is nearly shouting.

'But there's no space. Where are we going to put it?'

'We'll empty out a room. We've got too many anyhow.'

'That would look a bit suspect. No one will trust us.' My husband holds his head in his hard-working, clever hands.

'Things like that usually take place in basements . . .' My daughter, too, is often quite perspicacious.

'Cool! Life is sacred!' my husband and my son exclaim.

I fry the defrosted meat, dipped in egg and breadcrumbs. I fry and enjoy this moment when, for the first time in fifteen years, my husband is talking to my son the way people should. Never mind the fact that they are talking business, never mind that this business involves freezing living people, never mind that all these frozen sick people are going to lie in the cold-storage room under our house awaiting better times when people who haven't been frozen will have discovered some antigen against cancer and other yet-to-be-discovered bugs. Good luck with that! Let them have something in common so they can finally become a father and son, let them be united by the vain hopes of strangers, by money. I'm going to sleep . . .

. . . And I'm taking a cart loaded with rubbish across the bridge. I'm throwing rubbish on to the cart on one side of the bridge and disposing of it on the other. I push the cart and watch the sun setting on its far-away, deceptive line. I remember my childhood friend, the literary character Crazy Dauka, who couldn't have been more wrong when he thought he could row right up to the horizon, that he could reach it, that he could simply resolve to do so and enter the sun. He drowned because of his silly ideas. He entered the sun by going the other way, the way absolutely everybody goes. It's quite obvious that there's no other way to reach the sun. Just as there is no other way across the river apart from crossing this stone bridge. I take rubbish from the left bank over to the right, dump it, then gather rubbish on the right bank and take it over to the left, dump it there and pick up what's left on the right bank . . . And so on every morning, as if a sunset without stinking rubbish was an absolute impossibility. Have I deceived the gods in my wish to escape death?

'Look, you dropped a Maxima shopping bag.' I hear a very familiar voice at my back.

'So what?' I answer without turning around.

'If Sisyphus had let his boulder run back down the hill it would have been the end of him!'

'He was done for anyhow . . .'

'I wouldn't say so. He was the happiest person on earth. Pick up that bag!'

I turn around, and my back is wet with nervous sweat. The Green Crow.

'Wake up, please. I can't have a proper conversation with the sun rising to my right and your rubbish bin stinking right under my beak.'

I open my eyes. Darkness and warmth surround me. I hear voices downstairs, see a smouldering glow in the corner of the room.

'If we are in our house . . .' says the Crow.

'. . . then we won't be allowed to smoke. How did you get in? What do you want from me? And keep your voice down so my husband doesn't hear you . . .' There are times when it seems that it is actually the Crow who is the father of my clever son, and that my daughter ended up in my body accidentally.

'Yes, they are the questions I would like to ask you.'

The Crow strikes a lighter, and I suddenly see her beak, which smells of bone.

'Don't worry, it's an e-cigarette. My friends gave it to me so I don't get lung cancer. The magic lighter serves no practical purpose, it just warms my soul. I got in through your daughter's window

– I tore my cape, but my wings are fine. Your idiot husband and children are all downstairs, discussing their business plan and posting ads for opportunities for eternal life. They are otherwise engaged,' the Crow caws, sneering. 'They have named their new company Lazarus Ltd. They might as well call it Jesus_Christ. He wouldn't take offence and the name would have carried far more weight. Nowadays youngsters searching online for ways to freeze or do in their elderly relatives wouldn't even know who Lazarus was, whereas everyone's heard of Jesus –'

'Crow, what do you want?' I cut the Crow short mid-sentence, hoping she won't take offence.

'Nothing in particular. I came to see you. I heard you'd done well for yourself.'

'Please, go away.'

'Do you remember our last meeting through that barred window?'

'Don't!'

'I can't face New Year if we haven't sorted things out between us, OK?'

'But it's only June!'

'It is. But for us crows New Year is in July according to the Chinese calendar, in August according to the Jewish calendar, in September according to the Christian calendar, in October according to the Orthodox calendar and in April according to the skylark calendar! Over the space of a year, us crows don't have much time to make peace. You humans will never understand that.'

'We haven't quarrelled.'

The Crow pulls a candle out of her cape pocket, strikes a light and fixes it to my husband's expensive mahogany table by dripping wax on to the surface.

'In the days when you didn't have to wipe your children's princely bottoms clean. Do you remember the morning you woke up in jail?'

'I've never been in jail.'

'Well, we still have quite a way to go before that!' The Crow rises from her chair and paces the room, back and forth, her wings folded behind her. 'Have you got a drop of mulled wine maybe? Merlot or a Bordeaux would do just as nicely.'

There will only be wine downstairs if my husband and children, in the heat of their animated business talk, haven't already necked the lot. Having your mind full of money-making matters seems to wipe out all other thoughts – it's the best form of meditation. If I nip downstairs now and bring a bottle of wine up to our bedroom, my husband will accuse me of being an alcoholic – only alcoholics wake in the middle of the night and reach for a bottle. If I don't go downstairs, the Crow will get in a huff.

'Wait here,' I say, not trusting her in the least. The Crow is the sort to blithely cross the boundaries of commonly accepted norms of conduct without the slightest prick to her conscience. It's her feminine side.

My family is sitting at the table surrounded by dirty dishes, cold potatoes and my ashtrays. They are peering at the screen of the laptop and chiselling away on a sheet of white paper with their pens.

'How many years are we going to freeze them for?' my daughter pipes up.

'Ten years on the budget package,' my son says.

'And on the most expensive package?'

'A hundred,' their father replies.

'We won't live that long ourselves!'

I sneak up to the table. I'm invisible, inaudible, but I want to say this – or rather plead it – just the same. 'I would like to have grandchildren,' I say loudly, without really knowing why. As it happens, I don't want grandchildren at all. I don't like children. My husband and children turn their heads.

'That is what you need to do.' My husband looks at our children, his eyes gleaming.

'Have children so Mum can raise them to continue our business. Besides, she once told me that she felt her life was meaningless. Let's help her out!'

'Ugh, I don't want to have children, but if I have to help Mum . . .' my daughter grimaces.

'Makes no difference to me, but if Mum raises them and it helps give meaning to her life . . .' my son says.

I go to the wine, schnapps, brandy, whisky cupboard and withdraw two bottles of merlot. I pour a river of red into a pan, throw in some spices and warm it through.

'Mum, you won't make much of a grandma if you drink,' my son muses.

My husband runs me up and down with his eyes, his look a cold blue. Steam rises from the pool of wine, and I take the pan off the hob, pick up two mugs and leave.

'Why did you take two mugs?' my son calls to my back.

I stop in my tracks and, for some reason, feel angry. 'Has it ever crossed your mind that one mug might break and then I would have nothing to drink from? There's two of you, you and your sister, in case one of you dies. Nature has been kind to us, your dad and me, and I'm kind to myself. I make sure I don't have to stagger back downstairs and get another mug if that one falls and smashes. I can't drink wine straight from the pan! Don't they teach you anything at school?'

The family falls really, really quiet. They don't know that there's nothing wrong with wine straight from the pan.

The Crow has settled herself comfortably in our bed, an e-cigarette glowing in her wingtips, the sheets dirty, the air smelling of bird.

'Finally!' The Crow snatches the steaming pan from my hands.

'Why do you smell of hummingbirds?' I ask.

'It's in vogue this year. Big birds always want to appear smaller and small birds bigger. Small birds get chased by big ones, but big birds get shot down by humans. I never know which is worse. Big birds use the scent of small ones, and tiny birds go crazy for the scent of sea eagles or eagle owls. What kind of scent would you prefer?'

'Stop talking crap, I'm not a bird . . . What did you want to tell me?'

The Crow dips her beak in the steaming pan, then wipes it clean under her wing. 'Hen scent would suit you pretty well.'

'Hens aren't real birds.'

'Exactly. Hens don't live in the wild, and they never know when their owner is going to take a knife and cut their heads off. Without a cock hens find no meaning in their lives; they don't see light without light!' The Crow falls back on to the bed, crosses her legs, takes a drag on her plastic cigarette and somehow stares serenely into my face.

'If a hen runs away from her owner she ends up in a fox's belly. Tell me, why are you here?'

'I miss you and want you to apologize to me for what happened sixteen years, two months and four days ago. If you don't, I'll continue to experience intermittently a sense of inferiority, despite knowing how wonderful I am. So, tell me, how wonderful am I?'

'You are wonderful, of course, but I can't see you any more. Your being wonderful is contagious, and I can't be wonderful – I have to be miserable for my family to love me. Wonderful people are not loved; happiness is despised. I was happy once, but then all my loved ones grew unhappy. You have to be incredibly egotistical to keep on being happy when everyone around you is unhappy. Try smiling at a funeral – go on, just try it!'

The Crow hasn't taken her eyes off me throughout my speech, her beak hard and immobile. 'You need to apologize, and then we can carry on with all your nonsense.'

'What do I need to apologize for?'

'Do you remember that morning when the forest thrushes gathered in front of your house, watching the young earthworms that had crawled between the paving stones? That morning, as the sun rose, it caught on the oldest apple tree and snapped off a branch, but later you decided it had been the wind that caused the damage. You didn't believe it was the rising sun. Remember? A pair of storks flew over your house in search of a place to build their nest, but you didn't notice them at all. Greenfinches, bullfinches, redwings? All of them fussed around the barred windows of your house, begging you to look at them. The Green Crow was there as well. She checked over every square centimetre of the house, looking for a crack, a hole, that you – her best friend – denied her, because you had started your new life.'

How can a bird make so much out of nothing? You shouldn't take her too seriously. It was nothing. Just a minor incident – nothing more. 'I didn't have the keys, and the windows were barred, that's all. I couldn't let you in! Your beak got stuck between the bars wrought by a great artist, but none of it was my fault. It was the artist's fault – he had made the bars so strong. Then you started screeching like the Devil himself, the kind of sound that could unhinge a person. I was scared.'

'You sawed off my beak because you feared for your life!'

'I'm sorry.'

'How could any bird forgive someone who sawed off their beak?'

'I told you, I'm sorry.'

The day that the Crow showed up and got her beak stuck between the bars was the first day in our new house. She is always sticking her beak in where she shouldn't, but I couldn't disclose her existence to the man I loved. Keeping secrets from a partner is a betrayal of trust – that much is clear. Besides, I couldn't ruin the beautiful bars, so I sawed off a piece of the Crow's enormous beak instead, which hadn't been made by any great artist. And we escaped from the man I loved. On balance, I thought that the Crow had laid it on a bit thick, screaming in pain like that. Can bone hurt? Bone is not skin. Bone is not a heart.

'Did it hurt?'

'In the same way it hurts if a piece of flesh is torn from you; but you wouldn't know about that, as nothing has ever been torn from you, you've just been grown on. Abscesses don't hurt as much; they just fester and stink.' The Crow stops speaking and dips her beak in the cooled mulled wine.

'Is there any more?' She turns her red beak towards me.

'Yes, but . . .'

'Please, for old time's sake!'

'You are not speaking Bible-talk. Remember how you spoke Bible-talk that time you got drunk and were totally straight with me? It would be nice if you spoke in verse again, like in the Bible.'

'No, I can't do that any more. I've become a Buddhist.'

What a shame that the Crow has converted to Buddhism. I pick up the pan and go. No, I can't refuse the Crow, whose beak I sawed off in the foolishness of youth, I just can't. I go, step, crawl to the wine, schnapps, brandy, whisky cupboard in the kitchen. Dawn is about to break.

My children and husband are still engrossed in their conversation about corpses.

'We should definitely get a doctor on board. People tend to believe doctors, just like policemen and opera singers. Any ideas?' My son is jotting something down on a piece of paper.

'Mum's coming . . .' my daughter mumbles and looks at me. Everyone is looking at me, and even I start to look at myself.

They are talking to me. No, they are talking *at* me. They call me a drunk. They wonder why it is that I take no interest in their business, why it is that I am only capable of spending money earned by others. They are fond of me all the same. I make delicious pancakes, and they forgive me everything. If only I would stop drinking, as I have the parents' meeting to attend at school tomorrow and my mouth will stink of booze, etc. They love me and so on and so on.

I pour the Crow some wine, etc.

We talk until dawn breaks. I push the Crow out of the window when I hear my husband approaching the room.

The Crow isn't injured; she can fly.

'A fascinating story, but that's enough for today. You may leave.'

The doctor seems hasty and harsh. Thank God he doesn't have electric sea serpents in his room and my snowy paths remain mine.

NOBODY WANTS TO GO TO HELL

Here in the hospital, time is measured as it is in America. From breakfast to lunch, from lunch to dinner, from dinner to breakfast. I'm very confused. Every story about the Crow leaves me stranded outside space and time.

'Let's go to dinner,' I say as I step into the room. The corridor smells of food, and the illusion is saturated by a darker sun.

'Fine . . .' Fright replies, and tears start pouring from her ugly eyes.

'I've already told you . . .' F22 approaches me and pushes me towards the bed.

'What's the matter with you two? Someone die?'

'What's my name?' Fright kneels in front of me.

'And mine?' F22 sits down next to me and puts her arm around my shoulders.

'Fright and F22,' I say.

'Where are you?' Fright is sobbing.

'In the nuthouse, of course.'

F22 goes over to Fright, hugs her, and they both start weeping loudly.

'The care assistant told us you would be brought back in a wheelchair and would be a completely changed. A vegetable . . . And then . . . and it would have been dreadful if we never got to hear the rest of your story about the twins and the Green Crow. We would have risked dying of boredom, do you realize that?'

'I do. Once I almost died of boredom while stuck between four walls.'

'With the Crow?'

'No. You can't die of boredom when you're with the Crow. It was a very long time ago, at a time when the Crow had stopped coming to visit me . . .'

We are driving. It's dark. It's drizzling, warm rain, the drops falling and dripping incessantly down the windows. A quarter of an hour ago I asked where we were headed, and he answered that it was a big surprise. I've known him just two months, but already I trust him. Maybe he is taking me somewhere to kill me. That would be a big surprise, for sure! Like every other regular person, I'm afraid of pain, cancer, the dark, angry dogs, aeroplane crashes, heart attacks, bailiffs; everything that might result in death. Yes, I'm afraid of death. Only of death.

We met in March, the time when all regular people meet. He was a wealthy man, a businessman; I was just a girl not wearing a bra. That day I was going to a shop to buy some potatoes so I didn't die of starvation; he was riding his bike so he didn't die of boredom. And that is how we saved each other's lives, just as people do. Later he admitted that he had taken me for a hooker and thought it might be interesting to stop and chat with a hooker, something he had never done before. He had thought I'd be an easy lay, seeing as I was walking around braless, possibly knickerless, too, but he got that very wrong. It took four entire days before the moment came when, panting loudly, we merged into a single salvaged life in an Old Town gateway.

I fell in love.

He was married, but I guess he liked me more than his wife, as a month later he got divorced. 'You do realize I got a divorce because of you, don't you?' he said.

'Yes, I do, and I'm delighted that someone has done something because of me. Any regular person would be,' I answered.

So he put his wife's belongings out in the street in a twelve-metre-long shipping container, so she could journey over the sea to hell and never return. His ex-wife begged him and cried, threatened to turn to prostitution as she would never again find a man as good as him, no one would love her so easily and with such stamina, but he would not be moved. Maybe he even hoped that she would indeed become a whore, as that way he could pick her up as a streetwalker and fuck her without the hassle of having to be the least bit gentlemanly.

I carried boxes containing his wife's possessions out to the container that was to be dispatched to hell. Since meeting me he had completely stopped liking his wife, likewise her corals and silks. I didn't put up any opposition. I rather enjoyed browsing through his ex-woman's belongings. There were multi-coloured butterfly-like skirts, hair clips with fine blonde hair caught in the clasps, shoes that didn't fit me – she took a thirty-seven and I a thirty-nine – a half-empty bottle of body lotion, some Venera cream for down below, some jeans that were too tight for me around the waist, art books, hats and knitted socks. That evening I cried. His ex-wife's things were beautiful, sophisticated but all too small for me and therefore out of reach, despite sitting right under my nose in the container outside the house.

Thank God it was set to travel over the sea straight to hell. When the house was put up for sale the container was left right where it was beyond the fence. His ex-wife came around every day, putting on perfume and Venera cream, trying on her hats. In her misery she had become a whore. There was a sign with 'For Sale', written in English, hanging from the balcony, just in case any foreigners happened to drive past; but some wag had sprayed 'Fuck Me' on it in white in the hope that someone might take up the offer.

We lived in his pick-up truck for nearly a month. He bought a mattress to fit in the back when the seats were down. We switched on the radio and made love, drank wine, got out of the car to pee, made love again, went to show the house to prospective buyers as soon as anyone called him.

Three days ago he had sold the house.

'At last we're free,' he said.

We are still driving. Songs are playing on the radio. I don't like this kind of music, but I keep quiet. I always keep quiet if I don't like something, as I don't want to go to hell. I still don't know where he's taking me. We've been driving for two hours straight. It's dark outside. Everything generally recognized as being beautiful – trees, walls, clouds, concrete, colours, women and advertising hoardings – flash past the windscreen. There's only darkness outside. I don't have to see to know.

'Do you love me?' I ask him. Thoughts of death are always closely followed by those of love.

'No, you know what, I don't.'

He is getting upset. And I realize that he does. I calm down and imagine us, hand in hand, dying together in sixty years' time. No, better make it forty – he is fifteen years older than me and might not live that long, men tending to die earlier as they have to work so hard.

We come to a stop.

'Here we are,' he says. I want to get out, but he grabs my hand. And looks at me. And doesn't let me go. And I'm scared.

'What are we doing here?'

He lets me go and shoves his hand in his pocket. I close my eyes.

'Let's go,' he says finally and puts a black blindfold over my eyes. 'Let's go and see what the surprise is!'

We walk hand in hand. Beneath the weight of our feet, snails' homes crack, molehills tremble and branches snap, creating a path for the two of us. I calm down. I believe that at least he will be tender as he kills me, as he loves me he will try.

'You know', I say, 'the stars are shining through the blindfold. They're almost blinding me.'

'Never mind. You are allowed to look at the stars as long as they don't take you away from me,' he says. 'The one blinding you is Sirius, the brightest of all. Children learn about it at school.'

'Oh, right. I did home economics at school not astronomy, so –'

'How about this?' he interrupts. 'Sirius is my star – you need to choose another one for yourself. The Pole Star is pretty cool, too.'

'All right then, I'll take the Pole Star,' I say and am very happy about it. There is an old belief that whenever someone dies a star tumbles from the sky, although I've never heard of the Pole Star falling. It's a shame Sirius is already taken. It's very beautiful and never falls out of the sky either. I still have the blindfold on, and, from this day on, I shall be eternal and never fall.

We continue walking, the stars following us like devoted immortal dogs.

'This is it.' He stops in his tracks and tears the blindfold from my eyes. It's dark, and I can't see a thing. He takes me by the hand, and, as if by magic, a light comes on, flowing along the white seams of brick before disappearing into the expanse of a wall that stretches in both directions.

'What is it?' I ask.

'Surprise!' He waves at the wall. It moves, and a slit opens in the middle of it. Dry light sticks to the wall, but the slit is dark and damp. He pushes buttons on his miraculous remote control, and light pours into the opening, flowing over the path and lawn, revealing a kennel, a fountain and a house with enormous windows like reading glasses.

'You shall stand up there and wait,' he says, pointing up at the balcony and evidently talking nonsense, 'with your plaited hair reaching right down to the ground to help you descend. This is your house now.'

I'm lost for words. At times like this I usually am.

'Let's go and have a look inside your house,' he says and pulls the keys to my house out of his pocket. He unlocks the door and puts the key back in his pocket.

All very sophisticated and airy. Like something out of a film – and not of the worst kind. Maybe my house *is* out of a film? Maybe my house is the film itself – with stone-tiled floors, the kitchen that hasn't yet been messed up, a bar full of bottles, a pool that fills with bubbles at the press of a button, bedrooms with four-poster beds? In this film we will have children – I see a boy and a girl – and a St Bernard who will live in a kennel outside and sometimes mooch through the house with muddy paws, but we will all just laugh because we are happy.

'Will I be allowed to live with you in your house?' He kneels.

'Why?' I ask and look around. Is it possible for life to change like this in the blink of an eye? Other people save up and work until they drop, almost killing themselves, to get a house like this. But me?

'What . . . Why?' His eyes scan my face.

'This house . . . I thought you were taking me into the forest to kill me; that was going to be the surprise. Death always is a surprise, isn't it?'

'Silly girl. I want you to live for ever, with me, in this house. We will have a baby, a daughter who looks just like you, and she will run around the house in a white linen dress, and we will be happy. That's happiness, just as death is a surprise.'

We have only known each other three short months, yet he is already wishing for a daughter who looks like me and for eternal life together. I want to weep. I feel ashamed and don't know how I'll ever be able to repay him. I won't be able to give him a CD bought in the market for his birthday and make *karbonāde* and an apple cake for dessert. I will have to come up with something totally unique, unrepeatable, as expensive as this house. I will do a course in *cordon bleu* cookery and learn to tell a truffle from a dust ball, marjoram from oregano, a salad fork from an everyday one. I will borrow money from the whole wide world and get him a red Ferrari for his birthday. Can I really do it?

'All right,' I say, 'we *will* have a daughter, but she will look like you.'

He disappears off somewhere and comes back bearing a bottle of champagne, which he pours into glasses. We drink it before making love on the sheepskin rug in front of the fire lit by remote control. A couple of times during the night I sense him pushing buttons to add more logs to the fire. They fall from heaven and burn with earthly flames, warming us. When he is asleep, my nipples pinched between his fingers, I gaze at the tongues of fire and ruminate. If this were life, I would wish never to die. How could I separate myself from this house, which over time I would make into a home, from our daughter, who would look so much like her father, from these warm flames? How would I draw my last breath without knowing that it was my last? Such a beautiful house levies the obligation of eternal life. And it's not easy.

No one knows what eternity is, but everyone knows what night is. And the night passes. I wake up alone. He has dressed and covered me with a blanket – without the warmth of his body I'm cold.

'There's food for breakfast in the fridge, coffee on the shelf.' He kisses me tenderly. 'I'll be back this evening.'

There is a thud as the door closes, and my house is a Buddhist temple where the sound of silence can be heard. I run to the window to wave goodbye to my beloved, but, with a loud clunk, bars slide down over the windows – clearly custom-made, a carefully wrought masterpiece.

Soon I don't know what season it is outside; the beautiful bars are overgrown with climbing plants, the sun is shining. The twins had their birthday a couple of days ago, so it must be summer. Yes, definitely, it was summer when the twins were removed. I don't know if it can be considered a birth. With a birth, suffering is endured as it is with a death, but the twins were simply taken out of my incised womb like Caesar and his noble sister. My husband wanted to continue making love to a tight, unstretched vagina and accordingly paid the doctors so the babies would spare their mother and not destroy our sex life.

The day before yesterday was the twins' birthday. The four of us celebrated together. My husband's parents are both dead, but mine are alive. I never invite them to visit. My husband says that outsiders destroy family life – they talk too much and, in turn, make us talk as well. They make us notice, criticize, undo, advise. Who needs that? We know how to live, he says. He's right. My parents are over there, on the edge of a precipice – they stand there and wave at me, both wearing hi-vis jackets so I can see them: my cellular next of kin, chromosome donors, nappy changers, potato peelers, nightshift workers. I wave back at them, shouting to them that one of these days I will learn to take proper care of the climbing plants, cut them back so they can see me through the bars.

'No, not really. It's not as cool as the one with the Crow. It's quite an ordinary story. We all have stories like that to tell. A domineering husband, always putting money first and so on! There's nothing unique in this. Only the thing about the house. How long did he keep you locked in for?' F22 bites into a chocolate bar.

'Until I started hanging out with the Crow, because then the fact that he didn't talk to me any more, that he'd turned his back on me, didn't seem to matter. I had the Crow.'

'What happened when the Crow disappeared?'

'I didn't want to go back to my family. I didn't want to live with them, make meatballs, raise children, do as I was told unquestioningly . . .'

'I beg to differ from what F22 says about there being nothing special about being locked up in a house. It's a violation of human rights.'

'But she wanted it. She doesn't need defending. That would be like saying that it's the brewers' fault if the nation drinks itself to death. It's up to us to choose what we are.'

'What about your voice then? You want a currant bun, but the voice demands a kosher meat pie . . . Is that your choice?'

We are heading towards turning the room upside down – as the discussion becomes increasingly heated, Fright is edging closer to the wall-mounted button used to call the care assistant. That would lead to F22 being sent to a room where there are many more electric wires than those coming from a phone charger. We are saved by Snow White. She speaks for the first time in a week, and we all immediately fall silent.

'My son is in charge of this ward.'

'Then why did he lock you up in here?' F22 is the first to find her voice.

Snow White continues, 'You've got it right about the pancakes and the children. He wants to make pancakes using just one egg and raise his children as he sees fit. Don't you girls agree that pancakes made from one egg will come out tasting of nothing and that children can't be raised by people who are still children themselves?

Fright is fidgeting on the spot, as if wanting to add something but only as far as pancakes are concerned. F22 also becomes restless: the voice would definitely have something to say here. I, however, have never been able to make pancakes.

'So who is the young man who visits you?'

'My other son.' Snow White wriggles on her back, but her arms, bound as they are with tight restraints, do not allow her to turn over.

'Why don't you tell your youngest son all about it?'

'He thinks I'm mad. And his twin is the boss . . . I don't want to hurt the younger one.'

'Twin brothers? Good heavens! They don't resemble each other in the least,' Fright exclaims.

'The younger one's hair is longer and he has a moustache. Other than that, they are as alike as two peas in a pod.'

It is as if by thinking of him the three of us have summoned Snow White's younger son. He comes in, followed by a fresh breeze that seems to have impregnated his grey overcoat. He sits down next to his mother's bed. He asks, 'How are you doing?'

'I'm fine, son,' Snow White answers.

'Do you need anything?' He gently strokes his mother's forehead.

'Common sense,' she whispers.

'Don't worry, Mum. The scientists are already working on that.'

'I know, son.'

'Well, bye for now, I have to go to work. See you tomorrow.'

'See you tomorrow.'

Whenever her younger son is expected Snow White is released from her tight restraints, propped up nicely on her pillows and a smile discharged on to her face, whether through medication or threats, goodness only knows. To be made to lie in a psychiatric hospital, tied to the bed and still smile would be beyond the powers of even the Buddha, Jesus or the Muslim god.

'Why does your son wear such a heavy overcoat when it's so hot outside?' F22's voice asks a tricky question.

Snow White gives out a heavy sigh. We wait.

'He's cold. Permanently cold. Maybe it's all my fault . . . Once, when the children were small, I had an argument with my husband. To tell you the truth, we each loved a different child; the parents of twins have this advantage – that they can love just one of them.

From the time of their birth I had chosen the elder, my husband the younger. It really isn't the case that all children should be loved equally; it simply isn't true. Some childless philosopher must have proposed the idea, and everyone takes his word for it, afraid of not loving.'

At the word 'philosopher' Fright makes a slight move but doesn't say anything.

'It was late one winter's evening. The children were crawling about on the floor, and I was knitting a jumper. My husband was listening to Ella Fitzgerald. Everything was precisely as it should be in an ordinary family until my husband started singing. He must have been head over heels in love with Ella Fitzgerald, seeing as he listened to that same record every single day. And he knew very well that I didn't like her, didn't like voices like hers, skin colour like hers and body shapes like hers. But he just kept listening to it over and over again . . .'

Snow White sighs and clicks her tongue against her dentures.

'But listening was not enough for him; by the third song he started singing along. Can you imagine? Singing along! I had had enough. At first, I asked him, nicely, to stop, as he was tone deaf and I didn't want our children learning to sing out of tune, but he took no notice – or maybe simply didn't hear me, as he was so smitten with Ella Fitzgerald. At that point I picked up the record player and smashed it against the wall, yelling at him to get out, to run to his Ella and never return, to go to hell . . . And he walked out; put on his coat and left. The children started crying. The older boy climbed on to my lap, but the younger one crawled over to the front door like a little dog, dirty little nails peeling the paint off, all the while screaming 'Daddy, Daddy!' Then I opened the door and screamed after him to come back for his child. He hadn't got very far, just to the courtyard gate maybe, and in a jiffy he ran back, picked up his child and was off again . . .

'The following morning I made some coffee, some porridge and went to fetch some firewood . . . My husband was buried in the snow, frozen to death. He had his back propped against the woodpile, his legs pulled up to his chest, but something was moving under his coat. It was our younger son, wrapped up close to his heart, buried like Ella Fitzgerald.

'When the boy turned eighteen I gave him his father's coat and an Ella Fitzgerald record. So my younger son grew up rather sensitive to frost.'

We are all sitting on our own beds, each of us quiet. Maybe some of us no longer resent an older son making pancakes any way he pleases. Perhaps F22 is now trying to picture the oval of Snow White's husband's frozen face, the strains of Ella Fitzgerald's 'All by Myself' on his half-opened lips. I'm sure Fright is suffering and not allowing the question 'Was your husband handsome?' to pop out of her mouth. As for me . . . I'm sorry Snow White's husband didn't have a Green Crow. She would never have let him freeze to death. Never.

'Four walls on two floors plus a pool, plus champagne, in exchange for this?' F22 looks at me as if I were mad, my stories a light southerly breeze in comparison to the icy whirlwinds of Snow White's.

'No one wants to go to hell,' Snow White murmurs, following our thoughts, and falls into a deep but not eternal sleep.

JUST ASK, PEOPLE WILL INVARIABLY HELP YOU

It is evening at last. Fright has been collected by the fat care assistant who said she had a check-up. We await her return.

'You know, if I had loads of money I would pay for Fright to have plastic surgery. A nose job, get rid of that hump, do her teeth for her . . . like in that American TV show.'

'And?'

'Fright would be prettier. Maybe then she would be known as the Little Princess!'

'My husband has lots of money, but he wouldn't give any away. He likes to feel superior . . . Once, the mother of a friend of mine fell ill. She was practically dying. The medication the doctor had prescribed was no longer helping, and she needed something stronger for the pain. She called me, even though we hadn't been in contact for more than a year . . . hadn't spoken on the phone, that is. I promised to help her, knowing my husband had more than enough money. She needed it quickly. I went to him and explained the situation, but he just looked at me, his eyes icy cold, and said, "You are aware that my parents died when I was twelve. My dad was hit by a car while we were waiting at a bus stop. He died from a blood clot the day he was discharged from hospital, and my mother slowly wasted away, dying in hospital a year later. And you know what? Nobody helped, we had nobody to turn to.

So, can you tell me why it is I should help a total stranger? Everyone must face their own destiny."

'"Don't you feel the slightest bit sorry for someone who is dying and in terrible pain?"

'"Yes, of course I do."

'"So why won't you help?"

'"As I just said. To each his own. That's what it said over the gates of concentration camps, *Jedem das seine*! Exactly that. That was one clever wartime nation!"

'The money was needed as soon as possible. I had to come up with something.

'"Then give it to me, not my friend."

'"Why to you?"

'"If you love me, then give it to me. Then I can do whatever I want with it!"

'"I'm not giving you any money." He left the room abruptly, vanished.

'I waited all day long. I sat in front of a blank TV and waited. I thought with extreme regret about my forest – what a terrible shame it had burned down. It would have been just the place to go while waiting for someone you know to die, trying not to think about how painful it must be, trying to get your head around the utter hopelessness. He came back late at night, asked if there was anything to eat, watched TV for a while, had a couple of beers and went to sleep.

'This time I started it. I didn't speak, didn't look him in the eye, didn't smile the whole of the following day.

'"What's the matter with you?" he asked with his eyes.

'I didn't answer and even felt a small sense of satisfaction – at last I have the right and a good reason not to speak, to pretend that he's not alive and has never actually existed. Two days went by. He came into the bedroom and put the money down on the bed. I then turned into the most flamboyant *prima donna* after her opening-night performance – I embraced, kissed and thanked him profusely, coming to understand the sort of person he really was. Turns out that hatred can come as a huge relief.'

F22 tears open another chocolate bar. She speaks, her mouth full.

'So? He gave you the money? What's to hate him for?'

'Don't you understand? Ask your voice. Ask her.'

F22 turns away a while, stops munching.

'My voice is asking how you would have behaved if you were in his shoes, if your dad had kicked the bucket and you, small and helpless, had been left to watch your mother die without being able to help her.'

'But what about mercy, compassion?'

'Why do you think that being merciful implies buying someone morphine to send them into oblivion? Wouldn't it be more compassionate to pray and be glad that a person should die while still fully conscious? Who says that the moment of death is not an adventure? What right have we to deny it to someone? Life and death are two cardinal points – both need to be experienced. As they say in film trailers, "Don't miss it! *Coming soon . . .*"

'I feel bad that someone should be in pain if I can help . . .'

'But it wasn't you, it was your moronic husband who could help.'

'But it was actually me who gave the money to my friend.'

'No. My voice says that your friend called because she knew your husband had money, not you . . .'

*

99

The doors crash, and Fright enters the room. She stops, her head hanging loose, her chin flopping down on her chest, her hands and legs trembling slightly. A cabbage. A vegetable.

'Fright, what's your name?' F22 calls to her.

Fright shuffles a few steps forward, topples on to F22's bed; she sighs and collapses, falling on to F22's feet.

'Bloody hell!' In a flash F22 is out of bed. 'A vegetable . . .'

The two of us, our cheeks puffed out with the effort, carry Fright to her bed.

We are not filled with pity because of the state Fright is in. We simply fear for our own fates. Fright was a whole lot more amiable than the rest of us: F22 was a schizophrenic with auditory hallucinations; I was friends with the Green Crow who, to the outside world, was no more than a figment of my imagination.

So we sit about, considering our own destinies in relation to the flaccid lump in Fright's bed. The nurse comes in with our medication, gives us each a glass of water and a handful of tablets. Seven tablets multiplied by three. But we are clever – we push the tablets into the cavities of our missing teeth, behind our upper lips, and later spit them out and rinse our mouths out, asking each other what on earth we are doing there.

'What the hell have they done to Fright?' F22 arranges the pillow at the foot of her bed so she can see Fright's face, her eyes staring and empty.

'In-su-lin,' Snow White says, pronouncing the word as if chanting a mantra. 'They stick a needle in you and wire you up to the system, then inject insulin into your vein until you're knocked out, then they wake you up with other drugs. With insulin pumping in, the mad ones calm down, don't go crazy, stop raging . . .'

'Fright never rages. She just grieves for her ugliness. She isn't aggressive,' F22 rushes to defend her.

'My son says that you can never really tell with people. Madhouses are created for that reason – to keep emotions under control. They say the best thing is not to think at all, that way you don't have any sensations, desires, opinions. My medication is working. I'm about to fall asleep. Earlier today I dreamed I was on the horse-drawn tram, going along Krišjāņa Barona Street. I was returning from the maternity home with the twins on my lap. My husband hadn't finished renovating our place, so we were staying with our next-door neighbours. Five people in a tiny room. It was horrible, although it's better to experience the past in your dreams than to build a horrifying future in your head. Enjoy your time here, girls! Good-night!' Snow White's head slowly flops to one side, and she starts snoring gently.

'Spooky.'

'Yes, spooky indeed.'

As I'm drifting off to sleep, the horrifying fear rushes through me that I might end up in the past without the Green Crow. If that were to happen I would have to start counting the years spent in vain, the years I drag behind me like refuse sacks.

'F22, do you want to hear a story?'

'Sure, go ahead! I can't sleep. Looking at Fright's glazed expression just makes me want to cry . . .'

Our country cottage is falling to pieces. It has been hollowed out by woodworm, just as cancer eats away at good people. My husband will never let it happen. He will fetch timber, bang in nails, smear on paint and slowly kill himself, but he will save the house, heal it. It was not for nothing that he had bought back his family's old home from the previous dishonourable, moneyed owner who had only bought it only to use at weekends, a place where he could show his sons how to kill a viper, light a fire without lighter fuel, how not to suffer any discomfort. The house meant nothing to him, nothing at all. Never mind the fact that my husband's great-grandfather had lost the house in a game of cards, his wife then being sent to the workhouse and he then choking on his sorrow like a drunk choking on his own vomit.

'It should be every man's mission to regain his family's property. To regain and safeguard it!' My husband cannot refrain from repeating this sentiment endlessly while cleaning the resin from logs. 'I will rebuild it from scratch – bigger and better!'

The twins are four months old. Two months each. While their dad and three toothless jacks-of-all-trades are rebuilding the house, the babies and I live in the sauna hut. I sleep on the sweating bench – as wide as a well-fed dog's back – and my son sleeps in a wicker cradle placed at the mouth of the wood burner. The planks are hard, but I am soft. I roll my daughter under one armpit and tie the cradle to my big toe with a string, so my son is gently lulled to sleep as if by the waves of the sea and grows up to be a great seafarer. The spirit of the sauna is called upon to bear with us for two months. I don't believe that he will ever have children – after the constant wailing and human milk splashing all over the place, only a fool would wish for children – but the spirit is clever. He is gradually driving us out – the bench becomes increasingly narrow and a viper pokes her head over the threshold with increasing frequency.

'We're moving out tomorrow; the big house is ready.' I whisper reassuring words, singing them to my children in songs so the spirit can hear, too, trying to appease him a little longer.

It is nine o'clock. Today the toothless cheerful workers will finish their job for good. Let them get drunk, throw up, spill their drinks and pee in our new house! As long as they get out and don't infuriate the spirit of the sauna. Once they've gone I won't have to make enormous pots of soup, peel potatoes, beat marbled pork, knead dough and wash dishes any more, all the while clutching the babies tightly under my soft arms. I don't want to smile and say, 'Enjoy your meal!' I want to go home, back to the city.

'When a husband is building a house for his wife, she must remain by his side. That way she can't say later that the house he has built is no good,' my husband repeats drily on the countless occasions I beg him to take me home. He puts up with my whims, satisfies them by driving at least once a day to the local shop thirty-nine leagues away to buy nappies, beer, meat and bread for the workmen. 'It's absolutely wonderful here,' he says, stretching his limbs. 'Country air is great for children.'

The planks beneath my back are not getting any softer, and the days are like photocopied sheets of paper. All identical, the colour occasionally paler in certain spots. It rained today, washing away the pale colours, too. Nothing is left. No joy, no love, no passion. Green, red, yellow. My sheet of paper is blank, and, despairing that I'm unable to fill it in, I stand there barefoot in ragged shorts, my shirt impregnated with milk, and feel like putting the babies into the wicker cradle, relinquishing them to the river and running away. If only I could, I would run away, my fat thighs wobbling along the banks of the river to the highway before coming to a stop in the middle of the road, my hands outstretched or placed as if in prayer, imploring someone to take pity on me and take me far away. Babies sent floating down the river in a wicker basket become kings sooner or later.

Look how the babies sleep! I watch them and can do whatever I want with my life. Today I don't have to cook dinner, and I can please myself. Namely, sleep. I don't have dreams, though. Or maybe they can't find me, seeing as I no longer exist. I am nothing but two swollen tits, blue-grey eyes, hands and legs. The dreams all go to my babies, my husband and three toothless workers.

Just a little longer, and I will fall into a warm hole through the boards of the bench as if they were goose down. And yet I don't. I hear shuffling steps. My husband appears in the doorway.

'Come on, let's get moving. We're going to grill some sausages.'

'Nooo . . .' I hesitate, then roll over, turning my back to him.

'What do you mean "no"? You're the hostess. You need to show some respect to the people who have worked so long to build you a house! Come, let's do it!'

'I want to sleep . . .'

'God dammit! I'm ashamed of you!'

He slams the door. I sit up quickly. Sleep has gone, my cheeks become heavy, the first tear rolls down. My right eye always starts first. A second later, it is joined by the left. I try not to sob out loud, so as not to wake the babies. If I don't go and eat sausages with the toothless ones, my husband won't talk to me for three days, maybe even a whole week. He will be as cold as a dead body, his limbs limp, his face wordless. I will sneak up to kiss him, but he will turn his head away. I will make soup, but he will say that he isn't hungry. I will cuddle up to his warm thighs, but he will turn his cold buttocks towards me and bid me 'good-night'. And so it will continue for many days, many nights, until my blame is extinguished through pain and not knowing. Then he will give a sign that I am forgiven, he will mark me with his seed and hug me tightly. Now, I have to figure out whether there is room in my body for more pain, whether I'll be able to bear it for so many days.

I opt in favour of the sausages, encircled by a fire with no warmth. I place the sleeping babies in the pram, and we are off.

Halfway there and I can hear them talking. The toothless ones are already well tanked up, telling tales of adventure from the world of construction, while my husband listens gravely, his thoughts on me, on my disobedience and lack of respect. He is in for a surprise!

When I emerge from the darkness, a black apparition pushing a wheelbarrow, the conversation peters out. They fix their eyes on me.

'Oh, our hostess!' the boss of the toothless gang roars.

I sit down and remain silent. I don't smile. I don't eat. I am not having a good time.

'Ah, why is our hostess so miserable?' one of the other toothless guys chips in, his attitude offering a clue as to why his teeth might be missing.

'Angry about something, are you? Yeah, there's no pleasing you women,' the third one offers.

'Right. Good-night everyone!' My husband gets up and leaves.

The band of toothless men squint from under their brows, following my husband with their eyes, but they dare not look me in the face. The boss is the first to get up.

'So, good-night . . .'

Their shadows disappear into the darkness. Are these workers the sort of men who look after their children, watch television, sleep, cry, try to understand the world around them? My husband says they don't need much for two months – a tent and a hole for a toilet will do. Their steps can be heard shuffling away quietly in the darkness towards the grove of trees where they vanish into tents as if into large lurid flowers, then fall asleep and breathe. As people do.

A two-litre beer-filled plastic container shines beyond the flames. The workers have left behind their strong seven-per-cent friend. I also used to drink.

Cheap wine in the silent kitchens of my friends, schnapps straight from the bottle in blocks of flats . . . I drank with a man who later dived into the darkness, slack as a dead body. We drank, and we were friends, the three of us. Now I don't drink, my breasts are swollen with milk. I now take a DD, my husband's favourite size. If I start drinking, my boobs will become droopy, my husband unhappy. Beer is my heroin, the sap of poppies, death. I begin, but it is for the beer to conclude, to decide when I am to fall into the darkness, grind my teeth and snore. No, no . . . I can't.

There's one here and another one there. Two plastic beer bottles containing the fortified liquid are sitting on a stump of wood. I'm afraid they might melt, so I get up to rescue them. Just to move them away from the heat, just to move them, that's all. Like any good hostess would. The way they live, the way they die. I focus my thoughts, as you might gather saliva before spitting, on how the toothless workers' gums must have rubbed against the neck of the bottle, how bits of sausage must have come away from their teeth and now drift in the deep lake of beer, how the toothless ones have been with cheap whores from the Central Market, how their tongues have greedily licked the slits of those whores. I imagine how the DNA of their lives floats, attached to the bubbles of carbon dioxide, how I will swallow it and get sick, how I, too, will become a toothless worker and fornicate with whores from the meat hall of the Central Market . . .

The bottle is warm and heavy. Almost two litres. The lid is on tightly. Exactly, the lid. It sweeps clean, wipes away all the germs, squashes and kills them – so long as they are not like Highlander, who can only be killed by having his head cut off. For germs the lid is a kind of guillotine. Open and close, open and close. The heads of germs shall roll at the feet of the busty housewife.

I take my first sip.

It makes me gag.

Those toothless workmen, what great guys, they have even left me some ciggies. Cheap and malodorous. Along with the smoke and noisy pulls on the beer comes understanding. It's not advertised in shops nor mentioned in the instructions for use, otherwise everyone would just get used to understanding everything all the time. And now I understand it all, all that the world has ever doubted. I suddenly gain an understanding of how money-laundering works and how easy it is to cheat during presidential elections, how celebrities come to have such very white teeth . . . I'm an intelligent woman with milk-soaked breasts, a woman who is never going to be president, a celebrity, an African, a money-launderer. The plastic bottle, light as a feather, flies into the flames. The babies are still sleeping. The other bottle I saved from the heat leers at me from the stump.

I throw the second bottle on to the embers and leave. The babies are sleeping. With luck still alive. But I'll see whether they are or not when I come to unload them. There is an incline ahead of me. There's nothing to think about – I let the pram with my babies in it roll down. Let go! Books tell us that children are not the property of their parents, that they should be released like an arrow from a bow, that although they come into the world through their parents they are not *from* them, that we might resemble our children, but we can't make them like us.

I let them go. I want to resemble them. I want to be free.

'They weren't killed?'

'Of course not. The pram rolled down a little way then came to a stop. The twins woke up and smiled. Alive.'

'Certainly. Who wouldn't smile about being free?'

'Ugly people,' F22 frowns. 'Carry on . . .'

I put my babies to sleep: my daughter on the sweating bench, my son in the cradle. I light a candle and stretch out on the floor. I can't keep my eyes open; for a brief moment my mind lights up – we could die at any moment. Why shouldn't Death come now? And there she is, loud and breathless, running down the slope, straight ahead for thirty metres then veering slightly to the left, and there is a door handle and I'm in there. She opens the door and stands still. Maybe it would be better to wake up; not everyone deserves to die in their sleep. She stands there, observing how the cool air streams in through the door.

'Where's the beer? The workers are looking for it and can't find any,' Death says.

Death seems to be a little over thirty. Fair shoulder-length hair, eyes as icy as water from a mountain lake, a sturdy body a little under two metres in height, a checked shirt and balls between his legs.

'There's no beer,' I reply and close my eyes.

'What do you mean, there isn't any?'

'Sooner or later everything comes to an end. I want to sleep or die. Please, let me be.'

My husband, who, in fact, is Death, who, in fact, is my husband, comes in and closes the door behind him.

'Have you been drinking?' He leans over me and checks my breath.

'And what about you? You've been drinking, too.' Now it's not me speaking but rather my newfound understanding, which still needs to be slept on.

'Me? . . . Are you sick in the head? I don't have two babies. I'm free to drink! Uh . . . I mean . . . I don't have to look after them, take care of two-month-old babies!'

'And I do?'

'You are their mother, for heaven's sake! Filthy drunk! You stink!'

'Go fuck yourself!' Again, it's not me speaking. And the one who is not me starts screaming hysterically, shedding tears all over the place. The stranger snatches the wooden sauna ladle from the basket and, with all her strength, smashes it against the wall. The ladle bounces back and falls into my son's cradle.

And then my husband becomes another person, too.

'You bitch! You drunk! Do you want to kill your own children?' He grabs me by my hair, pulls me up and drags me out of the sauna hut, throwing me to the ground like a sack of potatoes without a face.

'Take that, you baby murderer!'

Thank God he is wearing the Nike trainers he bought a week ago to lose some weight. They are running shoes, not football boots with studs. I receive five kicks – three to my head, one to my buttocks and one in the chest. After that he's had enough and vanishes, walking away into the dark. Maybe he ran, trying to shift a bit of extra weight.

'And you stayed with him after that?'
   'Yes, we're still together now.'
   'And afterwards? Were you covered in bruises?' F22, head in hands, looks as if she might be crying.

The following morning I woke up with a headache. A hangover. He brought me my morning cup of coffee and, for the first time in his life, prepared breakfast. I drank my coffee and ate the sandwiches so as not to anger him, offend him. Then, again for the first time in his life, he picked up the twins and put them down to sleep, pushing the pram around the bumpy meadow. When the babies had gone off, he put his hand around my waist and led me to the place where he had kicked my head in, took my knickers off, fucked me and said he loved me. When he had finished he turned to me, saw my tears and asked, 'Don't you love me any more?'
   'I do,' I replied.
   'Then let's go and get the new house straightened up. We will never sleep in the sauna again.'

F22 is breathing rhythmically. My story has made her pretend to be asleep. At least that's one bonus for reliving my past.

ALL FAMILIES BENEFIT FROM THE ADDITION OF A NEW MEMBER

'I don't understand why you are here. If you want to leave your family . . . why don't you just get a divorce, leave the children and that would be the end of it?' F22 is making her bed and looking at me reproachfully, as if my not being there would allow her to breathe more easily in this room where memories inhabit the folds of the curtains, the folds of the bed linen, the round shapes of the lamps. And they can't simply be washed away, cleaned, bleached out because that's life, the bed is there waiting for the next lot of memories to come, memories that never cease.

'Honestly?'

'Of course. How else?'

'I want to be certified insane. Then I will go back to my family, and they'll all be scared of me. They will let me do and have whatever I want and leave me to hang out with the Green Crow, never telling me off and loving me because I'm sick. Sick people are loved and pitied, aren't they?'

'You really are insane. You'll never be able to get a loan, rent a property, you'll never be able to drive a car, become a Member of Parliament.'

'Freedom starts where rights and obligations end. I've been pretending to be insane for two years now. My husband will meet another woman, buy me an apartment and I'll be free . . . I don't want to leave my family and feel guilty for the rest of my life about having hurt them, abandoned them . . .'

F22 takes an intake of breath to continue listing everything I stand to lose but stops herself as Fright is sitting up in her bed.

'Love,' she says loudly, her eyes wide open, staring at the illusion on which the sun is shining. 'Love is like a small flower. In the blink of an eye it blooms and gives off such a fragrance, such a fragrance . . .'

Fright no longer looks like a shell-shocked soldier; she just looks like a very ugly woman.

'What's the matter with you?' F22 shakes her by the shoulder.

'He touched my shoulder, just like you did now, but he didn't shake it; he caressed it and told me that I was beautiful, probably the most beautiful woman in the world, and then . . . then he kissed me . . .'

'Who kissed you? You went to see the doctor yesterday. Tell us everything, right from the beginning. The fat care assistant came for you and led you away, and then . . .'

'Right, exactly. We walked along the corridors looking for the doctor . . . Oh!' Fright hides her face in her hands.

'And then we found him. He was coming back from an electroconvulsive-therapy session; as the head physician he has to be present each time, you know . . . So then the lovely care assistant took me to his office . . . and then . . .' Fright breaks down in tears again, 'and then he asks, "Why did you try to commit suicide? Don't you realize that there is nothing after death, just a vacuum devoid of thought and feeling?"

'"No, I didn't know that."

'"But I do, because I'm a doctor and have graduated from the Academy of Medicine, where we learned that people need to be saved from the vacuum. So why did you try to commit suicide?"

"'I'm so very ugly and nobody wants to have anything to do with me," I say.

"'And who told you that?'

"'Well . . . me, myself . . . I look in the mirror and see it for myself . . .'

"'Classic. Absolutely classic. Remember, you can always get a second opinion instead of tormenting yourself with questions you can't answer on your own. Ask me!"

"'What?'

"Ask me whether you are beautiful."

"'Am I beautiful?'

"'Yes, my dear! You are as beautiful as the sunshine, warm and affectionate, very much needed. If there were no sun humankind would be doomed. Are you following me?'

"'No.'

"'Close your eyes.'

'I closed my eyes, and then it happened. He removed my shirt and touched my shoulder, pressed his cheek to mine and kissed the corner of my mouth.

"'You are beautiful," he said. "Count to fifty and then open your eyes. Your life will be changed."

'I counted . . . I opened my eyes and saw the care assistant.

"'Let's go," she said.

'The rest you saw for yourselves. I came into the room and sat on F22's bed, but you moved me to my own.'

'Why didn't you tell us any of this yesterday?' F22 looks offended.

'There is nothing in the world more fragile than a thought. Compared with a thought a spider's web is like a brick wall. I didn't want to lose it by chatting with you girls, sorry . . .'

'We thought you'd turned into a vegetable, a cabbage . . .'

'No, no. I'm not a vegetable. I'm in love.'

Fright lies down with a stiff smile on her lips and doesn't move.

'Did you have sex?' F22 stands at Fright's bedside, her arms crossed.

'Sex?' Fright asks, like a child playing for time to think of an answer.

'Yes, sex.'

'No, we didn't.'

'Look me in the eye,' F22 orders. The whites of Fright's eyes, as large as a calf's, clearly give her away. Fright glances at me then looks away, hiding her head under the blanket.

'I've got it. Fright has never had sex. You haven't, have you, Fright?' F22 giggles.

'I have,' Fright answers, still hiding her head under the blanket.

'Then tell us what kind of sex you've had!' F22 is mocking her, and I, too, want to hide my head under the blanket. Direct questions like these are like the plague, they kill the infected and everyone around them, too. Life and death are topics to be discussed, laughed about, grieved over, whereas sex is a far trickier topic – certainly more interesting.

Fright is still cowering under her blanket. It's easier to talk about sex when your whole head is hidden from view. Everyone knows that.

'We lay on top of each other and moaned. The whole building shook, got it?' Fright screams as loud as her guts allow, but the blanket muffles the sound.

'Ha!' F22 exclaims. 'You've been watching too much TV! If you've never had sex, no wonder no one wants you, no one loves you. You have no fire inside. Fi-yer! Those flames are what set a grown woman apart from a flat-chested little girl. The males of our species are like freezing old men, out in the middle of a forest – light the right sort of fire and everyone feeling the cold will gather around it, full of clever talk, boasting, just so each of them can get a bit of your flame. Fright, if no man has ever warmed between your legs, that fire has nothing to get it started. Virgins are cold because they don't know what's going to be done to them. Sex is really the only reason men and women live together. I wonder why that doctor of ours kissed you. I really don't get it –'

'It was a form of therapy,' Snow White interrupts.

'To make her fall in love with him? Therapy?' F22 roars, her voice apparently having taken over the reins.

'Yes, it's essential that you understand . . . you see, my boy has come up with a therapy to be used on most of his female patients. He makes them fall in love with him and in so doing saves them from possibly committing suicide. Falling in love cures all manner of ailments . . . Your Fright tried to commit suicide, and, as luck would have it, she was allocated to my son, with whom she'll fall in love and then get better. The project is funded by the European Union, you know, to improve the suicide statistics –'

'Are these all lies? How will Fright react to this? She must have heard everything!'

'Never mind . . . People in love don't hear much . . .' Snow White looked at Fright, who had transformed into a flowery heap of singing snow. I wanna be kissed by you . . . boop-boop-a-doop . . .

'Does it make any difference how you fall in love – with the support of the European Union or in the half-darkness of a nightclub?'

'Fine, I get it, but what's going to happen when he dumps her?' F22 insisted.

'You can't dump someone when you've never actually been an item, can you?'

'No, haven't they . . . ?'

'No, of course not. They will speak on the phone, exchange letters, meet every so often, and all the while Fright will be getting better, doing her best to drag herself out of her situation. Later, to help soothe her further, another man will be sent to Fright – a very handsome one, by the way – and he, too, will be part of the European Project, and then another one . . . Fright will fall in love with each of them in turn, and her confidence will blossom. In two years' time you girls won't recognize her . . .'

'Does this project focus only on ugly participants?'

'No, not entirely, not entirely . . . Everyone could do with some European support . . . The most important thing is to attempt committing suicide . . . only attempt, mind . . .' Snow White's morning medication is starting to take effect. She is slowly drifting off, as per usual, after downing seven pills. She won't come round again until after lunch.

F22 sits on her bed and remains silent. I don't have anything to say either, my memories leading a life of their own as always, without my permission as always. Just memories.

He'll be waiting for me in bed. He'll be unable to sleep. He'll wait for me, naked and drunk. I know that he's waiting for me naked and drunk, but I'm sitting on his desk, pushing the all-important drawer open and closed with my big toe. A host of significant things have been thrown in there: contracts, waybills, our wedding photograph, my son's diploma, black shoe polish, keys for two cars and three motorbikes, photos from his army days and a crocheted red rose I gave him for his fortieth birthday. I also know that in the furthest corner of the drawer are my letters, between twelve and fifteen in number. I used to write them and put them on his desk. All bear the marks of time and space. Oppressive marks.

I move my hand about among the significant things and pull out a wedge of banknotes – ten, fifty, five hundred, some fives. I don't know how much there is. I stick it back. I didn't even know that the money was in there. I try again. I dig out a Christmas card. Made by me and written on by me. A white heart with a gingerbread scratch-and-sniff sticker glued to blue cardboard. 'I'm sorry that I'm not the wife you would have wished for, but I will do better. Believe me, as it's Christmas, I love you.' It was written ten years ago when the twins were not yet able to tell the difference between a television series and each other's clothes. I crush the white heart to my nose to breathe in the scent of gingerbread, but all I smell is burned roast pork. I hear the special Christmas lovemaking. On that occasion he gave me a ring, and I gave him a leather jacket with brass buttons. The ring was too small and the jacket too big, but we both wore them, smiling at each other and at other people, too. Later, I lost weight and he filled out so, now everything fits perfectly. In the drawer there is another card, this one with an Easter dog on it. The twins were about eight years old. I told them to make a card for their daddy. They drew an Easter dog! A white mutt with spots and big balls. I asked them why . . . Daddy will only throw it in his drawer, and we will still get our Easter gifts anyway, they said. What difference does it make? And that was exactly what happened. And that is how it is.

'We came up with a business plan.' The twins' heads are hovering at the crack in the door. They look very much alike, only my son has fuller lips and therefore also a large member. I haven't seen him undressed for several years and don't suppose I ever shall again. Their hair is the same length, they have the same eyes, similar physiques. Only their lips give them away.

'Mum, did you hear us?'

'Yes.'

'So, we are going to create a weight-loss programme. It works a hundred per cent!'

'Yes.'

'Aren't you interested in losing weight?'

'Not any more.'

'The best way is to . . .' They start wriggling about with laughter.

'To pull out all the fat person's teeth . . .' Tears stream down their cheeks.

'So the person will never smile again,' I say.

'Yes, that is, no. That wouldn't work. We'll have to think of something else. Life without laughter is no life.' My son is drying his own and his sister's tears. He slams the door.

Once more I dig my hand into the drawer, as if into a toothless mouth.

'Mum, why are you sitting on the desk?' The twins' heads are at the door again. 'Mum, why don't you let us sit on the table?'

'I don't let you drink. I don't let you do anything.'

The twins slam the door. I continue rummaging through the life written in my own handwriting. I unfold a note.

'Please talk to me again.'

After reading these words he had started to talk to me. He'd said, 'Let's go to the beach'. It was winter. Shards of ice. Cold snow cannon and warm people everywhere. The car was breathing in our faces. The car heater was warm. We didn't speak. We always went to the sea after disputes and disagreements. We would get to the dunes, look at the water for five minutes then leave. Always the same, except that first time when my husband enjoyed a moment of ecstasy looking at the sea with his trousers down and me attached to his direction indicator. I remember that time – I looked at the front of his trousers and the sea and couldn't decide which I liked best, which I had seen less, known less, loved less, taken inside, caressed, rejected, cursed. I wondered which of the two would be most willing to let me kill myself if I'd really had enough.

We turned on to the main street going towards the city centre.

'The sea is back the other way.'

'Oh, I changed my mind. Let's not go to the sea.'

We stopped in a quiet side-street.

He never took me to cafés, clubs, shops, gateways, park benches. Never.

'Let's go and see if they've got anything interesting in there.'

'Where?'

'There.'

In the gloom, blue and red lights pulsated as if it were the heart of the timid side-street. I knew that heart and always sneaked, drove, dreamed past it. Hearts such as those, the atria guarded by cupids crafted from blood-coloured diodes, are not to my taste.

'Let's go and take a look . . .'

We went down the steps. Neon cupids exchanged glances.

It was warm and sticky inside. Hidden away at the very back was the greatest thrill of all – cabins with a roll of toilet paper on the left and a rubbish bin on the right – between them a plasma screen and a stool. There was no soundproofing, just put a coin in and turn up the volume so as not to embarrass other customers.

Take us! Take us and abuse us, then wash us in warm soapy water and abuse us again, the dildos, neatly lined along a glass shelf, begged amid all the confusion. They had proudly straightened their powerful heads towards the ceiling. Black, transparent, flesh-coloured, red, big, ridiculous, enormous and miniature. All at the ready. The vibrators kept quiet, coyly feminine, but the blow-up doll on the top shelf raised her voice in a vulgar manner above the artificial phalluses, unable to keep her mouth shut. She didn't say anything sensible, just groaned and yelped in pleasure and pain. The black leather whip, excited, waggled its tails.

The left side of the shop remained mysteriously silent. For now at any rate, while the orgies hidden behind the sumptuous covers had, as yet, not found their other halves, capable of interpreting and revealing to the whole world the true nature of love between two men; women's expertise with their tongues, tasked with far nobler purposes than those of everyday life, probing the anatomy of hairless girls, the pride of well-endowed men; the trajectory of blows falling on the disobedient and uncompliant, as well as other ways in which silicon and bags of salted water may rule the male brain. The covers of the rental films were well worn, stained by love juices.

The doorbell jingled and another customer emerged from behind the curtain covering the door from the street. Silence fell. The dildos, out of respect or awe, lowered their heads, the rubber woman shut her gaping mouth, the whips pulled in their tails and coiled up obediently. The shop assistant put down his detective novel and smiled politely at the new customer (he plainly thought we already knew our stuff), ready to answer any daft questions posed by the new arrival. And yet the young man's lips let him down, the only thing he managed to get out being 'Hmm . . . well, this is a shop for intimate goods . . .' The elderly woman who had recently come into the shop and was now looking around, dumbstruck, didn't even hear him. She must have been at least eighty. The world of adult toys had such an almighty impact on her that she had taken off her glasses and just stood there, totally at a loss for words.

Finally, she grasped her shopping bags tighter to her and walked slowly past the shelves. The items displayed on them had assumed an exhibition-like status, at least as far as her life was concerned; a life where hormones only played hide-and-seek with each other and mortals scorned their inescapable end under a pile of earth in a cemetery. Ashes to ashes, dust to dust. Some time. Maybe tomorrow but not today.

The old girl psyched herself up.

'What's that for?' she asked, pointing at something that looked like two icicles melted together. One shorter, the other longer.

'Hmm . . . how can I put it . . .' The shop assistant blushed.

'Just spit it out, will you!'

She had already pointed at a dozen items, asking each time, 'What's that? What do you do with it?' The shop assistant's embarrassment mounted with each answer. There was plainly only one question he wanted to ask her but didn't dare, in view of her advanced years. However, when the elderly finger reached out to touch yet another glass showcase, the pointing digit accompanied by another 'Why?' and 'How?', the shop assistant took the plunge.

'Madam . . . what exactly is it you're looking for?'

'I'm looking for ecstasy, young man!'

'Do you mean . . . an orgasm?'

'Yes, damn it, call those sacred cramps whatever you like. I must have them and that's all there is to it!' the old woman shrieked. She turned away, a pink girlish expression flitting over her face.

The shop assistant froze, thinking it over, chin in hand.

'Well, for starters, you could try this.' The man bent down and came up a second later with a package he placed on the counter.

'What is it?' She was guarded – it didn't look anything like a dildo or a vibrator.

'No, maybe not, better try this.' Luckily, the shop assistant realized just in time that there would be no point trying to explain to the old lady how to use a vacuum pump and instead took a small semi-transparent dildo from the shelf.

'It's very easy to use. Just press the button and it'll start vibrating, then . . . you know . . . rub it on your . . . well . . . you can work it out for yourself . . .'

'No, I can't! What sort of shop assistant are you if you can't explain what to do with it properly?' she snapped nastily.

'I'm not a sex therapist! Do you want it or not?' By now, the shop assistant was riled, too.

When the old girl finally shuffled towards the door, a black parcel in her hand, the shop assistant refrained from issuing his customary farewell call, 'Look forward to seeing you soon!' Aware of the possible consequences of his usual customer care, he forced himself to keep quiet, as did the dildos on the shelves, wordlessly watching their luckless associate leave the premises in a shopping bag.

I stood there for a while, maybe considering my own future.

'And now, young man, back to us. My wife wishes to buy something.' My husband broke the silence.

We didn't see the sea that evening. In a black bag, identical to the one the old bag from my future had taken, two silicone go-getters were rubbing necks, one against the other. One was baptized Žanis, the other was simply called the Leg. In all honesty, it was called that by my friend's son who, playing in our bedroom one day, ran up to his mum with the forty-five-centimetre dildo in his tiny hand, asking, 'Mummy, why has the goat lost its leg?'

Undoubtedly this event served to make our family stronger. New family members invariably do. I certainly didn't give up writing letters to my husband.

Next time we went to the sea.

'Mum, why are you still up?' The twins are spying on me again. 'Dad has been snoring for ages already . . .'

'Do you want to send me off to bed so you can watch some porn?'

'Mum, what are you talking about?'

'Just don't sleep with each other. It'll ruin your childhood.'

I'm drunk. The twins are used to it.

'You mean we shouldn't sleep with each other like you and Dad do?' My daughter is putting on an act, pretending to be a five-year-old, giving me a sly smile as she sees how drunk I am.

'Just . . . always keep your eyes open . . .' I mumble as I jump off the desk and stagger towards the door. The twins make way for me, leaping back as if to the cardinal points of a compass.

I fall asleep without washing my hands after the colonoscopy of our life.

*

'The earth is flat. Easy,' F22 announces after listening to my story. 'As I've already said, only sex keeps a man with a woman. Sex and the fear of being alone. Your husband is trying.'

Fright has unwrapped herself from the blanket. There is no longer the slightest hint of calf-like whiteness to her eyes – they are now like big buttons on a granny jacket. She opens her mouth as if to speak and stays like that – her eyes wide, her mouth half open.

'This is what life with sex is like, Fright.' F22 smiles. Embittered yet tender. She starts telling her story.

'I was eighteen, nineteen maybe, I don't remember exactly, and I had a friend; he was exactly forty. A real gentleman: witty and, most importantly, intelligent. I visited him almost every day after college. He taught me how to treat a man. He said a good man was a happy man. We made love every time I went there. He showed me and taught me how to sit down on his dick properly, told me how to take it in my mouth, how high I should raise my leg when he takes me from the side, how to arch my back to look pretty when he takes me from behind. It was interesting. I haven't a bad word to say about it. In the end he gave me the keys so I could get in even when he wasn't expecting me – yes, especially then. We were basically living together. Six months went by. I was such a regular at the chemist's they didn't even have to ask, just put a packet of the morning-after pill on the counter.

'Then one day he invited his illegitimate nineteen-year-old son and his girlfriend for a day in the country – to help out at his house in the country. I was the same age as them and much better-looking than his son's girlfriend. We stocked up on beer and took off in the car. It was early springtime – you know, when the earth is no longer completely bare and it's beautiful, the time when last year's shrubs are still covered in snow and ice mirrors gleam like glue in potholes. This is an important detail in my story, and you'll see why later ... So, we were driving along, downing the beers. It was obvious that work was the last thing we had in mind. When we rolled up at his place we realized we hadn't brought enough booze for the four of us. My bloke was incredibly stingy, a real miser, and wouldn't let his son drive his posh car, said he'd damage it and then he'd have to pay for the repairs. And so the two of us went to the shop. I don't know why I insisted on going with him. Such a girly outburst. You know, I can't stand seeing men driving cars, their wives sitting at their sides like silly geese! I find that more repulsive than road accidents, when crystals of asphalt gleam through puddles of blood. Ugh. So, off we went, got to the shop, bought some booze and turned back. God knows why he was rushing! He was almost an old man – forty years of age – with a young girl who had seen every centimetre of his flesh, drunk his semen, swept under his bed, heard his godawful snoring, allowed him to take photos of her fanny ... So, what else was he after? Why did he have to show off and drive at such speed down a slippery spring road? What the hell? That was how it all started ... We flipped over, did a somersault that would make a top-ranking gymnast's effort look like a fart from a dead body. Who knows why the hell I'd decided to put on my seatbelt that time ...

'We had good and bad luck in equal measure. We came to our senses after the car had flown over the ditch, turned two somersaults and finally come to a halt on its roof. My man friend had somehow managed to get out, but I was hanging from the seatbelt. The wheels had stopped spinning, and the engine was dead. He stuck his head through the passenger window, which miraculously hadn't smashed, and said, "Are you alive? That's good. Just be careful getting out, don't break the windscreen ..." It goes without saying that I tried as hard as a terrified young girl hanging from a seatbelt possibly could. I tried but didn't succeed; the screen cracked like thin ice under rubber boots. It was then that he got angry, yanking me out of the car by my hair, yelling, cursing, throwing me to the ground and kicking me. There's something about men and their feet, isn't there? As if it wasn't enough to slap me across the face ... I was lucky that time, a car pulled up, so he stopped his assault, just spat in my ear, warning me not to complain as it was all my fault; I had broken the windscreen.

'Ten minutes later, and our car had been pushed out on to the road and the people who had stopped to help us vanished, taking their sympathy with them. Just the two of us left standing there. Rubbing my bruised ribs I told him I had had enough, I was going home, but he grabbed me, shoved me into the car, hit me over the head. We drove. Every so often he swung back and punched me with his free hand, saying that I was nothing but bad news, he'd only got involved with me out of pity, he had tried to make a woman of me, but I undermined him at every turn, acting like a schoolgirl, driving him to bankruptcy, ruining his life. He told me to keep my mouth shut and not to say a word of this to his son. If I did there would be trouble. And he was right, as always. Although I tried – I hid by the pond in the reeds in an attempt to hide my swollen face from everyone – I failed. When his son's girlfriend found me I simply couldn't hold it in and, without a second thought, told her everything that had happened. Just as I'm telling you now.

'After listening to my story, Kasītis (that was his son's nickname; I never knew his real name or even if he had one) made us hide in last year's haystack while he went into the house. All we heard at first was the bubbling of melting snow and the gentle whisper of a spring wind. Who knows why, but before he entered the house I called after him, "Don't hurt him! Go easy on him!" Kasītis was a few centimetres taller than his father, so about one metre ninety-five. At first the house was silent. Contrary to what the Bible tells us, namely that in the beginning was the word, we heard a terrible noise: thuds, a shot and then silence again. No words. That girl and I hugged each other tightly, clasped together – I never imagined I could embrace a girl with such force. We waited. Almost immediately Kasītis came out of the house holding a shotgun in his hand. Then he ran down to the pond, threw the gun into the water and joined us.

'"Let's go. We don't have a lot of time." At first we kept silent. Later, Kasītis explained in a matter-of-fact tone. "I asked him why he had raised his hand to a woman. He said I was young and didn't understand the first thing about life. He moved towards me and hit me. I hit him back. He pulled a gun out from under his bed and took a shot. I took it off him and knocked my dear dad's teeth out."

'It was dark outside. We still had sixteen kilometres to go until we reached the motorway. We were hungry, in shirtsleeves, coatless, tired. The road was empty – only trees, bushes, more trees and bushes. Soon, as can be expected in early spring, the darkness of evening engulfed us. We could no longer even see our own feet when a large house with lights in the windows emerged from the darkness. Kasītis said that he thought we'd better stop. If we wanted to survive, we would have to ask to be taken in, like travellers of old.

'The house was pretty posh; beautiful, very tastefully furnished. Like something out of a film. It seemed odd that a house like that could suddenly materialize at the side of a country road. Its owner, a short, taciturn man, was polite and hospitable; he agreed at once to let us spend the night. He fed us and asked where we were headed. We had nothing to hide, so, eating greedily, we told him our story and were shown to our beds. Kasītis and his girlfriend went upstairs, and I remained downstairs.

'I thought I would just dive beneath the covers and fall straight to sleep, but how wrong I was. Quite the opposite. I tossed and turned and couldn't get off. Besides, I didn't have to wait long before the owner of the house presented himself in front of me, stark naked, saying that our lodgings weren't free of charge after all. Despite being just eighteen or nineteen I understood what he meant by that. I tried to keep my dignity; I got up from the bed and said I was leaving. "Then take your tired friends with you!" he said, and I stopped to think it over. Well, what was there to think about? I was young and tired.

'"Fine," I told him. "Let's do it." Can you imagine? What a scumbag. He had listened to our predicament, heard it clearly enough, but no . . . no sympathy whatsoever. What a creep!

'Then I lay on the bed, spread my legs and . . . it was all over in an instant. He came inside me then politely bade me good-night. As he left, he said, "In the past all travellers paid for their lodgings."

'I've never had sex like that in my life. Over in about two minutes and the smallest dick ever – about the size of my thumb, honestly! Poor man.'

'Did you tell Kasītis about it later?' Fright takes her chance, the first time F22 pauses to draw breath.

'No, of course not. He was worried enough as it was about his father's teeth . . .'

'And what happened later, with that man of yours?'

'Nothing much. I heard he got hooked on gambling machines;

they couldn't care less how many teeth you have in your mouth when you smile, lit up with their green and yellow lights. I never saw him again. Thing is, though, I never knew which of them was my son's father. Although my boy is very well built, tall, he has got a very small dick.'

'Is that when you started hearing your voice?'

'No, Fright. That started last year when I realized that the earth was flat and life was completely meaningless . . .'

'Seeing as we're talking about sex, I'd say my story was better, though.' I dig into the junk of my past again.

'Just be careful not to finish Fright off completely.'

'Better for her to be killed by a story than by cancer or her family.'

It's noon. I'm woken by the sun. It's stuffy, the room full of dust whirls and smells. It smells just as it does at night when, ashamed in case the sad, lonely moon face sees me, I withdraw to the edge of our enormous bed. The springs squeak less there, the moon doesn't see me, the children don't hear. Ninety kilos plus sixty-five is as much as a baby hippo. All night long, my husband and I were a baby hippo, straining the bed springs, moaning, snoring, rolling over, jumping and, finally, making the bed wet. In the morning the whole room smells to me of this baby animal; it's just that we wake up as humans. I push my husband's limp hand away from my wet crotch. I get up, wanting to make sure our children haven't drowned, burned down the forest, died of boredom or bleached the dog's fur. Nothing more.

'Where are you going?' My husband grabs me by the hand.

'We do have children.'

'Of course.' He turns over, annoyed at having to live in close proximity with our children. 'Come back soon. I want you,' he shouts out when I'm already downstairs, checking that our children haven't died from some unforeseen misfortune. If our children did die, my husband might not even notice for several days, whereas I would be aware of the fact immediately because of the previously unexperienced peace and quiet.

Our children are eight years, four months and eighteen days old. My son is extremely bright, he reads encyclopaedias and journals. My daughter knows how to listen. They enjoy each other's company.

And there they are, alive and well, lying in the sun on a blanket by the river, talking peaceably as always.

'Spread your legs wider,' my boy says and grabs his sister's leg.

'Ouch, you're going to break my leg!'

'Hang on a second, will you? I just want to work out where the clitoris is . . . the book says it's here . . .' The boy is staring between his sister's legs, now and then referring back to the medical encyclopaedia that, in our house, is used to diagnose ailments and locate organs. If one of us has a pain in the lower abdomen, right side, we hastily pick up the encyclopaedia to find out what is there that might be hurting. Not knowing and no desire to find out is the worst that can befall someone.

'Hey! What on earth are you doing?' I scream at the top of my lungs as my son stretches his hand out towards his sister's vagina.

The children jump to their feet.

'We . . . He . . .' my daughter stutters.

'Is it correct, Mum, that the little mound between the small labia is the clitoris? And every woman has one of a different size? And when a woman rubs it, she feels the greatest pleasure in the world, greater even than that produced by D&G shoes?'

I stand there as if someone had doused me in cold water, sliding my hand into my pocket so my son doesn't come to know that a clitoris smells just like my fingers, as observed last night out of the corner of the moon's sad eye.

'Yes. That is all correct,' I hear myself saying.

'See, I told you!' My son punches his sister, who is as red as a beetroot. I confiscate the medical encyclopaedia and walk away.

'Yesterday's soup is in the fridge. I'm going back to bed for a bit...' As I move away, I hear the little ones giggling and whispering. You are never fully alone in this world.

All is quiet up on the first floor of our house. I bend over my husband's lips to hear his breath. It does happen, people do die in their sleep. All of a sudden, he grabs me, rips my shirt off and roughly pulls down my bikini bottoms. The messengers of joy are lined up on our bedside table: fat pink Žanis; the Leg, a full forty-five centimetres long; and the loser, Bobītis, thin and sickly, although equipped with an electric motor. Do whatever you want, just leave the Leg alone, I think to myself, but too late. My husband has already grabbed it and is aiming for my crotch.

'Do you know what the children were doing outside?' I try to distract him – I hate the Leg.

'The most important thing is that they don't touch my chainsaw; they could wreck the chain . . .' he says, and continues shoving the Leg inside me.

'No, no. Everything is fine with the saw. They were just trying to locate the clitoris!'

'Ugh, what's that?' My husband straightens up.

'Pass me the encyclopaedia.' I point to the book on the floor beside the bed.

'You know I don't like medical stuff.' He grimaces.

'Oh, well . . .' I take up a position and open my legs, 'Look, here, that small mound there . . .'

'Can we change the subject? Let's just make love.'

I wake up in the afternoon. My husband is caressing my behind and poking at the screen of his laptop with his finger.

'You can find all sorts of stuff online . . . Look at this, a hook-up site for couples.'

'So what?' I'm still not quite awake.

'I thought you might want to try this . . . this kind . . . of thing . . .' He stops mid-sentence and looks at Žanis, the Leg and little Bobītis.'

'What . . . thing?'

'I . . . thought we could meet up with another couple. Have a sauna together and, you know . . .'

'You're not right in the head.' I'm telling the truth.

'Yeah, well. Do you think I can't tell how much you enjoy Žanis, Bobītis and the Leg? You shouldn't suppress your desires. You think I don't notice how you moan and writhe about . . .'

I touch myself under the covers. It has stopped. It doesn't hurt like a raw wound any more, hiding the truth. It has stopped.

'All right, if you don't want to . . .' My husband shuts his laptop and moves away on to his side of the bed. I touch his shoulder, but he seems to be sleeping like a log. Maybe I have killed him?

Usually, I could bear it for a week. Let him not speak, let him turn his back on me in bed, let him watch television all evening, let him treat me as if I were nothing. Let him.

Ten days go by, and I start to long for human warmth, human breath on my forehead, words, curses, noisy indifference, thoughts.

A human being is a hippo following the herd. I register on the hippo-herd website, creating a profile with a caption reading 'Looking for a couple to share fun times with', posted a photograph of myself standing nude in front of a mirror with my husband taking the picture, gave my telephone number. All I had to do was sit back and wait – for forgiveness, warmth and two naked willing hippos.

'You shouldn't have done it if you didn't want to.' My husband finally embraces me tenderly.

'No, I want to. Of course I want to.' I'm ruining my family life by lying.

They come soon enough. Over the telephone they say that nothing will happen the first time. They will just have a look at us, like beautiful gods, have a chat and leave. They ask if it will be our first time. I say it will. Very well, they answer.

The woman, Odeta, is over forty. A bounteous, no, enormous, bosom, just the sort my husband likes and I don't have. Dyed black hair, red-varnished fingernails, slim legs and a plump tummy. The man is over forty, too. Bald, round glasses like that poet of Riga street life, Aleksandrs Čaks. Very much like Čaks. Odeta is named after a character from an opera or a ballet, but Čaks is just called Ivars, Andris, Guntis or something similar, without any special associations.

We sit and drink beer. We are sitting on the terrace by the sauna and having a beer. We talk about everything under the sun. We are emulators, sex maniacs, obscure people with no idea of how this encounter will play out. We are hyenas who watch and people who imagine. I drink and wonder how Odeta's enormous breasts look naked, and how they might grant me forgiveness. I have a plan, and Ivars, Guntis, Andris – or whatever he's called – has no place in it.

We've been chatting away for hours, gulping each other down. It's getting dark. For the first time in his life my husband lights a candle to make it more romantic.

'We should make a move home,' Odeta says, but my husband still hasn't seen her naked. I get up and slowly go over to Odeta. The beer wells up in my throat, I swallow it and sit down by her side.

'I want to kiss you before we say goodbye,' I say.

'All right,' she smiles.

Can you believe that the woman's lips are like ground granite, her saliva distilled water, her tongue gentle and wise, her hands warm and dry? She opens her eyes and whispers in my ear, 'Look at them both watching.' And watch they do. Frozen to their seats.

Finally I touch Odeta's enormous breasts. I don't like them. Heavy. I don't like heavy things. I want to let them drop. I want to grab Odeta's heavy breasts and throw them away, thus relieving her of them.

Soon we are both naked from the waist up. We kiss. I would have liked to add a pinch of salt and pepper to Odeta's saliva, rub an emery board over her tongue. It seems too soft. It's because I'm kissing a woman.

'OK, fine. We can stay a while longer,' Odeta says to the men, detaching her lips from mine.

We go into the sauna. We sit down on the bench, encased in pale slimy logs. I remember how I peeled the bark off them, drank vodka and kissed a man who has since disappeared without a trace. His place has been taken by another, completely different.

Bald Čaks moves closer to me; Odeta squats on the lower bench and caresses my husband's leg. My husband is looking up at the ceiling, sweat dripping from the corner of his eye, a lot of sweat, a lot, as soon as Čaks touches my breasts and pushes my head down until my lips touch the tiny Čaks, standing to attention very questioningly. My husband's manhood, diminutive at best, shrinks back further, tiny and sick, the salty sweat from the corner of his eye dripping down on to its small head. Odeta glances about, her leery eyes looking for a chance, her fingers feeling around, her breasts flopping. She rubs herself against my lap and pleasures herself. Čaks starts wheezing, Odeta moaning. Our sauna hut changes into a henhouse when the fox has got in. Čaks's groans of pleasure are so comical that I smile. At that moment my husband looks at me. He doesn't smile. I mustn't smile.

'I'll go and check on the children, see if they are asleep.' He darts out of the sauna. A cockerel bitten by the fox.

I follow him, but it's dark and quiet outside. I have a beer while Odeta and Čaks wait for the biggest pleasure in the world to come and go.

A while later I see our guests off and watch them drive away in their red Mercedes.

'I'll call you,' Odeta says before leaving and kisses me. I wash down the distilled water with a Pilsner.

The sad moon is no longer peering in at us in the bedroom. My husband has curled up in bed, wrapped himself up in the covers.

'Want to talk?' I put my hand on his shoulder.

'Get lost,' he shouts, and slaps my hand away.

I do get lost. I get myself lost down by the river. I want to drown myself. And I almost do. After the fifth bottle of beer I fall into a vortex. It's dark. Just as I'm about to meet my death, a strong hand grabs hold of my knickers and hurts me. When my husband's steps recede into the distance, everything is dark again. I drown in the wet grass and in my own tears.

In the morning I pack my bags and hold my children's hands.

'We are leaving,' I say to my husband.

'That might be for the best. I'll never be able to kiss you again.' He gives me a sad smile.

'It was what you wanted.'

'No. I wanted you to be better.'

I knew that he wouldn't actually let us leave. He loaded us in the car and drove us to the bus stop, then said, 'Who says two people who love each other have to kiss anyway?'

'Big deal,' F22 starts giggling as I come to the climax of my story, but Fright remains quiet. Very, very quiet. F22 opens her mouth to add something, but she doesn't have time to do so before the door bursts open and my family is standing in the empty hallway, enveloped in the smell of the corridor.

'There, I told you Mum wouldn't be tied to her bed. Only the violent ones get tied up!' my son roars. Goliath, our cat, is asleep in his arms. My daughter is tactfully keeping quiet; there must be something of me in her. I want to shout at her always to say what she thinks, wherever she is, but then I get scared, picturing my daughter in one of the rooms along this corridor. She is such a gentle girl with beautiful eyes and an excellent figure, perhaps she would do better to keep herself to herself. Maybe she doesn't actually have anything to say.

'Hi!' My husband squeezes stoically past the children and takes up his position by my bed. He stares at me but doesn't kiss me, just puts a carrier bag full of food down on the floor.

'We have our first clients. So far so good . . .' he says and looks around timidly. F22, Fright and Snow White are not looking away.

'Yes, Mum! We've frozen one man already, very well-do-to in his own right as well as benefiting from an inheritance. We've made mega-money. Two million for twenty years! It's just like storing a sausage in the freezer.' My son pulls a sausage out of a carrier bag. It's cold and hard.

'We could go for a walk . . . Goliath looks frightened.' My husband is still looking around nervously. He doesn't know the first thing about Fright, F22, Snow White and me.

'Fine,' I agree and put on my dressing-gown.

Meanwhile a care assistant comes in. 'You are wanted in the doctor's office,' she says, looking at me.

'But I have guests . . .'

'Never mind, lovey, family is no substitute for a doctor. Quite the opposite, my dear, quite the opposite.'

We go. Through the maze of corridors and silence. If I were to ask, Fatso would say that we were going to the electric chair. There's no reason to get upset, she says it to everyone. You can get so used to a certain expression that you no longer sense or understand what it implies. But if squirrels, when cracking open nuts, can tell empty shells from full ones, people should also be able to distinguish meaningful words from empty ones, even if the speaker is not family.

Mine stayed in the room. They will wait there until we can go for a walk around the hospital grounds.

'Sit down and tell me how you are doing.' Today, the doctor is exceptionally kind.

'I'm fine.'

'Good, good. Loosen up a little. How are you getting on with your fellow patients?'

'Very well.'

'Schizophrenia generally involves outbursts of differing natures, did you know that? A sane person, for example, would experience a strong dislike, so to speak, for imaginary voices, various fictions, the beautiful lies would get on your nerves . . .'

I really don't know why, but I cry out that it is he who is the liar.

'Is that so? Then do tell me what I have done to be worthy of such an accusation. Why don't we have a coffee? Then our little chat won't seem so dry and sterile.'

'All right. Milk and sugar.'

'Very well.' The doctor makes a note of something and switches on the electric kettle.

'First of all,' I begin, 'despite the European funding and so on, I don't believe it's fair to cheat Fright like that . . .'

'Fright? European funding? How interesting. Please elaborate.'

'Fright is that ugly woman from my room. Short, hunchbacked, crooked teeth, well, you get the picture . . . And the European Union is giving you money to deceive her, mislead her . . .'

'I really wouldn't know how to respond to that, but I don't believe that any of the patients in your room match that description. You are all, maybe not beautiful, but pretty at least . . . And what's this about the European Union? What has it ever done to you?'

He pours some ground coffee into a cup without asking how strong I like it, adds some water and milk and pushes the cup towards me. Brown flecks float on the surface.

'Well, from what I've been told your job is to charm the women who've attempted suicide, improving their quality of life by getting them to fall in love . . . and these services of yours are funded by the European Union in order to reduce the number of suicides.'

'Who told you that?'

'How . . . Who? Your mother, of course. She also told me all about a rather sad event from your childhood . . . I'm sorry your dad froze to death saving your twin brother.'

'I see. Yes, of course. As doctors, on occasion we change our lives completely in order to assist you, the sick. And what do we get in return? Nothing but lies and works of pure fiction on the scale of literary masterpieces. My mother is not in your room, of course, and I receive absolutely no EU funding . . .'

'But . . .'

'Let's get back to your problems. Tell me, did you meet up with the Green Crow at any time between childhood and adulthood?'

'The way you ask makes it sound as if the time in between was occupied by an indefinable vacuum!' I feel my blood slamming like a tidal wave into my head. I never could stand liars. Now I shall answer with a butcher's knife, no more poking about with a nail file.

'It's called puberty. And it *is* something of a vacuum.' He goes to the sideboard and retrieves some golden liquid, which he places between us. 'Here you are.'

'Yes, we did meet.'

'Tell me.'

Idleness. Pavements like a half-eaten wafer. Crazy birds. A deceptive impression.

The sausage smells as strongly as a woman does. What a disaster, shame on God for creating both sausage and woman (he should have thought twice before blowing growth hormones into the pig). I zip up my bag. I don't want a sausage. I don't want a woman.

I'm waiting for a being that is also a creature of God. Simply superb. She always has extra cigarettes, and some of them she shares with me.

And there she is. Green, 100-per-cent polyester wings, a chest broad enough to take on nearly the whole district, eyes like a geisha, shoes of the sort Russians wear.

I stagger to my feet from the kerb to stop her flying past me. She sees me and rushes over, smothering me with her polyester wings and asking what we should do. Let's have a smoke, I say. She agrees. So we shall. I'm glad. Lately cigarettes have come to mean more to me than my mum, dad and monthly travelcard. Not the cigarettes themselves, perhaps, more the smoking. I ask where we're going to smoke, but the Green Crow just carries on flying with me under her wing. We fly through the cage of the tram shelter, over gateways, many wonderful moments passing unnoticed. We fly along the pavement past the bakery and the shop selling punk accessories, whizz past the ice rink, the Russian school, on and on. How much further? I can't take any more.

The Crow pushes me into a narrow street. We are quiet. I know what the Crow is doing. She is kind, and I trust kindness. Caff-aaay, she suddenly caws, and we stop. A red neon sign – 'Café' – glows above my head. The Crow says it is a very cheap place, 'Very cheap, you'll see.' I really don't know why she is telling me this, but I trust her kindness.

We go in. We are assailed by the smell of old sea-dogs' fantasies, by the thickest of brewing storms, dated disco music blaring from appallingly low-quality speakers. But we soldier on. Or rather I do, almost tearing her wing off with my overwhelming compulsion to light a cigarette. The Crow remains cool; she stands her ground and doesn't drag me anywhere. I know that such persistence is deceptive. I have an urge to laugh out loud. I laugh. The Crow digs me in the ribs and tells me not to laugh. She says that laughter is a sign of irresponsibility and being under age. 'Look how quiet everyone is.' I look around. Indeed. I feel embarrassed and shut up. The people in the café look at us through a fug that has probably mutated out of the leftovers of oxygen. Some even manage to turn around. The bartender stares, too. I feel embarrassed, but the Crow doesn't – not in the least. She goes up to the bar, almost knocking over a clingfilm-covered bowl of pistachios and a tag reading '30 santīmi' with her green wing, then pulls her wallet out of her pocket and starts muttering, all absolute nonsense. Mulled wine! She demands mulled wine! And now everyone in the bar has turned to look at us. They are watching the Crow's and the barmaid's every move. Then the most appalling thing happens – the barmaid, with her aquiline nose, actually pours her some mulled wine. The old men growl in satisfaction and follow us with their eyes. There are no seats left at the tables so we make ourselves comfortable at the far end of the bar, next to the crackling sound system, a bowl of garlic crackers, marked up at '25 santīmi', a covered plate of smoked-sprat sandwiches at '20 santīmi each' and an ashtray. The crow gives me a cigarette and an explanation. Many years ago her mother had suffered terribly on this very date, and, if we assume that time doesn't actually exist, then she is still suffering now. I am confused, but the Crow looks at the clock on the wall.

'I must time it with the radio,' she says and lights a cigarette. I, too, light up. Our smoke rings mingle with other rings of smoke and the clove oil in our mulled wine. On the radio an Italian ballad starts playing. So, so whiny. I immediately feel like getting drunk. We are not drinking yet. We listen to the song in silence. The radio jingle follows. *Pam-para-ram-pa-ram.*

Someone announces that it's one o'clock. The Crow picks up her mulled wine and raises her green wing, solemnly extending the glass.

'Let's drink to my mother's torment being over.'

'Did she die?'

'No, I arrived,' the Crow explains.

We drink and smoke in honour of the Crow and her mother. I like the Crow, but the bar stools are incredibly uncomfortable. I start fidgeting. I want something to lean back on. Why can't we settle here for ever, I wonder.

'It's great here,' I say to the Crow.

'Yes,' she agrees and gets us each another glass of mulled wine. I leap down from the high stool and throw my bag on a free seat at a table. The Crow takes another. Someone else is sitting in the third.

We introduce ourselves to the Scientist.

He is drinking schnapps, taking tiny, elegant sips. We light our cigarettes. I keep quiet because I'm not sure what I can talk to the Crow about in front of the Scientist. The Crow doesn't realize that I don't know. We sit in silence for a while, then I jump to my feet.

'History starts in half an hour,' I say out loud to the Crow. For the first time the Scientist sets his glass down and looks me in the eye.

'Do you have relatives in Mongolia by any chance?' he asks.

I answer that I have a test on Trotsky in half an hour.

'History is always here. The present never makes it in time,' the Scientist says.

'And what about the future?' I ask, still thinking about history.

'I don't have a future.' The Scientist drinks with elegant sips. We try to do the same.

'Spit on Trotsky,' the Scientist says. And we both secretly spit on the floor. I notice that red spots have started to appear on the Crow's cheeks. I smile. Soon the Crow will start saying 'actually' after approximately every sixth word, and I will replace 'approximately' with 'almost', because it's much easier to pronounce. I really like the word 'actually'. A good combination of letters, it sounds almost magical.

'We could, actually, get another mulled wine.' The Crow has started.

'If you drink too much you'll become scientists.' The Scientist leans in closer.

'In which field?' I ask.

'In the field of science,' the Scientist answers.

'And how's that?' the Crow and I exclaim, almost in unison.

'You will forever be wanting to know things,' the Scientist says. 'Only scientists and professors come in here. I'm already a scientist, but those guys over there are still professors,' he explains.

A black-and-white cat jumps on to the table. I want to say, 'Look, a black-and-white cat,' but I say, 'Look, it almost looks like Batman.'

'As I said,' the Scientist continues, 'if you know too much you might end up like the professors. They keep quiet the whole time. They are afraid.'

'Afraid of what?'

'Of themselves and of each other. They are afraid of saying something stupid,' the Scientist whispers.

I feel quite melancholy again. I see that the Crow feels the same. To become a professor on your birthday, no way, it's too early. The Crow shoos Batman off the table. One of Batman's hairs has got in my glass, spotty as a quail's egg, light as life.

'Listen, let's not be afraid of all this nonsense,' I say, realizing how important it is.

'There is a solution, you know. It's fine to ask a silly question, but you mustn't give a silly answer,' the Scientist says. 'That's why the professors keep quiet.'

We have run out of cigarettes. I go to take one but the packet is empty. The Green Crow has run out of money, while I never had any. I do not want to leave. I've already said to the Crow how nice it is here, and no one wants to leave a place with such a pleasant atmosphere. It's just a shame that kindness alone doesn't suffice when you want to smoke, want to be able to stay in a nice place. I get up. The Green Crow does the same.

'Sit down,' I say. The Crow obeys. I go over to the table furthest away from us. I feel the Crow's eyes following me; I distinctly sense the Scientist's goodwill. He is a very elderly, very experienced man. He understands how a young girl feels when she has to leave a place in which she feels happy. I have to pull myself together. I feel slightly embarrassed.

'Professors, could I possibly ask you for a few cigarettes or, better still, some money for cigarettes and mulled wine,' I say in quite a loud voice so the white-haired heads on the other table can hear, too. 'Today, the great suffering of the Green Crow's mother came to an end,' I add.

The effect is immediate. Everyone stretches their necks to get another look at me – the turnover of customers in this nice place is both rapid and frequent. They come in as students and leave as tenured professors. And yet none of them gives us any money, the bastards. They just stare and give us nothing.

'How much do you girls need?' the one sitting with his back to us asks.

'We need a fiver,' I say.

'Do you, indeed? A fiver!' the Professor says and turns around.

'Mephistopheles!' I scream and lurch backwards, despite never having met Mephistopheles before.

'I thought he was Mephistopheles, too, at first!' the Scientist yells from our table. 'No, he is not Mephistopheles, oh no! He's a long way off – he's left it far too late for that.'

'I'm an artist. Somewhat below a professor,' Mephistopheles says and lets out an incredibly awkward laugh. More of a sneer. 'Actually, my friends – mostly women – call me the Old Buck. I also initial my paintings with 'O.B.', and this can be interpreted in a variety of ways – Old Being, Omniscient Being; I have also heard O. Bama – but the Old Buck is my favourite. Bucks never grow old, do they? Always the wisest and fastest, are they not?'

The Green Crow and I require a moment or two to absorb the fact that Mephistopheles is the Old Buck. The wisest, the fastest, the oldest. The Old Mephistopheles Buck. I want to speak to him, but it's not a good idea as he lends us a fiver and joins our table. The Scientist is none too pleased, says he feels sorry for us.

The Crow, starting on a cup of coffee, enquires why it is that he feels sorry for us. The Scientist smirks. The first impression is generally the right one – the world, too, was created spontaneously.

'You'll become a real woman, and then what?' he asks.

'What's wrong with that?' the Crow caws.

'It's too good. And too good is no longer any good,' the Scientist says.

The Crow and I are just fine, always fine. And so I say to all present that we are fine just as we are.

'Crows and people don't ever get enough,' the Scientist sighs and takes another sip, drinking so elegantly that such unfettered beauty makes me want to cry. I tell him so, as when you're having a really good time it's impossible to keep your thoughts to yourself; you have to share them. A tear drops from the Scientist's eye. He starts spinning a yarn about how very hard he has had to work to achieve such beauty, streaking his white stubble with tears and sobbing as he does so. I pass him a napkin from the holder on the table. He starts crying even harder.

'Stop making such a fool of yourself!' the Old Buck barks.

'Better a fool than not,' the Scientist snaps. 'I'm sorry that someone will suddenly come along and pluck these roses blooming here before our pile of shit, and then we will go back to being just a pile of shit.'

'Actually, what is he talking about?' The Green Crow leans in towards me, her breath smelling of mulled wine.

'About shit and roses,' I answer.

'He's quite right, actually, you don't get decent roses without shit,' the Crow says loudly. Too loudly. The Scientist starts crying even more bitterly than before. I pass him the last napkin.

'Don't make a fool of yourself,' says the Old Buck in the Scientist's ear, leaning over across the table. He thinks we can't hear him.

'You, Old Mr Buck, are much younger than the Scientist, and, besides, you are not even a professor, just some sort of artist. Actually, thou hast no right to dictate to him what he should or should not do,' the Green Crow says. I wasn't expecting that from her. Not at all. She has now moved into Phase 2, following the blushing and the use of the word 'actually'. Now she is starting her Bible-talk. So, she won't just say 'Pass me a ciggie' but 'My dear creature, canst thou pass me a cigarette'. I'm used to it. I like the Crow.

'I'm a cubist, not just any sort of artist,' the Old Buck responds, so icily you'd think he wanted to freeze the Crow's cheeks.

'I have heard say that you are known as the Old Buck,' the Green Crow cuts in haughtily. I am also of the opinion that the Old Buck is the Old Buck and not some sort of cubist. I agree entirely with the Crow – a person can't change their name and the skin covering their name at a single stroke – change a name, change the skin and all the rest changes, too.

'Why are you telling them that you are a cubist?' the Scientist asks.

'Because I *am* a cubist,' the Old Buck exclaims, probably a little too loudly, and the heads sitting at two other tables turn slowly in our direction.

'Just a moment ago you were the Old Buck. Now you are a cubist.' I feel angry, I don't like liars.

'You are so naïve, so incredibly naïve. People change all the time,' the Old Buck says and orders another round of mulled wine. He has completely forgotten about the fiver he lent us.

'You are a cubist, a chimney sweep, dust, a potato, a professor, the Old Buck, the Green Crow. You can be whatever you like. It's nothing to us.'

The Green Crow and I, we've had enough. It is sometimes the case that you have had enough of a certain topic, and this is then replaced by silent musing – an odious habit, especially if your friend has started using Bible-talk and you have no idea what tomorrow will bring.

'Old Mr Buck, a.k.a. Mr Cubist, pray forgive us our foolishness, as we forgive others,' the Green Crow croaks. 'Actually, let's have another drink.'

I dip the end of my nose into my mulled wine. I don't think anyone will notice me sucking it up through one nostril and blowing it out again through the other. I swill out my nasal cavity. Such a secret place where both nostrils meet. My father starts every day in just the same way – he prepares a light salt solution and runs it through his nostrils. He leaves the mulled wine for the evening.

Now both my nostrils are red.

'Thou hast the juices of life pouring from thy nose,' the Green Crow says, mildly excited.

'The capillaries on my insides art breaking.' I want to mock the Crow, I'm sick and tired of her Bible-talk, beautiful as it might be. Thank God the Old Buck doesn't see. He would say that it was time for us to go home, that he wouldn't offer us any more mulled wine and cigarettes. We don't want to leave just yet. It's nice here.

'You have to give blood in order to start living,' the Scientist says and looks me straight in the eye, which gives away the fact that my ancestors are from Mongolia.

'Will a glass of blood suffice?' I laugh.

'Maybe . . . maybe . . .' the Old Buck answers for the Scientist. 'If you're wondering what the Old Buck has in common with the cubist, I'll invite you for a short sitting.' The Old Buck is staring straight at me and, out of politeness, at the Green Crow, too. The Crow has folded her wings and rested her beak on the edge of the table. She is about to fall asleep. I get up and approach the Crow from behind. I tell her that she is not allowed to fall asleep here because then she would wake up as a professor. The Crow doesn't move.

'Which came first, the chicken or the egg?' I ask out loud.

'Crrr-oooow!' The Crow wakes and flaps her wings.

'Let's go,' I say to the Green Crow. 'We need to clarify what a cubist is.'

The Scientist, his head propped against the wall, carries on sleeping. There's too much knowledge these days. Cheap and within everyone's grasp. The Old Buck pushes us out of the door. How irritating such an abundance of oxygen can be! Soon the sun will drop very low to let us rise high enough.

'Go straight on and don't look back,' the Old Buck whispers, and he walks away.

'How?' I protest, but the Green Crow keeps quiet as it's quite complicated to ask 'How?' in Bible-talk.

'Straight on and then turn right behind the house, its roof tiles hit by the wheel of the Plough then straight on again, and then you'll see.' The Old Buck's voice grows distant. The Crow is staring at me, but I'm staring at the Buck's back, seemingly straight, seemingly quite noble. This time we are walking, the Crow's green wings are not carrying us because I have to carry the Crow.

During the session with the Old Buck, during which we attempt to get to the bottom of cubism, I can do no more than coax the Crow, tempt her with small treasures and trinkets, tell her to pull herself together as Crows are heavyweights. I say that starving tomcats and spoiled children live down the alleyways – all just waiting to pull her claws out one by one, poke her eyes out . . . I say phew, I say it would be a crying shame, but there would be no getting out of it.

'Oh, taketh me yonder, towards the sun and happiness, changeth me from Crow to human form,' the Green Crow whispers, still in Bible-talk. But she doesn't give up, she stays by my side, leaving her footprints behind on the path to our session on cubism.

I love the Crow from the very bottom of my heart; I just can't stand her Bible-talk. I wonder how we have so far escaped the phrase she usually churns out on such occasions: 'And the Lord God caused a deep sleep to fall upon him, and he slept: and he took one of his . . .'

So what? I just don't like Bible-talk, I really don't. I don't think we need that sort of language – it takes you longer to understand the world. If absolutely everyone measured the road as the Old Buck does – that is, following the stars – everything would be great and there would be peace on earth. I light a cigarette and feel proud that I'm going for a session with the Old Buck.

'Oh, wouldst thou be so kind to share thy cigarette with me?' the Green Crow rasps. I pass my cigarette to the Crow and light a new one. We are at the corner, the stars of the Plough are not yet falling on our heads, we have to turn right, and there he is with a plastic bag in his hand; rather saint-like, so unruffled and indifferent. I wave but am at a loss as to what to call out. I tell the Crow that we're almost there, that the Old Buck is in the distance waving, that we should hurry so the Buck doesn't run away. The Crow wants to flap her wings, but she's in no fit state to fly. I grab the Crow by the wing and drag her along. As the Buck sees us moving towards him he paws the pavement for a moment, then races away, glancing back at us every so often. We follow hot on his heels, not wishing to be late for the session.

'Oh-oh-oh. Nature doth exercise her temporary effect over me, granting me momentary serenity.' The Crow stops and refuses to move any further – meanwhile the Buck gains distance on us. In my agitated state it takes me a moment to translate the Crow's Bible-talk. Serenity, serenity . . . nature doth exercise, I think. What can nature make you do?

'Just tell me in plain language what you're after,' I shout at the Crow, 'and I'll try to help.'

'Oh-oh-oh, then both my flesh and spirit shall be alleviated,' the Crow croaks. And I understand.

'Do you need a wee?' I say, watching the Buck, who by this time is about to disappear around the corner. Instead of a Bible-talk 'yes', the Crow caws. Her cawing is heartbreaking, so heartbreaking that I almost tear my eyes away from the Buck, by now far in the distance. I tell the Crow to get on with it. She squats down, and the world is patient, serene. Drinking elegantly is one thing, but even more fascinating is when a bird relieves herself.

Softly, softly.

The Green Crow finally rises.

'You are beautiful,' I tell the Crow, but she just caws. I think birds caw when they are happy.

In the distance, the Old Buck is waving his plastic bag. I embrace the good Crow with tenderness and urge her on towards him. We are drawing closer, but the Buck darts away through a gateway on his right. We follow until we meet in the yard of a grey house. The Buck doesn't speak; he just looks. We look, too. We don't just look at the Buck but the bag in his hand as well. Through the yellow plastic we can make out two vitally important words: *Glüwein* and Marlboro. I smile. A couple more glasses of mulled wine and the Crow will not speak any more; she will just sit with great poise. The Old Buck is far-sighted. How else could he have reached such an age in the forest where the eyes of hungry wolves leer from every angle?

'So you girls haven't changed your minds?' The Buck leans closer to us. The Crow caws before I have time to answer.

'So you are the Old Buck and not the horrible wolf who wanted to get his paws on Little Red Riding Hood?'

'Of course I'm the Buck, of course,' the Old Buck replies.

'The air, then, is actually clean.' The Crow grabs me by the elbow.

The Old Buck digs about in his bag then hands me a packet of cigarettes.

'Have your cigarette down here, then come up to the fourth floor. I'll wait for you there.'

The Crow wants to caw, but I grab her green wing, signalling 'Shhh'. The Buck probably has to clear away some dirty dishes and iron out the creases in the tablecloth; the Buck has to get in the right mood for the session. He, poor guy, hadn't been expecting us, hadn't been hoping for us. 'Let's just make it a quick one!' I say to the Crow, but she can't smoke quickly; she stands there with a cigarette in her beak reciting a psalm in Bible-talk. I don't understand a word. I just keep saying, 'We're having a good time, a really good time, aren't we?' The Crow's beak is beautiful despite being a sooty black. I have a mad urge to kiss the Crow. I tell her to take the cigarette out of her beak. The Crow just stares and doesn't take it out. 'Please, take that cigarette out,' I repeat. She doesn't say anything, but I answer anyway, 'Because I want to kiss you, you idiot!'

The Crow spits out the end of her cigarette in a flash and turns her sooty beak towards me. I stroke the Crow's wings and press my cheek against her beak – it's warm and dry and can't be pursed – and why should it be?

'Crow, you are my home,' I say and touch my lips to her beak

– it smells of tar and bone. 'Let's go. The Old Buck is waiting for us on the fourth floor. Did you see he had some cold mulled wine in his bag? With any luck he has a kitchen with a saucepan. Come on, let's go!' I push the Crow through the door. 'If he doesn't have a saucepan we can drink it cold, can't we?'

'Caaaaaaaaaaaw!' The sound escapes from the depths of the Crow's little heart.

'Obviously it doesn't really matter if there's a saucepan or not.' I try to catch my breath on the third-floor landing. 'Crow, what's the fastest-swimming fish in the ocean?' I ask, just to say something.

'The cachalot is the fastest,' the Crow says. I don't reply, never having heard of a cachalot before.

'What's a cachalot?' I ask the Crow.

'The fastest fish in the ocean,' the Crow answers. We have an excellent understanding, the Crow and I. I knew that she would say 'a cachalot', and she knew that I didn't know what a cachalot was. It's wrong to say that a common language can't be found; it's not like that. It really isn't. Anyone can talk, always and about everything.

The Old Buck, having put on his slippers, is now standing in the doorway smoking. Once more I feel like screaming that the Old Buck is Mephistopheles, he looks so composed and sagacious. I find I want to renounce our session in favour of some sort of revelation, but then I glance at the Crow. Some quality time with the Buck presiding over it could be just the thing to get the desperate bird back on her feet. I decide against crying out 'You are Mephistopheles.'

'Everything is ready,' the Old Buck says quietly, then, instead of ushering us in, pushes us into his lair. There is no denying that this is rather dubious behaviour, but I say nothing to the Crow. I have no wish to agitate her further, to no avail. In no time at all the Crow has become frustrated, as there, right in front of the entrance four small, male rhinos are sitting on a wall, their snouts extended towards us. I, too, am frustrated. Unbelievable.

'This is realism,' the Old Buck smiles.

'I can see very well that it is realism. I'm not blind,' I snap.

'Realism is reality, yet reality is not realism,' the Old Buck says. He does not seem to be particularly at ease with the Crow and I standing on the threshold. I think it's rather poor manners to welcome your guests with realism. We squeeze past the rhinos.

'What else around here is realist?' I ask.

The Buck responds that, as yet, he himself is not but that his apartment, in its essential sense, is pure cubism. We are relieved to discover that the rhinos are no more than a painting, although their horns are real.

'Have you got a horn?' I ask the Buck.

'Yes, I have,' he answers in all honesty.

I like honest people. The Crow seems to be placated, too. The Buck shows us into his room. Everything is quite normal in there. A sofa, creased bed linen on the floor, a badly renovated rococo-style table, a television, a lamp with a dusty shade, a broken bottle on the floor, a pair of women's knickers over by the cupboard. The smell is not the nicest, and there is an ashtray on the rococo-style table. Everything is normal. The Crow and I are able to relax completely. I light up, but the Old Buck darts over and snatches the cigarette from between my fingers.

'But we are indoors! You are not allowed to smoke in here,' he says and then notices his ashtray on the rococo-style table overflowing with cigarette ends.

'All right then, just this once, OK?' he says. I light a cigarette for me and another for the Crow – all this vexation has not done her any good on her birthday. Her beak is looking quite slack, and it worries me. The Old Buck invites us to sit down on the sofa. He urges us to be careful, not to burn holes in the furniture, but we are in no frame of mind to mark the sofa; we want to get on with the session and find out what's what. We don't like to rush the Buck – he has hurried his whole life, running away, hiding and all the rest, probably, only to meet us and arrange a session for our benefit. This can provide life with meaning – there is nothing to laugh about. I don't know why the Scientist was so set against us going to the Buck's. The Old Buck is just the Old Buck.

'Isn't that so?' I ask the Crow, realizing immediately that she can't answer as she hadn't heard the question. And even if she had, her exacting Bible-talk standards wouldn't allow her to respond with a plain 'Yes'.

'Never mind,' I say, 'everything is good today, absolutely the best. I didn't say a word, and you don't have to reply to anything.'

The Buck hurries away, most likely to the kitchen, as he hasn't offered us anything yet. Our treat should be coming soon, smelling sweetly of cloves and cinnamon, although . . . oh, what difference does the smell make?

'Do you think that mulled wine should smell of cloves?' I ask the Crow. She says nothing, looking grumpy, until the Old Buck, our cubist host, appears before us bearing two steaming, half-litre jars in his hands. The Crow smiles. Of course, she would do when mulled wine is just a wing-stretch away. A simple truth is suddenly revealed to me – even if the mulled wine were to stink of old socks we would still drink it.

'Let's get started,' the Old Buck says and pours himself a glass of schnapps. We have jars, he has a glass – this is something that I do understand. What makes the Buck such an excellent host is that his glass holds two hundred grams, whereas our jars take a full five hundred.

'The session is starting NOW!' the Buck cries, a television remote visible in his hand. I sulk, and, unfortunately, I believe both the Buck and the Crow notice – she searches me constantly for some kind of explanation as to what's been happening to the Buck and to her. She sulks, so I sulk, too.

What's the television got to do with anything? What? We have come to find out, to prove beyond all doubt, who the Old Buck is and what a cubist is. I feel like leaving, dragging the Crow along with me by the wing. The Old Buck needs to do something dramatic, take all his clothes off maybe or pull a dead hare out of a vase, make the clouds move, turn into an ugly old crone who might actually turn out to be very kind-hearted – something at least as impressive as that. What a complete and utter disappointment, and there's enough of that in the world outside! We were expecting some sort of message from the deep, from the very core of his inner being!

Out of politeness we don't get up to leave while half a litre of mulled wine still swills, unfinished, in our jars. Turns out that the Old Buck is nothing but an insensitive narcissist. Seeing our indignation, he just turns on the television, meaning we have to keep quiet, who knows how long for.

The session gets going with a wide-open human eye being slashed with a cut-throat razor, followed by a hole in the palm of a hand with ants crawling out of it. It's not as dull as I expected it would be. Tolerable enough. Some guy, maybe French or Italian, is in the film. We see him dragging pianos with dead donkeys inside them and loving a woman in every which way imaginable. There's a severed human hand, a man on a bicycle in a nun's outfit and a woman mown down by a car.

The Old Buck tries to stir our interest, exclaiming, '*Bravissimo! That's what I call living!* Yes! Fuck her harder!' However, the film has its down side – it drags on too long, for one thing. I see the Crow starting to yawn. I ask the Old Buck to bring a drop more mulled wine for her. He asks irritably how we can think about drink at such a pivotal point but puts the film on hold and goes to the kitchen to heat up the potion. The film has been paused at a point showing the caption 'I spit on my mother' beneath a painting by the leading man, the great artist.

I read it and think. The Crow has stopped sipping. I know that she is thinking the same thing as me. I gather saliva in my mouth. I hear the Crow doing the same.

'Actually it's not as simple as all that,' the Crow speaks unexpectedly.

I amass saliva and spit – *we* spit. It hits the floor.

'I spit in my mother's right eye, but she turns her left to me and asks if I can hit that one, too,' the Crow says.

'I hit my mother right on the mouth, but she licks my spit from her lips and smiles. I'm horrified.'

'If we can spit on our mothers we are free,' the Crow continues.

'Yes, we are free, here in the home of the Old Buck,' I agree.

Soon, the Old Buck comes back with two steaming half-litre jars in his hands.

'Salvador Dalí, a cubist,' he says. 'A great artist.'

'Was he someone who would spit on his mother?' I say, wishing to know if his greatness came from being able to do this. 'Did you spit on your mother, too?' I ask the Buck.

'No, she died,' the Buck answers and laughs at Salvador Dalí's shoes.

The Crow and I, we are still enjoying the honesty that seems to radiate from the Buck. Especially the Crow. She places her head on the Buck's shoulder. I feel uneasy. I also place my head on the Buck's shoulder. The film becomes really dull – no naked bodies or blood. There is an ordinary scene where the famous Salvador Dalí is having an argument with his father. As if that wasn't as commonplace as spitting on your mother.

'What is a hero?' the Buck asks, standing up abruptly. I fall on to my right side, the Crow to her left. Our heads bang together at the point where the Buck had been sitting. We pretend that it doesn't hurt in the slightest.

'A hero is the one who saves the world,' I say.

'The only hero is Jesus, the Son of God,' the Crow preaches.

'No, my dears,' the Buck says coldly.

The professors are quite right to keep quiet. They plainly don't wish to sound silly.

'A hero is anyone who stands up to his father's authority and trumps it.' The Crow's esteem and mine for the Buck rises. The topic of mothers and fathers is always an interesting one – it resonates with everyone.

'Which comes first? Spitting on your mother or standing up to your father's authority?' I ask the Buck.

'If Jesus had cast off his burden . . .' the Crow chips in with a rhetorical question.

'In that case, he would be a hero,' the Buck says, although it is clear that he has something more important than Jesus on his mind, something emanating from his inner self. All the same, the Buck says no more and sits back down on the spot where the Crow and I had knocked our heads together. The Crow places her head back on the Buck's shoulder. I start thinking that the Crow would willingly allow the Buck to fondle the underside of her wing, which I have heard is incredibly silky and beautiful. The Crow can be won over with honesty. That alone, naturally.

The Buck flips to a music channel. There is a little mulled wine left in our jars. Cubism is perfectly clear to me now, although I still don't know who the Buck is. I want to initiate a conversation about the essence of things, but I feel frustrated for the second time that evening. This time it's because of the Crow. She presses her beak to the Buck's ear but not to whisper; instead she sticks her tongue out – which I am surprised to see is forked like a snake's – twirling it around the Buck's ear as suggestively as a woman in a film. What Bible-talk is she going to whisper in his ear? I'm genuinely concerned. For the time being, however, she does no more than tickle the Buck's ear with her tongue, the same tongue that a second earlier had defended Jesus. I feel a bit awkward. I don't like the way this is going at all. The only logical explanation is that I'm hallucinating. The Buck is not reacting in any way; he isn't sticking his tongue out or trying to touch the underside of the Crow's wing. Something here is not quite real. The Crow seems to sense this, too, and stops wiggling her tongue around.

'Any more mulled wine going?' I ask.

'I only have schnapps left,' he replies, thus confirming that it is all real and for real. I don't object, telling him to pour me some schnapps, but the Crow stands up.

'I thank our host and go in search of pastures new,' she caws. I, too, get to my feet.

'You must journey alone down the long road,' the Crow says,

looking me straight in the eye, her beak curved in a smile. I like the Crow very much. I sit back down next to the Buck. The Crow spreads her wings and flies away, revealing briefly the underside of her wings. The Buck waves her farewell and locks the door.

'Who are you?' I ask the Buck.

'I'm the Old Buck,' he answers and passes me a full glass of schnapps.

'And who are *you*?' he asks me.

'I'm me,' I answer the Buck.

'Pleased to meet you.' The Buck extends his hand, which is large and clammy, but the schnapps is sweet.

I'm enveloped by a foetid warmth. It smells of freshly mixed concrete. I'm unable to open my eyes. I hear the dust on the lampshade, I feel a broken bottle piercing the linoleum, I feel the breath of the rococo-style table on my foot and the sofa cursing at my temple, I smell the knickers on the floor – now there are two pairs. I recognize my own smell. There is an advertisement on television for mobile-phone rates at two santīmi a minute. The door creaks and water runs. Someone touches my shoulder – yes, it probably is my shoulder.

'This is for you,' the Old Buck says. I stretch out my hand and take whatever it is the Buck is handing me. It's a glass. Oh, merciful gods. I keep my eyes closed and feel the rim of the glass; saltiness touches my lips.

'Ugh, what's that?' I spit.

'Your blood,' the Buck says. No way could there possibly be a whole glassful of it.

I open my eyes.

*

160

'So you gave up your innocence to that arrogant artist?' The doctor has emptied the bottle of golden liquid, and, in its place, an almost half-empty bottle of schnapps has appeared on the table.

I dare to say, 'You are drunk.'

'That's really none of your business. What happened afterwards?'

It is a long morning. The longest of my life.

The Buck is kind. He doesn't rush me. He just watches as I roll out of bed and crawl to the four bull rhinos in the hallway.

'The mirror is behind the fourth one,' the Old Buck calls out from the bedroom. I count the bulls. One, two, three, four.

'There is no mirror, Buck,' I say, 'none whatsoever.'

'There always has been one there,' the Buck shouts back.

I count again. Now, I start from the rhino in the middle. One, two, three, four. There is still no mirror, none.

'You are counting the wrong way,' the Buck calls out, but he doesn't come to my rescue. 'Start with the first rhino and end at the fourth.'

'How am I supposed to know which is the first and which is the fourth? Tell me which the first one is,' I demand.

'Just start with the first. That's all there is to it.'

I don't have the patience to question the rhinos themselves as to which of them is the first. I take hold of the upper left-hand corner of surrealism and rip it. It comes off quite easily, tearing neatly around the horns. They remain on the wall. The mirror really is next to the fourth horn. I should have counted from the one closest to me, but you never know which that is. I needed to see myself, which was why I treated realism so harshly. I edge up to the mirror sideways on. There is emptiness.

The mirror is beautiful when you are not right in front of it. I take a step to the side and scream. Red nostrils, red eyes, red hair.

'Why am I so red?' I ask the Buck.

'There is nothing to be ashamed of. It happens,' he answers. 'You need some mulled wine. Red on red makes white. Take my word for it. I'm an artist, a cubist.'

'Where is the mulled wine?' I ask, trying to cover my whole body with my hands, but they are too small. I pick up the piece of realism featuring the bull rhinos and cover my head with it. I sit on the floor.

'Get dressed. Let's get going,' the Buck calls from the bedroom. Good Old Buck.

'Have you ever been to Venice?' I ask the Buck.

'Of course! I am an artist after all, a cubist.'

'You must have a mask then.'

'No, I don't have a mask.'

'Shame,' I say. 'Everyone who goes to Venice brings a mask home, so why don't you have one?' The piece of realism covering my head quivers, troubled by my breath.

'Because I'm the greatest mask-maker of them all. I can design and fashion any mask whatsoever,' the Buck says.

Wonderful Buck, my Old Buck! Everyone should have an Old Buck like mine, then everyone could go around behind a mask, and it would be just beautiful.

'What kind of mask would you like?' the Buck calls from his room.

'That's easy. I want a woman's mask.'

'Women are all so different.'

I shout back that I want to be a beautiful woman.

'Fine,' he says, 'but there are so many beautiful women. What kind of beautiful woman do you want to be?'

'Well...' Here it gets a little tricky. What a wonderful opportunity to be a woman! Wonderful! I'm touched. 'Well... I don't really know,' I shout back to the Buck.

'You must have some idea of who you want to be.' The Buck is clever.

'OK, fine...' I'm quick enough to sense that she should be around thirty with an aquiline nose and blonde hair, even if it is dyed.

'Everything is dyed here,' the Buck says soothingly.

'Good,' I say. I shrug the piece of surrealism off and go to the bed and hide under the covers.

Meanwhile the Buck starts work. I hear the pencil scraping, the paintbrush dancing. Clearly, very, very clearly. The Buck is fast, both in the forest and in life, where danger is ever-present.

'Ready!' the Buck finally shouts from his cubist studio.

Again, I am moved. The Buck is extremely kind, drawing me absolutely free of charge.

'Here it is!' The Buck snatches away my blanket and extends my face towards me. I press the mask on to my face. Face to face.

'You are beautiful,' the Buck says.

'Yes, thank you, Old Buck.' I shove my head back under the covers to hide my tears of joy from the Buck. Now it is safe for us to walk down the street.

'I need some string,' I say.

'What for?' the Buck asks.

'To attach the face.'

'*Ein Moment!*' The Buck picks up the pair of knickers left near the cupboard and removes the elastic from the waistband. 'That's it,' he says. 'Let's go.'

'Let's go.'

The Buck pushes me out on to the landing. He slams the door shut. I stand all alone with the face of a beautiful woman. Buck, are you ashamed of me? I address my question to the door. No, you are ashamed of yourself, comes the answer. Where are we going? I ask. We have to find new knowledge! I shall be the invisible man, right by your side, but then I will become visible again, all right? Very well, Old Buck, I'm going. But why do you want to be invisible? You are too beautiful with the mask I made for you. You must see that. Yes, I see that you are old and ugly. Do you have more questions? No, I say and make my way down the stairs. I know the way to the temple of science, I tell the Buck when we reach the ground floor. The Buck doesn't answer. It clearly must be hard to be invisible *and* talk at the same time. Don't talk, just be by my side. You know, Buck, I, too, want to be great. Yesterday I spat on my mother, and today I shall counter my father's authority and trump it. I know the battle will be long and hard, but fathers can be such tyrants – it's all very bad. What was your father like? Did you trump him? All right, you can tell me later when you are visible again.

I feel Buck's hand in mine. Buck, would you like to be my dad? Buck, would you like me to have your children? Buck, Buck, my Old Buck. Wait for me here, I'll just nip in to the chemist's, just in case you say that you don't want any children after all. I let go of the Buck's hand. What is it like, Buck, life? You are old, you must know.

So true. Life is indeed long. The Buck would have to live another lifetime before he could answer that, I get it. When you are as successful as Salvador Dalí you'll make a film, won't you? Then it will emerge that your life lasted just two hours. The invisible Buck doesn't reply, but I know that he heard me. Sometimes people need an immensely long time to think. I smoke and trust the world, in its goodness, in the goodness of others. I trust that everything is good, I feel good. The older you get the worse the world seems. That's because it has to carry so many lives on its shoulders, always remembering that the one-to-one ratio remains unchanging. One person: one world. No, not really, I don't really believe that the world belongs just to one person. And who would that be? The Buck? The Green Crow? The Scientist? Me? No, the world belongs to everyone; we are put here to live. I smile under the 'Café' sign, clapping my hands like a schoolgirl, exactly like a schoolgirl. I dive in through the smoke and am pierced by the aquiline nose of the barmaid, caressed by the eye of the Scientist.

The Green Crow! The Green Crow is sitting next to the Scientist! I want to embrace her, my joy scattering left, right and straight ahead, but the Crow rises from her chair.

'Hello, Crow,' I say, but she turns her beak away from me.

'What's the matter?' I ask, but the Crow touches her wing with the tip of her beak.

'Yesterday you fractured my wing.'

'How?' I can't believe it, I love the Crow so dearly, am so very fond of her.

'It probably happened when you were dragging me off after the Old Buck,' she says. 'I could hardly fly home, something I didn't *actually* realize until I'd slept off the effects of the mulled wine.'

Actually . . . the Crow is back on the mulled wine.

'Please forgive me.'

'I don't know if I *can* forgive you. In zoology class we learned what happens to birds whose wings are damaged.' The Crow is staring at the wall but speaking to me. 'Chapter eighteen, paragraph five: "When birds become human",' the Crow quotes. 'Why did you want me to become human?'

'I didn't want anything of the sort, you are so, so dear to me,' I tell her sincerely.

'Your mother clipped your wings, too. Remember that?'

'Yes, I do. It was awful.' The memory returns.

It was indeed horrible. My dad held me down while my mum got to work. That evening I had flown to see the Crow, we drank beer and listened to Pink Floyd. I flew, flew. All we wanted was to be ourselves. I might have been wrong in flying back home so late, but when I got there my parents were waiting for me, scissors in hand. Your great-great-grandmother clipped your great-grandmother's wings, your great-grandmother your grandmother's, your grandmother mine and I shall clip yours, my mother said as she did so, feather by feather. Only once did my dad raise any objection as he was holding me down. Her wings, they are so beautiful, he said while my mum carried on snipping, her fury growing. It's some sort of affliction, she said. Humans are supposed to walk, their feet on the ground, not fly.

'I don't want the Crow to be human. There are enough of them already, and they mutilate crows. I'm sorry, Crow, I'm sorry. Just keep loving me, won't you?' The Crow tosses her head and stares at the wall where the café's licence hangs. She doesn't speak.

'Which one of your two faces is speaking?' The Scientist enquires.

'Mine,' I answer. 'The one with a heart.'

'Do you mean that the woman hanging around your neck – who looks quite real, by the way – doesn't have a heart?'

'The Old Buck didn't draw one,' I answer.

'Didn't *paint* one . . .' the Scientist corrects me.

The Crow still isn't talking to me or looking at me. I need her to talk to me, even just to look at me, but she won't. I want to tear off the mask of the beautiful woman drawn – no, painted – by the Old Buck, but the knicker elastic gets caught around my ear, and I can't get it off.

'I did warn you,' the Scientist says and drinks so elegantly – as if he could do otherwise.

'The Buck should become visible again soon,' I say. 'Then he can take it off for me.'

'An artist is he. Never shall he remove his artwork,' the Crow caws, much to my surprise, once more in Bible-talk.

The Scientist rises from his chair and staggers over to the bar, picks up the bowl of pistachios and crawls up on to the pile of shit on which we – the perfect, the fragrant – are sitting.

'Have you read Tsvetaeva?' the Scientist asks.

I shrug, but the Crow nods her beak up and down. Of course we've read Tsvetaeva – in Russian literature class. I'm purposefully obstructive as I don't recall the name. I can only remember Blok, as I wrote an essay on him. The Scientist says that he doesn't like Blok – such a masculine individual for poetry, far too masculine. Poetry is a woman, he continues. Rhyme, trochaic tetrameters and iambic pentameters serve to create a rhythm of the sort that can only be dictated by a woman.

The Scientist blows his nose and continues to drink elegantly. The doorbell chimes, and the Old Buck comes in. I throw my arms around his neck, my hands feeling the touch of 100-per-cent polyester that then vanishes with the wind. Migrating birds gain height when flying into the wind. Crows do, too.

*

'So, after this little incident, the Green Crow didn't show up for a while?'

'Exactly. Shortly afterwards I met my children's father, and the Crow didn't appear again for several years.'

'And what happened to the Old Buck?'

'After I dumped him the Old Buck turned Orthodox and started painting cubist Virgin Marys.'

THE NEXT CHAPTER

We separate in silence. He waves me away with his hand, indicating that I should go, and I obey, keeping the most exciting part of the Buck story to myself. The doctor is drunk, and drunks can't tell pearls from shit. They are like Burgundy snails; changing sex for the mating period, adjusting, vanishing, staggering and in the morning throwing up on the whole world. I've already told him that I won't report him, won't tell anyone that he's been drinking on duty.

'Your stories about the Crow are so exhilarating, so convincing, it's as if the Crow genuinely is real, whereas your family are total crap, like all families in any good drama. It's just not possible to listen to this stuff sober. Sorry.' I take advantage of his moment of weakness to ask about his family – his mother, wives, daughters, twin brother. One moment the doctor seems on the verge of telling all, then his eyes come to rest on my chequered hospital gown, and he demurs. He doesn't need healing, being a doctor himself.

If I enquire after F22 and Fright, he replies by reciting the hospital's motto – 'Our inmates know no boundaries'. He tells me to think it over, not to believe anyone. Poor doctor. At the Academy, maybe they didn't teach him that faith and love lie at the very base of everything.

Mulling things over, I haven't moved very far. I stand, leaning against the wall, surrounded by voices, the muffled clanging of metal, fast-paced footsteps and the motto 'Our inmates know no boundaries'. In the room along with F22, Fright and Snow White sits my family. Goliath is purring on my son's lap. I don't want to see them. None of them. When they came into the room my heart flutters slightly but then calmed back down. As with virgins. The first time, when a man's coarse hand probes about and strokes, they tremor with pleasure, fear and ignorance. Years later there is only pleasure, then just a sense of obligation and, in the end, nothing but weariness. My family is a hungry man with rough palms and a swollen member, but I am no virgin. I am weary and have a lover – the Green Crow.

No, I won't join them.

It's fifty days ago. A Sunday.

It is said that God worked for six days and on the seventh He rested. I never managed to do that – quite the opposite, in fact, as my husband had informed me that he would stop loving me if I went out to work. He told me I wasn't God, just a sinner. It would do me no good to try to emulate God. There are many folk observing different laws, all in fear of God. Maybe it's only far away in England – where cars drive on the other side of the road and, instead of schnapps, they drink tea in the afternoon – that things are different. They don't have Sundays there at all, and God is not as strict and furious a master as my husband.

'Aren't you dressed yet? We're leaving in five minutes!' My husband rips the cover off me.

'I don't want –' slips out truculently from my lips.

'The children are already in the car. Don't keep us all waiting. Oh, and don't forget to wear a skirt.' He slams the door.

I've owned four skirts in my entire life: a long flowery gypsy one; a short denim one like a first-rate whore's, which is gorgeous but intended for entirely different-shaped thighs to mine; a black one for funerals; and a blue velvet one for my trips to church. When the world announces that God is dead I will finally be able to burn them; for the time being I'm struggling to pull them up over my bottom for the delight of the God-fearing church elders.

We drive in silence. The children don't like church. They would much rather laze about in bed, fighting back the hot rays of morning sunshine.

'In the past families used to drive to church on carts.' My husband looks over his shoulder. There's a long queue of cars, probably caused by an accident on the bridge.

'It's not the past any more,' my daughter says.

'The church used to be the only place where young people could meet and fall in love,' my husband continues calmly, as if giving the youngsters a history lesson at school.

'But, Dad, you already met someone fifteen years ago!'

'All the same, church is still the safest place to meet someone.' He is watching the road ahead, careful not to shunt the Land Cruiser in front.

Who knows why, but his words give me hope, and I imagine myself sitting on a church pew, murmuring the words of a psalm. I notice a man in the row of pews next to mine – he can't take his eyes off me. He is wearing a black jacket and white shirt, his cheeks covered in soft stubble. He looks rather like Dr House. I redden and stop myself. I don't, I really don't need someone like that in my life!

'We will pray for eternal life,' my husband continues, having taken a reverent pause while I dream of Dr House.

'You mean our business, don't you?' His chain of noble thoughts and words is rudely interrupted by our son.

Without realizing it we have driven into the Old Town, where the mighty church tower – its spire topped by a golden cockerel – rises above the mosaic of pastel-coloured walls.

'When I'm sick and tired of everything I go up the church tower and look over the city from on high.' My husband launches into the story – we all know how it unfolds and ends – that every Sunday is augmented with some previously unheard-of detail. Generally, the story goes like this: 'Once, in the craziness of youth, I married my first wife. After a quarrel I decided to go out for a walk on my own. I walked and walked until I ended up in the Old Town, and, as people often do in similar situations, I decided it would be a good idea to go into the church. There was a service in progress, so I sat down and listened. The pastor spoke of forgiveness, patience, mercy – it touched me so profoundly that I went back home and forgave my wife for going off in my car to the seaside with her girlfriends. And so I still come to the same church every Sunday. Never miss a week.'

The children listen patiently. They are still young and tolerate their parents' stories, aware that each time new aggrandizements and as-yet-unheard-of events are to be expected.

'That day a stray cat came and rubbed himself up against my legs. I gathered him up under my jacket and took him home. We kept him for two years. A lovely cat.' My husband embellishes today's version of his story, and the children's faces light up – their dad brought home a stray cat. Their dad is kind-hearted.

'Tell us what happened to the cat next.' I can't stop myself. My husband's face turns dark, while the children's faces shine, their childish cheeks glowing, curious.

'Yes, Dad, tell us what happened next!'

'Your mum has got the upper hand again . . .' He looks at me like a wolf in a zoo – too well fed but furious about his fate. 'Around the time I took the cat, Goliath, home my neighbour's wife had a baby. When the little girl was about two she tried to stroke Goliath, but he scratched her cheek. The cat was not fond of non-believers, probably some sort of complex left over from his church days. My neighbour raged like a madman. He said he would dry out my apple orchard if I didn't find Goliath another home. I didn't really take him seriously. A month went by, and Goliath disappeared. That bastard of a neighbour had murdered the poor pussy-cat . . .'

'Then it's all your fault, Dad. I read somewhere that you become responsible for ever for what you have tamed, or something like that . . .'

'How did the neighbour kill Goliath?'

'I don't know. He simply disappeared.'

'Goliath probably didn't die at all! He probably just ran away. Animals – people, too – can sense when someone wants to kill them.' My daughter is looking at her shoes as if she has wanted to kill someone at some stage but was found out.

'Yes, exactly. He ran back to the church and hid in the basement so no one would be able to take him away again. Millions of people have sought and found solace in the church.'

Surrounded by the tavern, street café, art gallery and stalls selling colourful wooden Stalins, wooden spoons, wooden lighters, wooden trees, wooden wallets and wooden faces, the grey bulk of St Peter's Church looms like a tall Latvian in his natural linen clothes. Grey but with a golden soul, close to heaven. It would appear that our Pēterbaznīca – or 'St Peter's Church', as stated on the brass plaque by the entrance – will endure for ever, allowing people to look down over the city every Sunday or whenever they have some time to spare. It's hard to believe that Goliath might have lived here, but, if he did, I doubt any of the churchgoers would have noticed such a tiny little thing. I know full well what will happen as soon as the twins step foot in the church. They'll kneel down – ready, steady – then race off to see who can find Goliath first.

'Goliath disappeared seventeen years ago,' I say before going into the church, hoping to prevent my children from looking for the living among the dead.

'Cats can live as long as twenty years, especially if they live in a church.'

'Or for ever.' My son terminates our conversation and disappears into the fusty interior.

'You had to go and ruin this wonderful Sunday, didn't you?' My husband pulls me to one side by the entrance – I almost put my foot in a beggar's hat, a wealth of coins glittering within.

'What have I done now?' I feel my eyes once more submerged in saltiness.

'Work it out for yourself.'

I can no longer see the church vaults, the rows of pews, the figure of Christ, the martyrs, my children or today. Thoughts, like the tangled lines of anglers, knot together in my head. I fail to see how a person as ordinary as myself can suddenly do something capable of ruining Sunday, a day created by God and the Son of God, a painted representation of whom hangs before me, both in a frame and from the nails piercing his soft palms. I can ruin a white shirt by putting it in the machine on a 95-degree wash with a red blanket – but not a day. A day belongs to all of us. Really I shouldn't have asked for the cat story to be continued, knowing as I did how it was going to end. Bloody Goliath.

I stand alone between the pews, between people accustomed to occupying a certain place in life, on the pews, in their places, in heaven, on trams, in their families and in conversations. Somewhere, all mixed in, are my children and husband and Goliath from many years ago. The organ wheezes into life, and the pastor takes his place in the pulpit.

'"Not by might nor by power, but by My Spirit . . . What are you, mighty mountain? . . . You will become level ground,"' he begins, literally shrieking. The hubbub of conversation is transformed into a satisfied murmur. 'Do you think Christ had it easy? Christ was David, Goliath the evil snake, the temptress. You come across the snake every day. Goliath, that colossal, evil mountain which we must seek to transform into level ground, comes to you all, even in your dreams!' At the words 'colossal mountain' the most powerfully built men and women attempt to shrink smaller, casting worried glances at those around them.

'Today I shall speak in the name of God about happiness. Nowadays the wrong meaning is assigned to the word "happiness". Have any of you, reading the Bible, ever come across the words "happiness", "happy", "made happy"? No, never, and neither shall you! I tell you this – stop looking for happiness then you shall not be unhappy at failing to find it. Instead of happiness you will attract nothing but Goliath and his brothers! Heed the words of Solomon: "Better the poor whose walk is blameless than a fool whose lips are perverse . . . Wealth attracts many friends, but even the closest friend of the poor person deserts them. The one who gets wisdom loves life; the one who cherishes understanding will soon prosper."'

The pastor's words disappear like grain into the black, wet, wide-open, fertile mouths of the congregation. They will swallow all of Solomon's cautions, to the very last syllable. They will go home, open their fridges, turn on their televisions, make love while their children are playing outside and continue looking for happiness, probably typing 'happiness' into an e-Bible search engine and think their computer has stalled when happiness is nowhere to be found there. Humans are not meant to be happy. The ones that are happy tend to be frivolous, not politically minded, smiling – and definitely not going to church on Sundays.

I look to my right and left, counting people like passing flocks of seagulls or squares, the longest side multiplied by the shortest. There are my children and my husband and Goliath, too, maybe with his brothers and sisters.

'Let's go to the Annie Lennox concert at the Concert Hall.' I feel the touch of a warm beak on my ear.

'Fine,' I answer. 'What time?'

'Six o'clock this evening. I'll wait for you at the entrance.' The voice grows distant and light steps can be heard, softly tripping away along the red runner down the aisle.

It's impossible to refuse the Crow anything. She is my lover and my home. After the service my husband and I meet at the door of the church. My husband is furious because we didn't sit on the same pew. My son is grinning delightedly, clutching a tabby cat in his hands. He has found Goliath. He is so like his father. My son looks at my daughter, and I, like the pastor from his pulpit, regard my own congregation. Fat and wet from the river of words that never reaches the sea. The clever words dry out and make their way back to heaven. My boy is wet with excitement, with the duty of taking Goliath back home just as his father once did – and, who knows, possibly also his grandfather and great-grandfather, too.

'Dad, look. It is Goliath, isn't it?'

'Well, he does look very much like him . . .'

'Have a good look, Dad. It's him, isn't it?'

'Where are you taking him?'

'Home, of course. He will never run away from me. I know he won't.'

My daughter crosses her arms across her chest, sneering. 'He's not coming anywhere near my room. Never.'

The rest of us keep quiet. My son is very pleased with himself for having found Goliath, his father is delighted with his son for having found Goliath, and, as for me, well, however this male succession thing shapes up, I couldn't really care less.

'I'm going to the Annie Lennox concert this evening. Can I have some money for the ticket?' I ask, making the most of the moment's happiness.

'But it's Sunday. We have a dinner engagement . . . And who's Annie Lennox anyway?'

'A singer,' I say.

'This is the first I've heard of it . . . and on your own . . .'

'I don't know who she is, either.' My son is learning from this succession thing.

'At least tell us what kind of music she plays!' my daughter joins in.

I have nothing to lose. I move forwards, counting ten steps, go up on to my tiptoes like a ballet dancer and sing. Ta-da-da-da-da-ta-ta . . . No more I love yous, language is leaving me . . .

'What did she say?' My husband doesn't understand English. He went to a rural school and has a personal assistant who listens only to Gregorian chants – and no one has the faintest idea what language those are sung in.

'I don't love you any more, I don't have anything else to say,' my son translates.

'Is that so?' My husband gets angry, pursing his lips and breathing in sharply, his nostrils flaring.

'Your nostrils are like the cover of that King Crimson album, *In the Court of the Crimson King*,' I say.

'Who's King Crimson?' he asks, moving his lips as if they were heavy doors.

'A cult progressive-rock band, Dad.'

'Fine, how much do you need?' In the eerie shadow of St Peter's Church tower, he pulls out his wallet. I draw breath to speak, but he has already put it away again.

'If this Annie Lennox sings songs like that, you're not getting any money for her concert from me. Let's go home.'

And we are three children again. My daughter, my son and me. I follow my father.

'What's for dinner? It is Sunday after all!' my husband asks, cheering up.

'I'm doing green crow in a red-wine sauce!'

'Green crows are a protected species!' my son exclaims.

'Where can you buy it, and how much does it cost?' My husband pulls out his wallet again.

'A hundred lats. At the market,' I answer.

'Right, we'll let Mum out at the market and go home to tidy up for Sunday lunch.'

Shortly afterwards the car pulls over and I get out, leaving my mobile on the car seat.

*

No way, no. Far better to let them sit in the room and wait for me. I would much rather roam the hospital like a lost dog in search of its lost soul. I'll spy through the cracks of doors as doctors attach electrodes to patients' heads and summon souls back from the crossroads of the Milky Way, failing to realize that the soul has nothing to do with the head and that they are, in fact, the greatest of enemies. I will watch and smile, rejoice for the vegetables – the carrots, tomatoes, cucumbers, beetroots. F22 and Fright are so scared of vegetables. They don't know that human souls come together at the crossroads of the Milky Way and decide where to go next. We are timeless voyagers – the psychiatric clinic just a common-or-garden earthworm that knows nothing of the pathways of stars and the lightness of the soul when it is on the right track. What is more, they have no inkling that the souls that have made friends up there will never be separated or held back by others. The Green Crow and I, we stood side by side when the world was created, when love-filled milk poured from heaven down to earth and created life. Now all that remains are a whey-covered way and a crossroads – the stomping ground of the souls of vegetables from our clinic.

That was the day I finally got to walk around the whole city with a hundred lats in my pocket. They let me out of the car near the Central Market, where the pungent smell of fish melded with the sweeter one of meat, the fragrance of strawberries, sweet plums and sticks of celery, the lulling tones of gypsies, the screeching brakes of trams, the sweat of the pavement. I was threaded into the throng of simple folk, interwoven like a ribbon in a sturdy countrywoman's plait. I hadn't walked around the market for at least fifteen years. The market is the poor-people's supermarket; St Peter's Church tower their television.

I bought some strawberries, scooped up in a gloveless hand, tossed into a pre-used plastic bag. I didn't die. People don't, in fact; they just start reflecting a little on life and death. That's what spring is for, to get you thinking about who you are.

Right now the gang back home is cleaning and scrubbing the house, looking forward to green crow in a red-wine sauce. They don't know that the bird still needs to be plucked, which will smother the whole house in drifts of feathers. They imagine a green crow wrapped in cling film, gutted, eyes removed, wings cut off. I will just have to put it straight in the oven and pour my Green Crow's favourite wine over it, preferably a vintage merlot with a dried-fruit bouquet. I will take a pre-plucked green crow home to them. Plucked and gutted. We are to meet in three hours.

The clinic is quiet and empty. I'm still standing in the dark corridor where shadow conceals shadow like gift paper wrapping the world's biggest secret – light. I'm expected back in my room by my family. I'm sick to death of it all. I don't want to unwrap it again and find out. The shadow, here in the darkest corner of a corridor in this loony bin, is enough for me. Countless different noises echo around me – stretchers rumbling by, the tired beeps of life-support machines, nurses' comments, flies landing, a printer chugging away. Keys jangle at the far end of the corridor, someone opens a door and a man in a grey woollen coat steps out of my doctor's office. It is as if he has been cold since the age of two when his father, huddled in the snow, died trying to keep him warm. The man in the coat calls the lift, and I run to him, doing my best not to look like a crazy lady in striped pyjamas. This is something all parents teach their children – don't fidget, don't get worked up, keep calm, never do anything truly heartfelt, do not shout, do you hear, do not shout or I'll take you to a doctor to check you're right in the head, behave like a human or you'll get no sweets. Children like sweets a lot, so they calm down. But the adults who end up in a nut house are terrified of the electricity on the third floor; they don't need sweets any more and no longer fear their parents smacking them. They know that life means living in a way that pleases others. So I stop on the stairwell and, running into the fat care assistant, bite my lip and stare into the distance. They like it when you stare into the distance. The fat care assistant stares into the distance, too, but not at God – God is right by her side. While sipping her coffee she gazes at faraway lands, wishing she could leave and get a better job, be able to buy all of life's necessities. When Fatso vanishes down the dark corridor I race downstairs.

The man in the grey coat walks, teetering slightly, a brown briefcase crushed beneath his arm. Once or twice he runs his fingers through his thinning hair and continues tottering unhurriedly along. I follow the doctor I share with Fright and F22, just as patients usually do, stopping at every tree pretending to read a non-existent newspaper, staring at the toes of one's shoes. But the grey doctor doesn't notice a thing; he is drunk. When I stop by a broad old linden tree and peer out from behind its rough trunk, I start to feel really nauseous. A couple of metres away my husband is sitting on a bench, looking out across the pond surrounded by empty benches. The pond has been dug out specifically for psychotherapeutic purposes; it provides patients with an artificially induced sense of peace. A hundred years ago there might have been a graveyard for psychopaths here, a pit for dead bodies following failed experiments. But now a tern is fishing here, flying in search of bigger fish. He needs the biggest fish of all. The Green Crow would tell you that terns categorically refuse to eat cachalots as they are the fastest sea creatures on the planet and they can't catch them. Therefore, the book on terns says they eat all kind of tiny things but are not partial to cachalots.

The face I have lived with for more than a dozen years is my husband's. His slim nose, its tip folded over from sleeping on it, his cold blue eyes, his thin lips, a shallow dimple in his chin, his protruding ears hidden by his long hair. I also know that this man, sitting on a bench to one side of the loony bin's pond, stutters and doesn't use toilet paper to wipe his arse, preferring his hand, convinced that it's healthier. And he has a lot of money and a wife who lives in the loony bin and a son who, God knows why, has a bigger dick than his father and a daughter about whom nothing much of interest might be said.

The doctor goes out of the gate and disappears around the bend of the lazy Sunday road. I want to throw a stone, hit my husband on the head – you never know what a crazy person will do next, and, anyway, they can't be held accountable and you can't take offence at their actions. But I don't have a stone to hand. They have all already been thrown. Over the past fifteen years stones have rained down like hail. And anyone who tells you that stones never run out on earth, since they were created first, is a liar. First, God created light – so we would do better to throw light at one another, as light is never-ending.

I clench my buttocks rock hard and run to catch the grey-coated doctor. If my husband had happened to look up just then he would have recognized me immediately. Once he told me that if I were ever involved in a terrible accident and covered in third-degree burns he would still be able recognize me from my bottom.

The doctor slouches slowly along the pavement. The street is as straight as a rule, coming to an end far off in the distance where the enormous shadows of tankers sway gently in the dirty waters of the port. I cross the street. I don't know what date it is today, just as I hadn't that day my children and husband waited for their green-crow roast while I had a good time, knowing that the sky high above me was my husband's eye, watching but unable to do anything to me. Only people who have recently had sex are followed by eyes like that. The Crow thinks that human sex is just a question of the domestication of flesh. It's different for birds; they make love to have chicks, as is God's wish, God having said 'Let birds be born' and tasking birds with continuing His work to prevent them from dying out. And so they fly about, setting an example to us people, filling the world with their love songs. Humans, on the other hand, buy scented condoms from vending machines.

The day that I walk around the city I look up at the sky and cry. I think about the birds, none of them aware that the sky is actually my husband's eye and that I shall never be a bird, able to relieve myself neatly in the very iris of the sky's eye. There are times when, looking up, I see love, and the raindrops that soak me to the skin are tears of joy. So I decide to go into a shop and buy a small turkey, which I can cook in a wine sauce and serve to my family, presenting it as the roasted queen of the green crows.

There aren't any people around the entrance to the Concert Hall. The pavements breathe peaceably. The Green Crow never lies. There's going to be an Annie Lennox concert tonight. I stop at the entrance and see that my husband's eye is laughing; clenched like a pig's arsehole, weeping tears of joy. 'You are small and will not succeed. Nothing will come of it. Better get home. I will pin your turned head against a famous artist's painting and fuck you. It will be great. It's nothing to me if you like it or not . . . I don't care. I'm so used to fucking you. I'm fucking you now. If you don't believe me, have a feel of yourself, you are so wet you're making a noise as you walk.' I shove my hand between my thighs. He's right, as always. It's raining even harder.

'Oho!' The Green Crow lands in front of me. 'Just look at you!'

The Crow has an eagle eye. One like an eagle, the other like a hen. It's her genes. I feel embarrassed.

'If no one sees you can get away with anything. Even murder. But you're not murdering anyone, you're just shoving your hand down your pants. Then again, birds don't rub their wing on their . . . well, you know where I mean. The underside of their wings is very delicate; if it gets damaged, they've had it. Birds' souls are located on the underside of their wings, so we're hardly likely to rub our souls against our rear ends . . . but maybe I'm just prejudiced!'

'Why is no one here? Is the concert still on?'

'Why do you people always seem to think that you can't have a concert without drunks throwing up over the heads of people enjoying themselves? Come on, let's go in!' The Crow nudges my back with her wing.

'Do with me as you please,' I say and immediately feel ashamed for having said it. Once I resolved to say just that to a man who I was planning on loving, as I do those mornings when I wake up feeling alive, like the tiny damp body of a newborn baby. I almost said those words to the wrong man. Instead I said to my husband, 'Fuck me any way you please.'

'Even if our wishes are not the same?' The Crow stops and looks me in the eye.

'Yes.'

We shoot upwards, splattered by raindrops, up, swirling in a vortex. I clutch at the Crow's soft feathers just as I did when I was little, but this time I'm not afraid as I know what a family is. I scream. We shoot upwards, past metre after metre of concrete concert hall and the glass portals designed to let light in as well be targets for stones.

'Are you enjoying yourself?' the Crow caws.

'Yeeeees!'

I think the Crow is about to fly with me across the city, which from above looks like the drawing of a madman. I imagine stopping by the shiny cockerel on top of St Peter's Church and him telling us on which church elder's lap Goliath has been sleeping all these years. I imagine circling the supports of the suspension bridge and chasing cormorants on the roof of the Press House, or steaming along at great speed a hair's breadth from the darkly swelling waters of the Daugava. But nothing of the sort happens. Instead, we fly straight upwards until the outer wall of the Concert Hall stops. The Crow rolls me off her back like a heavy sack of potatoes.

'Cling-clang, we are here, my dear,' she says, and I simply cannot comprehend how I have survived all these years without her. My cheeks redden as I recall sawing off her beak, stuck as it was between the window-bars of our beautiful house.

'And now jump please,' I feel the Crow thrusting me towards the edge of the Concert Hall's roof.

'Why? What are you doing?'

'You are forty-two years old and you have no investments, no savings, no debts. You are forty-two years old and you don't know how dragonflies mate or how cats cry. You don't know what love is. You have nothing to lose. Jump!'

'No. Please, no!'

'Really? Wasn't it you who said, "Do with me what you will"?'

It only takes me a second to appreciate the terrifying extent of the entitlement I have granted the Crow, but it's too late . . .

The grey coat, still staggering, lurches ahead of me. At least twenty trams go past, clattering away on the rails. The sun, like a raw egg thrown at the window of a querulous neighbour, slides down peacefully, leaving behind it the blurred traces of the day gone by. The grey doctor stops at the gate into the port, shows something to the guard and continues on his way. The gates close slowly, and I am left behind outside clinging to the railings. The notion of returning to my children, husband, F22, Fright and Snow White vanishes in an instant when I see the doctor lurching along the pavement on the other side of the railings. 'There *is* a God!' people tend to exclaim when their luck is in, when they can follow their psychiatrist and don't have to go back to their families. Soon the doctor stops, scratching his bald head as if at a loss as to where to go next. That yacht with the enormous sails has most probably been bought with the money from the European Union, granted to him for deceiving ugly patients.

The grey coat disappears into the cabin of the yacht, and I am finally able to read its name. *Fright*.

Along with the wind from the sea and the plaintive cries of the seagulls, a sense of peace enfolds me. Snow White was right. The only thing is, I don't know where to look for the doctor's twin or why he is wearing his brother's coat. Maybe he has murdered him and thrown his body into the waves for the cachalots? Oh, poor, poor Snow White! It's enough to make anyone mad.

'So, nosing around in other people's lives, are we?' I hear a familiar voice, serene and wise, at my back. The last time I'd heard that voice it had said, 'We can't choose whom to love.'

'Jonathan?'

'Of course, my dear, of course! And you are the one who is forty-two years old, has two children and has forgotten all about the Green Crow.'

A white seagull, maybe slightly smaller than the time before, looks at me from the top of the railing. If last time Jonathan was fourteen, then now . . .

'Yes, that's right. Now I'm forty-nine!'

'I haven't forgotten the Green Crow. She just disappeared.' I avoid Jonathan's eyes.

'You don't say.'

'What do you mean?'

'The Crow never simply disappears. Her only enemies are children and cats, either being capable of scratching her eyes out and leaving her to die on a sweet-smelling spring lawn.'

'Do you think the Crow is lying injured somewhere?'

'I don't. I'm sorry.' Jonathan flaps his wings and lumbers heavily into flight, as seagulls usually do. 'You humans think toooo much. Farewell!'

Slowly the seagull disappears behind the dull, pitch-covered funnels of the tall ships. I don't know if I will ever see these ships again.

Certain words of Jonathan's churn around my head, as if they constituted my entire life yet already lay so far behind me. Can I turn back? Do I have time to turn back? That road, as straight as a rule, ends at the sea and that grey coat, and, consequently, you don't notice the face rising out of it. You think . . . you think that Jonathan is a senile old seagull.

No way.

All the same, I knock on the window of the port master's office.

'That man in the grey coat, does he have a twin brother?'

'Lady, what are you on about? How am I supposed to know if someone has a twin if they're identical? Only those who know him can know that. I'm just a guard here.'

'Yes, of course.'

'Well, goodbye then. Not from the asylum, are you?'

'How did you know?'

'They don't usually think much and end up down here. Goodbye now.'

I could jump into the sea off the tall ship and drown, as I can't swim; I could take off all my clothes outside the guard's hut and be taken as his wife; I could sit with my back propped against the railings and wait for Jonathan, as I still need answers to some of my questions; I could just stay here while the Crow, her eyes poked out, lies on a velvety lawn as she dies.

I could go, letting the twins – those enormous, stupid, beautiful creatures – crawl back into my womb, splitting into cells, vanishing into our bodies and entering God again. Moreover, I could wish that the tits of heaven would swell with my husband's evil words, and, oh, how I would laugh when the whole lot fell back into his mouth. How he would choke and gasp for breath, claiming that he is now a grown-up and no longer needs milk from heaven. I will return to the evening of the Annie Lennox concert, save the Crow and never, ever think of it again.

But a Number 18 tram thunders over the rails, carrying the reflection of striped pyjamas into the city centre.

The Crow pushes me off the roof of the Concert Hall because I had said 'Do what you want with me'. It's not the same as fucking someone on a street corner. The Crow opts for killing me.

Time and time again. And every time I die in her soft wings. I plummet down and she catches me a couple of metres above the ground.

'I want you to learn to fly, do you understand?'

'Yes.'

'I want you to learn to fly, do you understand?'

'Yes.'

'I want you to learn to fly, do you understand?'

'Yes.'

I stretch out my arms as required, as if they are birds' wings, and then I fall. Each time the Crow catches me and then shrugs me off her back.

'My arms don't have flight feathers. That's just how it is.' I just about manage to get the words out, but the Crow keeps pushing me off the edge, time and time again.

'Please stop loving me, Crow, please stop. We're not getting anywhere . . .'

'Too hard?'

'After falling so many times I'd rather just kill myself and be done with it.'

The Crow catches me again, as tenderly as a mother catching her child tumbling from the ninth floor. However, this time we don't fly back up, descending a little instead and going in through an open window.

'Do you still want Annie Lennox?'

The auditorium unfolds before us. Pale moonlight shines in through the window.

I feel the Crow looking at me. I am aware of the smell of living bone.

'So do you want Annie Lennox or don't you?'

'Well, yes, I do.'

'Here you go then.'

The Crow flies on to the stage, throws off her green nylon cape and smiles, smoothing her bluish head with her wing. Even very experienced ornithologists are unable to detect a bird's smile, going so far as to claim that birds don't smile at all, considering that if you can't see something, it doesn't exist. Nobody commissions churches in honour of birds.

But now the Concert Hall roars with the bird's music. The Crow stands all alone, centre stage, fragile and smiling, illuminated by moonlight. She bows deeply for me alone.

I look up to the little bird . . . she begins, first glancing at the high ceiling of the auditorium and then at me, looking me straight in the eye. I know this song. It's 'Little Bird' by Annie Lennox. It's my first concert in twenty years. Twenty years of silence. And now – Annie Lennox all to myself. Tears stream down my face, but I haven't got as much as a daisy, not a single little daisy, to give her . . .

'What are you doing in here?'

The graceful performance is interrupted by a voice behind me.

Naturally I turn around and am confronted by a man, shiny buttons down his front, standing there. A shiny button for every concert he's slaughtered.

'I'm listening to Annie Lennox. Would you care to join me?'

'Please, come with me.' The guard smiles.

The shadow of a bird in flight gleams on the gently lit wall. It follows us across the walls of dark night-time houses and downtown shitholes, city-centre banking buildings, the bumpy cobbles of the Old Town, the puddles of Pārdaugava and the windows of my house. I would like to wave, but my hands are cuffed; my mouth, however, is stretched in a smile. I know the Crow can see it; the guard, too.

After the fifth ring on the doorbell my sleepy husband, wearing only his underpants, opens the door. I see his aroused dick, so it must be about three in the morning. That's the time he usually wakes me up to make love. If I'm drunk or fast asleep he doesn't let his erection go to waste – he just pushes me up against the wall and gets it over with very quickly.

'Is this your wife?' The guard pushes me towards the door.

'Yes, of course! Where the hell have you been?'

'I found her in the Concert Hall. She was standing there humming a tune to herself. Asked if I wanted to join her listening to the Annie Lennox concert. Annie Lennox must be over fifty by now. She doesn't tour any more, does she?'

'I have no idea. I really couldn't care less.'

'Point taken,' the guard mutters. He removes my handcuffs and heads back to his car. 'I think your wife needs help,' he says, his head sticking out of the window. 'As far as I'm aware, Annie Lennox doesn't tour any more.' His car vanishes into the darkness, its tyres squealing.

'You weren't on your own, were you?' My husband stares at me, his eyes cold.

'No, I wasn't.'

'How long have you been together?'

'A very long time . . . since before you knew me . . .'

BABIES EVERYWHERE

The hospital building is shrouded in darkness. Lights can be seen in some areas on the third floor. When I was small I always used to count the lit windows in the maternity home as my mother and I rode past it. 'There are babies up there,' I used to say.

'Yes, my child, one day you will be up there giving birth as well, screaming, while other little girls ride past on the tram and look up at the light in the window where you, exhausted, sit cuddling your baby, and they'll say, "There are babies up there." Goodness knows how many little girls will ride past your window. Goodness only knows!'

No babies, however, are born in the madhouse. Instead, there are many who were once beautiful newborn babies and are now taking around twenty-one pills a day to stop them returning to the crossroads of the Milky Way. They fear that their friends and relatives, as they look up at the stars at night, will say only 'What a beautiful night' and fail to notice their next of kin trudging along at the start of the road.

In the madhouse everyone is asleep, experiencing drug-induced dreams. The hospital garden lies silent and empty, although as I pass the old linden tree I think I see a man with a straight nose, the end of which has been squashed where he has slept on it. He is sitting by the pond, waiting for the bottom he could recognize even if it were reduced to ashes.

The main door is unlocked. Loud rhythmic moans can be heard every so often coming from the reception area. There are no handles on the first-floor doors. Sisters and brothers are all asleep. I wake them up by banging loudly on the door. They don't ask me why I'm so late nor where I have been. They are not my husband; the ends of their noses aren't bent over and they don't have a lot of money.

I'm taken to my room, a dozen pills under my tongue. I wave good-night, and the nurse leaves. F22 is the first to wake up. She doesn't turn on the light – we don't have bedside lamps, so that we are unable to slash our wrists with the broken shards of light-bulbs in moments of lucidity. However, F22 has a bit of candle and a lighter hidden away. I spit the pills down the toilet.

'You really are mad! Where have you been? Your children and husband waited for three hours! The nurse lied to them, saying that you had gone for treatment. She could hardly tell them that the real nutters just vanish from the hospital without a trace!'

'For three hours?'

'Exactly.'

'Not long enough.'

Meanwhile Fright has woken up, too. 'Is that you?' She sits up drowsily. 'You have such a cool husband and children. You know, we talked for a long time . . . All that stuff you told us about them can't be true. Can't be.'

'He is not a proper husband to me. We just live together. And he is *not* cool.' I start to get really angry.

'But he is so –'

'Shh, Fright, I think she is about to tell us something!'

*

The twins were three years old at the time. Three years each – making six all together. They didn't go to nursery or torment babysitters. They walked around calmly holding my hands, one each. They were learning to hit a pancake stuck on the ceiling with a boiled potato. They laughed at each other's clothes. They wanted a cat. As babies they woke up three times a night and snuck over, each latching on to their own tit – one tit each. They rolled over my sleeping body and switched tits, as if milk flowed from one and water from the other. Every morning I would take my sleeping daughter to the sofa in the guest room because she, just like any woman-to-be, always woke up first and her fidgeting would wake her brother up.

My life felt as if it were slowly turning into a vigil. A water bog with two beautiful cranberries, and me standing on the edge of the bog protecting my cranberries, ready to dive into the bog, fight my way back out and prepare to protect them again. There are no seasons in the bog. There's nothing in the bog, just a rotten stump to sit on while watching over your cranberries until they are ripe and ready to be made into jam to ward off cold and misfortune. And you, the peaceful guardian of the bog, don't believe that the cranberries will ever ripen. But then the day comes when, at ten o'clock in the morning, you start believing in God. You get a call from the Apple Tree Nursery saying that they have places for your children. You abandon the rotten stump on the bog's edge. You come out of the forest and see the sun. You are blinded by it and buy some sunglasses in the Central Market for a fiver, sunglasses just like John Lennon's. But even that isn't enough.

You see an advertisement in the newspaper for useless things that are up for grabs. You see that an old stolen bicycle is free to anyone prepared to collect it. Never, not even as a child, have I possessed something that was stolen. So I race to the other side of the city to fetch my new means of transport. I pump up the tyres at a petrol station and roll home, as fine as any lady. I name the bicycle Blue because it is blue in colour and needs a name to reflect springtime, which is coming to an end, and because of the stickers of bluish-capped snowdrops that are glued to its frame so securely that later, when driven by feelings of depression, I find they are impossible to remove even when attacked with a knife.

My bicycle is bad. My bicycle is a piece of alloy metal that takes me away from my family. I like it. I make the pedals spin, putting my heart into it, and roll away with butterflies in my tummy because I have six whole hours to myself with Blue before I have to pick the children up from nursery. We ride along silent streets lined with private houses, we stop for a quiet breather, we speed along and shriek with pleasure. I feel totally confused by the vastness of the world, that six hours can fly by like a happy outburst under a spring roof. Every so often I get a call from my husband. I answer him with a grave voice – I don't want my cheerfulness to make him upset.

'What are you up to?' he asks.

'Nothing special. I'm riding my bike. My legs are killing me, they're agony, my fingertips are frozen, I'm out of breath . . .' I reply.

'Where are you?' he asks.

'Just by the supermarket. I'm going to get some meat for dinner,' I reply.

'I can pick you up,' he offers.

'All right,' I answer, not wanting to hurt his feelings any more than I already have by saying that I'm having a good time. As fast as I can, I pedal to the supermarket near our house, stopping on the way to buy some meat of unknown origin in the market. As I glide up to the supermarket I see my husband's car is already in the car-park. I wipe off the sweat and wait for him to come out of the shop, trying to look calmly truthful. And here he comes, turning his head and looking around. He is looking for me, as if you could find a person simply by turning your head around.

'I couldn't find you. Where were you?' he says, staring at me closely.

'Down the other end. I was in the shade so the meat wouldn't go off,' I lie, raising a black carrier bag to eye-height.

'Did you get that here?'

'Of course,' I reply.

'That's not a bag from this supermarket. OK, let's get going.' He takes Blue and loads it into the boot of his car.

'Do you have any plans?' he asks as I'm pouring coffee and making sandwiches.

'I'm going for a ride and then . . .'

'What? Do you spend the whole day on that bike?'

'Yes. I mean no, just while the children are at Apple Tree –'

'But you hate it, you get tired, your legs hurt . . . Why are you always out riding that thing?'

'Well, you get a great sense of freedom on a bicycle . . .' I want to quickly add something about there being no chance of freedom without our two kids constantly clutching my hands, not relinquishing them for anything, that freedom without waiting for my beloved husband to come home is unthinkable, that freedom without not being free is unthinkable. All the same, my husband has left his favourite salami sandwiches on the table and gone to the bedroom. I count to ten in silence and then follow him. He is sitting in front of a blank television screen looking out of the window beyond which lies a blotch of bright, frozen white light – the window frozen in his blue eyes. I think to myself that it would make a beautiful picture – sensitivity set to one hundred, diaphragm closed, the switch on two hundred. He doesn't turn to me. He sips his coffee and looks out of the window. Cold is coming in through the window, just like in wintertime.

'I don't have any freedom either,' he says and turns to me. His face is as foreign as if it was sculpted from ice. 'Perhaps it's better if we go our separate ways? Why suffer in captivity?'

'What are you saying?' My heart is stuck in my throat. I sit down on the sofa and put my hand on his leg. I choke on my tears.

'Me? I'm not saying anything! I didn't expect something like that from you. No, maybe I did. All these years we've been living together, I expected it every day. I knew that you would say something like that, and I feared it coming. After all I've done for you . . .'

'I . . . love you.' Tears stream down my cheeks. Such proof of love. I clutch at his elbow, but he pushes me softly away and stands up. My eyes are crying, my lips whispering of love, but somewhere, between my stomach and heart, a poisonous primal flower is starting to bloom. Leave me, I think, leave and feel guilty that you have abandoned your children and the woman who is far better than anyone you'll ever be able to find again.

'I love you, too, but we must go our separate ways. You want that.'

No way. All I really want is to press him close to me, squeeze him so tightly that everything that we have accumulated during this life together runs down his leg. We-must-get-a-divorce is a mantra. It is enormously powerful. The whole time we've lived together we-must-get-a-divorce has been chanted at least fifty times, zillions of times less than the I-love-you mantra, but still . . .

'I'm going to the house in the country. That's it,' he announces, putting on his cardigan, the red and grey spots of which are as idiotic as he is himself.

'Fine. When you come back the children and I will be gone, and you won't find us again. I'm sick and tired of it all, too. I've had enough.' Someone replacing me takes his cup from the coffee table and smashes it against the wall, where the remains of ground coffee now tell our future. The heaviness recedes.

I let him walk out the door. My small husband steps into his small car and drives away, becoming even smaller.

I go out on to the veranda and kick Blue. What an unholy mess a stolen bike can cause.

Three hours later I'm bumping along in a van with the children. A massive bag, crammed with a random assortment of items, sits at my feet, all snatched up just to prove that I'm leaving for good. The twins' backpacks are loaded and on their backs – timely purchases bought in the sales for school. My son's is blue, my daughter's red. The twins are split and classified like plots of land, insects and taxpayers, tribes and gods. My son is carrying the red one, my daughter the blue. Their dad would never have allowed such a thing. He has a degree; he has learned how to box and do motor sports. He is a real man and knows exactly what kind of bag a future man should carry. We have quarrelled and separated. I still have a long way to go. My son has a pink backpack.

Half an hour later, and I have dropped off the children, as quiet and mysterious as Christmas presents, with a friend of mine. 'You do know that presents shouldn't be passed on, don't you?' I shout as I run down the stairs.

'You are coming back for them, aren't you?' my friend shouts back.

'Yes, maybe.' I bang the door.

Finally I'm out on to the street, each stride the length of an entire block, every word I shout a person, each of my smiles an eternity. And so on. I feel so happy that I call an old lover who, the last time we were drinking together, had said that he would always have me. I have a whole list of old lovers' numbers, disguised in my contacts under funny names such as Nursery, Water Supply, Police Inspector, Drain Engineer, Charity Shop and so on. While I lived with the father of my children I never needed them, although I neglected to delete anyone's number. True love doesn't need shit extractors, secondhand clothes, law enforcement or water; just wine, many bottles of wine. True love fasts and counts positions, it doesn't create shit. I call the Drain Engineer as I find I have a rank taste in my mouth and my ears are filled with a thick, warm mass that definitely isn't honey. We talk for less than a minute. I wait for less than an hour. Then he comes.

Elegant and polite, in the gateway where the fine spring rain can't reach us, just like old times he offers me schnapps from the bottle as he last did five years ago. In actual fact, the Drain Engineer is a philosopher. After the first sip I quiver and hear joy pouring along the gutters. The second sip brings the smell of him back to me, while the third takes us to the city centre, like children in search of ice-cream and drunks a bottle. It's a feeling that gives such comfort – that sense of knowing your final destination. The same reason why Buddhist monks are so serene, just like me and the Drain Engineer. The torment of austerity can be endured only when you are truly free.

Like soaked Buddhist monks we finally navigate our way into a pub, clinking glasses and touching each other's hands.

'Do you remember how we met back then?' the Drain Engineer asks.

'Do you remember how we parted?' I ask.

The Drain Engineer goes on about our first encounter while I think of our separation.

'It was pay day, and I was in the pub. You came in – a grey mouse, a cheerful mouse – although maybe more of a white rat. It was midday. I offered you a drink because I had plenty of money on me.' I recall it differently; it was almost midnight. 'It was lunchtime, we got to know each other but parted company in the evening. You met me once again. You had sex with me. I stayed because you fell asleep, squeezing me close to you. Back then I had a two-year warranty. You didn't know that, you couldn't have known, but I was honest with myself and left before I had time to poison you.'

We are sitting opposite each other, staying put, without searching for reasons or guilty parties, although after our fourth glass we should give it some thought. Outside the night has swollen like a giant black hot-air balloon. Unable to get through the pub door but, if it were to explode, we would hunker down and hold on to our glasses. Not waiting to find out if the balloon would explode, we take our unfinished bottle and go out into a night that is like warm black milk poured down the parched throats of hungry adults. The Drain Engineer is taking me to his room, a few hills of crossroads to the east, a few valleys of side-streets to the south.

'Look.' He points something out to me. 'Right above the entrance you can see a sextant. Nothing in front or to the sides. Look up higher. Look further.' The Drain Engineer grabs the back of my head and positions it in the right direction. 'That one up there is a constellation, Sextans. Can you see it? It was named in the seventeenth century. You know what a sextant is, don't you?'

'Yes,' I reply, despite not knowing or seeing anything. I only know what sectarian means.

'You've become older and wiser, eh?' the Drain Engineer mutters, mournful yet excited, and leads me through the doorway. To the left gleams a large bronze plaque reading 'University Services Building'. We go up a spiral staircase – a dark, damp throat of cement. My mobile vibrates in my pocket. A message. I open it and read. I return the phone to my pocket only to get it out again shortly afterwards and reopen it. At such moments I'd just like to crawl away, disappear, frighten anyone feigning polite lack of interest in the lives of others.

The Drain Engineer clears his throat and squints at me. I smile. I want to scream for joy, leap up the throat of the university service building right to the top, begging it to vomit me out and smear this night all over the ground with its stone foot.

'What is it?' the Drain Engineer asks.

'Oh, nothing much,' I reply. 'That idiot husband of mine has sent me a message. He's spying on me.'

'I see,' the Drain Engineer says. 'Switch him off and be done with it.'

'Yes, just a minute. I'll quickly reply first.' I write two words 'Yes, maybe' in reply to my husband's message, which reads 'Will you marry me? I want you to be my real wife.'

We have got as far as the third floor. The Drain Engineer is taking me along sticky corridors smelling of dirty old war veterans and books read cover to cover several times. We walk along a maze of corridors, across the brains of the building, eaten away by woodworm, incomprehensible. We could keep walking like this for a hundred years, so long as I had a message saying that someone wanted to marry me. I smile.

'Do you remember our apartment?' the Drain Engineer asks, misinterpreting my smile. I chase away thoughts of matrimony and remember: a small kitchen; on the right a light-blue bathtub, bare and cold; one step on, an antique table and bench, both painted with white window paint; a couple of kitchen shelves on the wall and a gas stove; a window with faded flowerboxes; and, leaning out of the window, an organic vegetable shop. When we met I was nineteen, the Drain Engineer forty-one. He was a professor of philosophy at the university, although he made extra cash as a private tutor for first-year female students of philosophy requiring further assistance in understanding Socrates and his followers.

The Drain Engineer preached austerity, his spiel motivated by reasons as to why his students shouldn't develop into materialistic bitches, counselling them to choose either money or knowledge, as no human being could have everything. In the morning, his hands trembling, he would make coffee for these girls, adding a pinch of salt to make it taste better. He would show them around his room, which was home to his bed, an extremely ancient desk and a shield, behind which his university robes were hidden. When he had meticulously shown them everything, he would make a pen-and-ink drawing of them in the minimalist Japanese style then show them out. While I lived there with him, an ink portrait of a minimalist me hung in his room and the bathtub was always full of dirty dishes, the remnants of his sophisticated goulash and the potatoes peeled by me.

'I do,' I say, 'of course I remember. Why don't you live in your nice apartment any more, and what happened to the Japanese minimalist-style me?'

We stop at a shabby blue door. 'Now you shall see for yourself.' The Drain Engineer unlocks the door and opens it on to his world, where the antique kitchen table and bench await us once more, only now painted in light-brown floor paint. The desk is there, too, but the bathtub has been replaced by a small sink full of dirty dishes. A heaviness, like a blanket patched over several generations, engulfs me, suffocating me. 'Welcome,' the Drain Engineer says, and I listen to him. I step over the threshold, thinking of my wedding. To tell the truth, I want to go and hug my husband, but because of all the drink I've had and the fact that it is now dawn I'm overtaken by indolence, laziness. 'Look, just like old times.' The Drain Engineer lights a candle set in the middle of the antique table. An old cognac bottle, ravaged by time, acts as a candle holder.

'Lovely bottle,' I say.

'Glad you like it,' the Drain Engineer replies happily, pouring drink into two dusty glasses. 'What are you going to do now?' the Drain Engineer enquires.

'What would you like me to do?'

I don't even hear his answer. I see and feel everything. His touch on my neck, then on my shoulders where he always felt around for the bones, evidence of my successful dieting regime ahead of the bikini season. Then his hand slides down my back and stops in the valley that my geography and economics teacher once referred to as the relief of the continent. His hands linger there a while and then glide downwards, grabbing the two peninsulas – as I would probably define them if I were my geography teacher. He presses me so tightly to him I can feel exactly who I'm dealing with, then puts his hands to good use again. They are stroking my inner thighs, then race past the promised land of my belly, which has remained empty all day, stopping at my heart and checking if it has served me well, if my nipples are as hard as dried peas. Although nothing about me is hard, I see him measuring the distance to the bed out of the corner of his eye, while he has fixed himself to my mouth as tightly as an American tourist to a bottle of mineral water in the Moroccan desert.

He sucks on my lips, licks my teeth, pushes me, pushes, lays me down and rolls over me. He unbuttons my trousers, finding himself at a loss when he can't undo the last one. He asks me how to undo them, which does absolutely nothing for me. I help him. Then he takes off his own trousers. We always keep jumpers and shirts on – the promised land and the conqueror's musket don't coincide with their coordinates.

'What are you thinking about?' He is shaking me by the shoulder, tweaking that bone which testifies to my skeletal figure and the promise of warmer weather. The candle on the antique table has died or been blown out, two beams of sunshine have sneaked in through the window. My phone rings.

'When are you coming to pick up your children?' my friend asks, and I hear my son and daughter either fighting or jostling one another. Back to reality. I had forgotten that I had children. I have dallied in purgatory, the sort of place where you're always overcome by weakness and thirst. I tell my friend to bring the children to the university services building. I know she is poor, I know she doesn't have much petrol, and I know that anyone would want to get rid of someone else's children as quickly as possible.

'You have children?' The Drain Engineer is flabbergasted.

'Two at the same time,' I say as he stares at me, weirdly silent, like a man who's just been told he's a father. 'No, no,' I laugh, 'they're not yours. Your children have long since been transformed into fertilizer for the city's linden trees, planted in a straight row by the Monument to Freedom. Now they are rotting cells, giving life to life. I was told how they fought back, called to you for help, but you just sat at home, head in hands, reading Heidegger. I was told that their hands, covered with pink tissue, clutched feebly at that metal monster. I know that one of them bravely resisted the vacuum pump, holding on to its edge with his little hands, his head already pulled into nothingness, ripped from within me. That day you took the trolleybus, then the bus, the tram, and later that evening you called for a taxi. Do you want to know their names? Max and Moritz, King and Goldilocks, the fictional step-sisters Maija and Paija – one lazy and mean, the other hardworking and kind. I came up with several alternatives and said sorry to all of them. Pour me a drop, will you? And, please, can you clear something up for me? Is it possible to say sorry to those now feeding the roots of the linden trees that blossom in summer? Bees will gather their nectar and beekeepers will sell honey conforming to EU standards. Do you like honey? I'm allergic to it; it stops me breathing freely. We might be raising your children. How old would they be?'

The Drain Engineer drops his head.

My telephone rings. I pass it over to the Drain Engineer so he can tell my friend the way to the university services building.

'Where are you going to live when you leave your husband?' the Drain Engineer asks, having told my friend how to offload my children.

'It doesn't matter where as long as I have my freedom,' I say, and I get to my feet to pace the room. I can't put off hugging my husband, my future husband, any longer. We will put our children to sleep and make love until we drop dead because we have had an argument. He will say a few tender words because we have had an argument. I can't wait. For the tender words.

'I still love you. I've always loved you.' The Drain Engineer stands in my way.

'Well, I stopped loving *you* quite some time back,' I answer, more for the sake of saying something, as in my mind I have already tried on at least eight wedding dresses and chosen a hairstyle.

'When did you stop?' the Drain Engineer insists.

'That night you came home and took me from behind and fell asleep without a word. You had been to your friend's name-day party and as things heated up had fucked his friend. You came home and fucked me with the same part of your body. Afterwards, much later, you tried to calm me down, saying that you had had her up the arse whereas you'd had me at the gates of paradise. You got it the wrong way round and left me feeling dirty. And your excuses, stories, begging, entreaties concerning anyone's inability to think straight when drunk, all taken from the internet, didn't calm me down in the slightest. I stopped loving you, but you didn't stop drinking. Let's have a drink, OK?' I raise my glass.

'It was a big mistake. Everyone makes mistakes.'

Straight, with his head shaved, that's what the Drain Engineer – who is going to be forty-seven this year – is like.

'Look! Just have a look!' He gallops over to the bed and kneels down, stretching and grunting. 'Look! Look!' He is holding a piece of paper covered in dust with a Japanese-minimalist-style girl sitting on it. Black on white. He painted me on himself – black on white, yin-yang.

'I know you made a mistake,' I snatch the sheet of white paper. 'I know.'

The Drain Engineer empties his glass. 'Then do something! Forgive me and we will be happy!'

I don't want to tell the Drain Engineer how I forgave him, how I ripped out my insides and mended them again to get everything out that had happened, and a lot had happened. The Drain Engineer had locked me in the world of grown-ups, the only ones who lose faith in goodness and replace it with fear and mistrust. My world – built of white sand, embellished with shells, grasses and colourful pebbles, seagull feathers and other such childish rubbish – is transformed into a moated fortress. Once you've hardened like that, only Krishna, Buddha or Osho can save you, the parish pastor handing you an iron mask as a gift to enable villains to slap you on both cheeks, break your nose, cut your lips. Still, I'm a non-believer and don't wear a mask, but, all the same, my world is surrounded by a high wall and a cheerful smile. I forgave the Drain Engineer. I forgave him, forgave him but gave him nothing more.

'I forgave you.' I put on an ephemeral, saint-like smile. My phone rings. My friend wants to get rid of my children, now charging around at the entrance to the university services building. The Drain Engineer is putting on his shoes; he wants to act the kindly uncle, he wants to meet my children. I let him. I remain by myself and pour myself a little more to drink.

My friend has hooked the blue backpack on to my son's shoulders, so I switch it for the pink one. The Drain Engineer objects. 'Why do you make the boy carry a pink backpack?' he asks.

'If you don't like pink backpacks for boys, don't ever bother calling me again.' I take the children by their hands and leave. The Drain Engineer stays and later calls me almost every day.

We go out on to the street. I'm safe, back in the midst of the society that flashes past all three of us. I have to prepare for the wedding. I have to go home and embrace my husband-to-be as soon as I can. I have to choose my dress and hairstyle. I have to telephone some inexpensive but decent venue for the wedding – as always, I have to think of our family's budget. I have to ready myself to be a wife.

The house is a tip, but no one is bothered – we are going to have a wedding. We tell the children. My husband buys three bottles of champagne. We sit in the kitchen, but the children have fallen asleep on the carpet in the living-room. We drink all three bottles, and everything goes just as I predicted – we make love all night, he whispers the long-awaited words of tenderness. I melt and am set on fire. I don't want my children any more, just a wedding dress and a great hairdo.

Two days later he takes me to a bridal shop, says we are shortly to be married and his bride needs a beautiful dress and asks what they have to offer. I'm wearing ripped jeans and a T-shirt. My hair is loose and my mouth stinks of hangover. The shop assistants whisper among themselves and place three thick magazines in front of me and remain standing by my side elbowing each other, their arms crossed. After the first magazine my earlobes blush, after the second I feel envious, but towards the end of the third I have resolved upon a two-week crash diet.

How can you even think of getting married when you are not remotely beautiful? My husband is sitting next to me, totally at ease among the magazine brides.

'Have you chosen one?' he asks.

'Yes,' I reply and immediately start crying. The people surrounding me pretend not to notice. All brides-to-be probably weep while choosing dresses from the catalogues. But it's not a question of the dress, rather my face and tits – which, after having the twins, are as saggy as two Finnish tomtits' nests. Nests like these can't go anywhere near an elegant dress like this. I can't touch it, no.

'Have you made your mind up?' my husband asks again. By this time I've gone off the idea of getting married, but, seeing as it's been decided, I open the second catalogue and point at the bride's chest on page 140, although whether I'm actually pointing at her chest or not is debatable as it can't be seen. The dress is a heavily draped protective covering, like a stage curtain. 'No, no way . . . absolutely not.' My husband shakes his head. 'I want a beautiful wife. You understand that, don't you? Choose the dress you like best. It's that easy. And don't worry about the price,' he adds encouragingly. Meanwhile we have shop assistants breathing down our necks.

I open the first catalogue at the second page, and Pamela Anderson's double leers at us. (I think to myself that it can't be Pamela herself as the dress isn't all that expensive.)

'Quite pretty,' my husband says, unable to tear his eyes away from her fulsome breasts, which are suffocating a small gold cross. 'Yes, not bad.' He continues staring at the heavenly beauty. 'But, no, it wouldn't suit you,' he sighs heavily. 'You don't have the legs for it. Pity, of course. A real pity . . .'

I'm near breaking point. I have one final option. If it doesn't work I might end up not getting married at all, not becoming happy and beautiful, not becoming a wife.

'Wait, perhaps you might like this. A slight twist.' One of the shop assistants hands me a leaflet. It's dog-eared and well worn, as if it has seen service somewhere people take reading very seriously, such as a public toilet or video booth.

'We'll take that one,' my husband declares.

'We'll take that one,' I echo. You would say the same if you were a woman about to get married. Any man or dog would say the same – the dress is adorable, the creation possibly of sorcerers or aliens. It's not of any colour children learn about at school; it's not of any material you might buy in a shop; it's not sewn by human hand or the finger of a machine; it is and it isn't, all at the same time.

The shop assistants, smiling, exchange glances – their smiles are not of the usual kind. They have probably set their faces into forced smiles like that to the thousands of others creasing the leaflet on the beautiful dress.

'So, you are taking that one?' they ask like twins in unison.

'Yes,' we answer together.

'Have you seen the price?' they say.

I squeeze my eyes tightly closed – my husband said not to worry about the price, but out of the corner of my eye I squint past my husband's elbow. 'Price?'

I notice my husband has grown pensive. In literature such a moment would be defined as the protagonist's inner conflict, in mathematics as infinity. The dress costs an infinity. There's no way we can buy it, which explains the shop assistants' giggles, why the leaflet is so worn. There is no point fighting inner conflicts. There will be no wedding.

'My bride shall be beautiful.' My husband finally speaks – roars. 'I have no need to scrimp. I'm expecting a money transfer any day now.' He pulls his wallet out, fishes for a banknote marked with the symbol of infinity. The shop assistants start crying, hugging each other, kissing each other's tears away. At moments of great joy we forget who we are and who others are, too. Half an hour later, when the deal is done and the shop assistants have more or less calmed themselves down, we learn that the shop is closing down and today is its very last day in business. Nevertheless, the dress, which costs an infinity and is made far away in England, will be waiting for us at the shop owner's house ready to be picked up on our wedding day. She extends a scrap of paper with the address, realizing as she does so that in two weeks' time she will no doubt be living the high life in a house with a pool. It is agreed that the shop owner will call and invite me over to her new place as soon as the dress arrives from faraway England.

The days drag by in despondent mood. My husband doesn't go to work. He has borrowed money against the expected transfer, and we drink champagne. In the morning I take the twins to nursery and on my way back home stop off to buy three – no, better make it four – bottles of the semi-sweet elixir. We make sure we love each other in every corner in the house – including the children's room and even out on the balcony. We fall asleep and wake up. We have something to eat then I rush off to the nursery. On my way there I buy the children some sweets; that way they'll eat their sweets and leave us alone, but for us it's three – no, better make it four – bottles of champagne. Then suddenly, quite by chance, we come to our senses. The wedding is in three days' time, and we have nothing apart from ourselves. But weddings don't work like that. You need a dress, guests, food and drink, good cheer and a register office for a wedding. Yes, the register office.

'We can't get married – we haven't applied for a marriage licence,' I say, dishevelled and naked, as I roll off my sticky, slippery husband.

'Rubbish! That's not the most important thing! The most important thing is that two people love each other.'

I consider him, our children at the Apple Tree Nursery, the asphalt path in front, beneath and behind us, our chubby fingers on to which silver rings have been rammed with considerable difficulty and can no longer be removed, my friends nodding their heads and gesticulating jubilantly, looking for some frame of reference.

'What does it mean to get married?' I ask.

'The paperwork is not the most important thing. You do realize that, don't you?' My husband takes me in his embrace, pushing me deeper into the mattress, stroking me as if I were a cat, combing my hair, cleaning out my belly button, looking at me in such a loving way that I could die right here and right now. The sense of bliss achieved through righting your consciousness, the opening of the third eye – I leave all that to those underestimating the power of loving the one you are with.

'What's the most important thing about getting married, and what does it mean to get married?' I insist. I don't want to spoil the moment, but I desperately want to learn the truth.

'Tell me, do you want to put on the dress I paid an infinity for? That infinitely beautiful dress?' His words warm me. I'm no longer myself – a woman in an alien's dress, with an alien's hairdo and an alien's eyes. Every woman, at least once or more in her life, should feel like an alien.

'But why did you say you wanted to marry me?' the down-to-earth, guileless woman in me speaks up.

'So you can say your vows in that dress,' my husband says, lying down on my legs and propping his chin on my pubic mound of shame.

'But what about our friends, our parents? What are we going to tell them if we don't invite them to the register office?'

'Leave it to me.' My husband is on top of me, once more a propeller in my brook. 'I will enlighten them to the fact that true love vanishes along with paperwork, just as it was with me and my first wife. We got married three days after we met. We registered our marriage at the register office, and it then took a mere fifteen years for the divorce papers to come through. You just have to be beautiful. That's all.'

While we are making love my thoughts drift elsewhere, far away to my friends' doorsteps. I'm thinking what I'm going to say, how I will persuade them to come to our wedding. I want everyone who cares about me to come, to see my dress and alien eyes. Almost everyone has accepted. The wedding is in three days.

It's a widespread custom that the groom shouldn't see his bride on the day of the wedding – the preparations must be made in complete secrecy. So, on the morning of the wedding day, my dad comes for the children. He's not coming to the wedding itself as he has to work that evening. I go to a friend's. She is pregnant; her second child is due any minute. My friend is excited, delighted about the wedding. It makes sense. I understand her. What true friend wouldn't be delighted for me, marrying a wealthy, good-looking, well-educated man? A real friend would be glad if the wedding chased away the conjectural Green Crow she had once met during our teenage years, deciding in the blink of an eye that the Crow was ruining my life. Interesting how anyone can be so judgemental without even talking to the Crow, without taking the time to find out about her views on life and death, her principles. I agree, the Crow can be a bit scary-looking, but my friend isn't the sort who never reads fairy stories and fables about gentle souls trapped in Quasimodo-like bodies. Even so . . . she disliked the Crow intensely.

'You're settling down at last. I'm so happy for you,' she shouts from the bathroom. She's washing her hair so she'll be beautiful for my wedding. 'What time do you have to be at the register office?' she asks.

'We won't be going to the register office. Maybe in the future. We were late getting our application in,' I lie.

'Are you mad?' she shouts over the noise of the hairdryer. 'It doesn't make any sense if you don't do it properly!'

'I love him,' I blurt out.

'Love? Of course you do, but why organize this whole circus for the sake of love alone? Getting married means putting your signature on paper, making your love official. He talked you into this, didn't he?'

'No, I made my own decision,' I lie again, not wanting to exercise her further in case she gives birth here and now on the kitchen floor. 'Let's talk about it later. Don't let's ruin my wedding day,' I say to my friend, who just stares at me in silence.

'Fine, let's go.'

It's hot outside. I'm hot inside myself. It's hot in the car. It's hot at the hairdresser's. It's hot in the cheap eatery. Sea waves are frozen in my hair, where white and pink plastic roses, fifty santīmi apiece, have also blossomed. They told me the waves should last until the wedding night, but it would be best to take out the stemmed roses before going to bed in case they prick the groom and put a blight on my life. On top of all that, I have a new set of nails with rosy-pink and white spots, longer than my friend's. A woman becomes a wife with acrylic nails like these so she can remove a speck from her beloved husband, scratch his back.

For a while we just stand, beautiful as we are, in the cheap eatery. My friend orders a well-done steak as her baby needs the iron. I'm having a coffee, no sugar, because I need an empty, flat tummy. Just the make-up and dress left to go. Time: four hours. My friend has been chewing on a piece of steak for several minutes, too embarrassed to spit it out and put the inedible remains on her plate.

'Just the dress and that's it . . . that's it . . .' I repeat as we race down the road, as if it had been laid specifically to transport me to the dress for infinity. 'You'll have to go down the next part of the road on your own.' We stop, and a feeling of solemnity comes over me, as if preparing for a ceremony of consecration, because there is absolutely nowhere to park. I get out and walk, clutching the piece of yellow paper in my hand. The women who sold the dress for infinity to my husband have opened a new boutique. From the balcony over the head of an angry lion I read the name 'Hestia' in pale lettering.

I take a seat in the centre of the boutique and freeze so they can make me beautiful. I don't blink, I don't smile, I don't cough, I don't exist. The Hestia women fuss around me, every so often feeding another log into the enormous fireplace that breathes heat in my face.

'This fire hasn't gone out since we opened the boutique the day before yesterday,' one of them says, catching my eye.

'Hestia was a powerful woman. She never married, so her house was always warm,' the other says. I want to ask why the bridal boutique was named after a spinster but can't speak for fear of it interfering with the beautification process.

'Do you have children?' the main make-up artist asks. I put up two fingers. 'Two? Girls or boys?' I put up my middle and little fingers. 'A boy and a girl? That's nice. Just don't let them sleep together. It will ruin their lives. What is your husband-to-be like?

Gentle? Does he ever do the dishes? Does he complain if you snore at night? Has he got a driver's licence? Will you stay together to the end of your lives? Are you getting married in church or at the register office? You are wearing a dress for infinity; you really should get married in church. Before God. That's probably the case, isn't it? When my grandmother got married she wore a yellowish cotton dress and, as a wedding meal, the two of them opened a tin of smoked sprats they'd stored away a long time before. It was wartime. It was how things were.'

The principal make-up artist speaks without stopping to draw breath, and I listen without drawing breath. Her grandparents had lived happily for the longest time, a good sixty years – although last year they had gone through a bad patch. Her grandfather had tried to kill his wife as he couldn't recall whether she had been a virgin when they married. Her grandmother had then tried to commit suicide after sixty years of virtuous married life. The old couple had died, one after the other, in separate hospitals, each clinging to their own beliefs. The urns holding their ashes had stood side by side beside her grandfather's bed for a few days before being put in a plastic box purchased at the supermarket and buried with solemnity at the cemetery. Her grandmother had had an eye on that storage box for her salted crackers but in the end had not got around to buying it as her legs weren't strong enough to walk the distance to the Rimi supermarket.

'Don't cry or all my hard work will go to waste. Well, let's see now.' The make-up artist pushes a mirror under my nose. The sad tale of the sixty-year marriage evaporates as if it had never been and is replaced by my beauty. I can't help myself; a few tears roll down my cheeks. The make-up artist dries them carefully, helps me to me feet, drags me off to another room, opens a red curtain, pushes me into a small storage room and gives me a pat on my back so my breath is not cut off when I come face to face with my dress for infinity. It is embellished with various plastic ornamentations and dawn-coloured Venetian glass beads, as delicate as clouds. Silk roses and lilies as fragrant as real flowers have been sewn on to the dress with a golden thread; the ribbon on the bodice is of regal velvet. I stretch out my hand timidly to caress the pearls, roses, lilies, infinity. Then I notice a yellowish linen rag hanging just to one side of it. The curtains close behind me and the empty linen sack fills out with youthful breasts, firm arms, the bend of a back, a neck emerging from the neck line, grey-blue eyes, short curly hair. A smell of fish fills the cubicle. A young woman in a yellowish linen dress offers me sprats straight from the tin. My mouth is watering, but I mustn't eat today so I can keep my waist slim. No, thank you. The dress grows droopy, the woman disappears, sprat oil has formed a stain in the spot where the heart should be. Thank God it hasn't marked the Venetian glass and roses for infinity. I hear steps on the other side of the red curtain.

'Strip off!'

'Why?' I ask.

'It's time to put your dress on.'

I do as I'm told. I get undressed. I wait.

'Knickers, too?' I call out.

'They're the most important. Let's get you washed with rose water, rub on a little almond oil, put these knickers on that have shielded the gates of paradise of the greatest Venetian courtesan. Let's get these stockings on, once worn by a virgin, my neighbour.'

I'm submissive, doing exactly what I'm told when a silver washing bowl is placed in front of me. I'm asked to spread my legs and squat down. I remain silent when a stranger's palm touches my gates of paradise and washes them clean. I remain silent when warm oil rains over me. I'm a racehorse, great hopes pinned on me; I'm a shadow of nothing; I'm a Venetian whore and a virgin whose stockings are cruelly cutting into her thighs; I'm a princess who can receive mercy or a death sentence in her dress for infinity. I'm ready.

'That's it then. Pay at the cashier's desk.' The dresser, washer, make-up artists, including the granddaughter of the spratty bride, hand me a slip of paper with the bill.

'Yes, one more thing.' She touches my elbow. 'During the ceremony, don't let anyone come between you and the groom. It's of the utmost importance. Goodbye now.'

We race away in my friend's black Jeep. The wedding ceremony is due to start in an hour's time, ten kilometres outside the city. The guests, breath held in anticipation, are no doubt expecting the arrival of the bride and groom. My friend's husband is sitting spellbound next to me on the back seat – he neither blinks nor speaks, but he does manage to open a bottle of champagne and pass it over. From him to me and back again. I need a wee so we stop at a petrol station.

'Don't go in there,' my friend says. 'Your dress will catch against the toilet bowl, and that will be that. Let's stop in the forest and you can go in the bushes.' But I don't listen to her. I squeeze past dripping petrol pumps towards the toilets. There is a queue. As they catch sight of me, the men calm down, the women peer at me and then turn away, the children point at me and smile. In fact, I don't need a wee at all, which is why the women who have once been brides themselves turn away in scorn. We know. The manager of the petrol station comes running up to me.

'We would be delighted to offer you our brides' lavatory, but unfortunately it's blocked. The best I can do is offer our standard facilities without having to queue . . .' A murmur of dissatisfaction rumbles through the crowd.

'Right, so she's going to block this one up, too. We won't let her through! We won't. *Everyone* has to queue! Who cares about brides and their special needs? We, too, we already-married people, have our needs as well . . .'

I don't know how it would all have ended if the sales assistant hadn't stepped in. 'Shame on you! Don't you realize she only needs to have a quick pee? Brides don't eat, you idiots!'

At this the crowd opens and allows me through to the toilet. I don't go anywhere near the toilet bowl, I just glance at myself in the mirror and leave. My friend's husband is standing by the Jeep, smoking and drinking champagne. I, too, light a cigarette and take a swig of champagne straight from the bottle. Passing cars wave at us, at me; they honk at my dress.

Twenty minutes later and we are there; our car is pulling up outside the wedding venue. My childhood friends are sitting in front of the entrance, smoking and drinking beer. Girlfriends from my school days are picking fronds from the bird-cherry tree to decorate the newlyweds' path. Everyone is waiting for the bride, my husband included, the father of my children. He sits in his car, waiting.

'Time to go,' my friend says. 'Out you get.' Before I do, I see how everyone is stubbing out their cigarettes, getting rid beer bottles and friends, rising to their feet and straightening their ties. The groom is getting out of his car, dressed to kill; everyone is waiting for me. I ask my friend and her husband to stand in front of me. I say that I'm embarrassed to be so beautiful. When my friend, who is one metre eighty-four, and her husband, who is one metre sixty-five, step away, the guests clap and start to move towards me timidly. But the father of my children and our children get there first.

'Your dress is beautiful,' they say, clutching at my voluminous skirt.

My husband comes and hugs me from behind. 'Your dress is really beautiful,' he whispers in my ear. 'A real princess's dress.' My friends echo his praise in concert, while my childhood friends swiftly finish their beers, plainly kicking themselves that they hadn't married me first.

'They are such a well-matched couple,' I hear aunts and uncles whispering. We wade through the fronds of bird-cherry trees, white and fragrant with tears. We take our places of honour at the table, where meatballs and potatoes sit, duly steaming; we tell the story of how we met and had children, we drink after every sentence uttered. Evening comes, and we exchange our vows, having removed the rings beforehand so we can exchange them in the presence of our guests, articulating words in keeping with the dress for infinity.

A friend of mine who has flown in from faraway Australia plays the flute while my husband and I stand facing each other next to an overgrown pond, the guests watching us. The sound of music dies, and the frogs on their lily-pad stage continue not with our wedding song but their own. The frogs interfere somewhat with our vows, making it harder to express the profundity of the occasion and speak with voices of angels, but I pull myself together. I swear on the lives of all those present, all those gathered for the wedding, that I will love and respect my husband for as long as I love him. I break down in tears as he slips the ring on to my finger. I took it off two weeks ago so the pale line would tan, so no one apart from my friend would guess that I'd been wearing the same ring for the past five years, ever since my husband gave it to me for Christmas one year. I felt great without the ring, absolutely great. Now I shall never be able to take it off again. Washing-up liquid will eat away at the skin underneath it, and rough strands of hair will get caught in it during lovemaking. And that's how it will be for as long as I'm able to wash dishes and make love.

The corner of my husband's lips twitches, too, as I force the ring on to his finger. It's too small to take off and too cheap to never take off. 'Now you are husband and wife!' a drunk friend from the crowd roars. Guests wolf-whistle and shout. We are handed glasses of champagne; the twins come running up to us, stand between us and start crying.

'What's the matter?' I ask.

'Your dress is so beautiful,' they sob. I'm crying, too. A beautiful dress.

'Oh, how exciting! I wish something like that would happen to me. Was your dress really that beautiful?'

'Yes.'

'When are you going to tell me some more about the Green Crow?' Fright asks, eager as a small child.

'They were all lies, everything I said about the Crow, and I'm sleepy now . . .'

'What do you mean, *lies*?' F22 jumps to her feet.

'Just like everything else. The whole world is false. Nothing but one big lie.'

Fright gets up from her bed and slowly comes over to me. Thank

God there are no empty beer bottles or lightbulbs in our room. The light from F22's candle distorts Fright's face, ugly enough as it is.

'So it is all a lie, is it?'

'Yes.'

'And your children are lying, too?'

'Always and about everything.'

'While they were waiting for you . . . well, we asked them some questions . . . do you understand? And they asked us some, too . . .' Fright takes a deep breath. 'And they said that on the night you were brought into hospital they had found an enormous bird with a green nylon cape. Their father had knocked it senseless . . . and they had put it in the life-preserving freezing chamber . . .'

'So, please, don't lie to us. The Crow *is* real! Your hus . . . well, that cool guy, he didn't hear as he had gone outside for a breath of fresh air,' F22 continues.

I want an argument. To take part with all my heart in a massacre. On my way back from the harbour where the doctor in the grey coat lives I thought over what he'd whispered in my ear about F22, Fright and Snow White being the truly crazy ones, that I shouldn't believe a word they say. He said that F22's voice was cruel and rasping, like a Mafia boss. It had told her to poison her husband's soup for no other reason than to see what a man drawing his last breath looked like. That F22 had a family – a husband and three daughters. And that Fright was happily married, too, with two children. She had ended up in the psychiatric hospital because she had been trying, without success, to write her dissertation for her philosophy degree. Frequently overcome by worldly sorrow for the idiocy of people, she had eventually lost her mind. She was told to keep a bucket of river water by her bed and soak her legs in it, thus proving that nothing flowed or changed and that it was possible to step into the same river every morning. She also joined an amateur dramatics group . . . but every year she spent a few months in the madhouse so she could listen to stories about the world that failed to flow anywhere or ever change. Only people changed.

I want to shout all that out loud, possibly beat Fright and F22 up because it is not only my family but them, too, all of them coming out with nothing but lies. But I won't. I need to get out and save the Crow. I don't even know if she is still alive or not. There is no point in me staying here. The Crow is back.

'I'm only joking, girls. I feel really sleepy . . .'

'You always have to tell the truth. Good-night . . .' Fright, yawning, disappears under her blanket, and F22 blows out the tip of the burning candle.

I'm afraid of the dark again.

It's early next morning, and I'm dressed, face washed, the collar of my striped pyjamas pulled straight and my hair neatly smoothed. F22 and Fright are still asleep. Only Snow White is rolling her eyes, the whites showing. She has never before seen me doing my hair or washing my face so early in the morning. She sighs heavily.

'Going somewhere?'

'I hope so.'

'We would all like that, but some things are beyond us.'

'The Green Crow says that everything lies within our grasp –'

'Forget the Green Crow if you want to get out of here,' Snow White cries out. 'Run while your legs still work, you silly cow! I'm old and have no wish to live on a yacht named *Fright*. I get seasick.

I'd rather die on dry land. But you still have time to say sorry and hand your children back to heaven as secondhand goods – they can then deal with them there, seeing as they gave you faulty products in the first place. You can wake up, smooth down your striped collar and follow any path your eyes light upon, seeing as you haven't lost all sight in them. Now go!'

F22's and Fright's blankets are now heaving suspiciously. They are pretending to be asleep, or maybe they are terrified at the thought that someone can just walk out of here.

'I know everything about you two,' I say loudly, making sure they both hear.

'Pleased about that, are you?' Fright's voice emerges from under the covers.

I don't have time for this. Conversations about happiness take up so much time, leaving no more than a brief flash, the anticipation of happiness.

'I'm glad I told you my life story,' I say, turning to the four beds and the illusion before leaving the room.

'Will you be back?' Fright sobs.

'If I don't save the Crow.'

It's six in the morning. The corridor is quiet, clean. The sun shines in through the windows, the bars splitting its rays, cutting slices of light and shadow like knives. There are no windows at the end of the corridor, just a wall and a shadow and a big plastic tree. In the mornings, when the sun is shining, I step only on the sun-filled patches on the floorboards, and if there happens to be a strip of wall between the windows I jump over the shadow. Nobody reproaches me or wonders why.

I steal a door handle from the nurses' room and run.

OH GOD,
THAT FEELS GOOD!

It's warm and dark. We are sitting by the fire, grilling meat and drinking beer. The children are drinking Coke; they are too young for beer. No one speaks. Everyone watches the skewered meat threaded spitting over the fire. Every so often someone swallows the saliva accumulated in their watering mouths. The meat smells good. Pork.

The dog rubs his flank up against us. He thinks the pork smells good, too. I don't eat meat. I like it but haven't eaten any for the last year. The aroma of smouldering fat, vinegar, onions, peppers and pork is winning me over, though. I feel I might start eating meat again, so I snatch up my bottle of beer and say that I'm going indoors to watch a bit of television. My family protests. It's no family reunion around the fire if the mother, back home from the madhouse for only a couple of hours, decides to go and watch telly . . . I stay. I try to stop myself from looking at the meat and thinking about the Green Crow. I reflect instead on the purity of the body, of medieval women roasted at the stake, the smell of their burning flesh seeping into the clothes of those witnessing their deaths, later to be taken home to their happy families. I contemplate deoxyribonucleic acid, in which the future of chromosomes boils, ideal material for any promising pig or witch.

'Chicken's better. I like its crispy skin,' my daughter says.

'Yes, and its meat is all white and juicy,' my son adds. They are twins with similar genetic character traits as determined by their genetic code, which is why they both like chicken.

'But pork is fine, too,' my son says, his mouth full of scalding meat.

'It's just that it gets stuck between your teeth,' my daughter says.

'Those are the myofibrils in the meat,' my son tells her and looks up into the sky where the stars are shining, doomed to order by the rules of the universe. Substance is and remains substance.

So, chewing away, my husband and both children spit out the burned myofibrils, which are then pounced on by the dog. I'm sorry I have nothing to throw him. I love my dog.

'Thread some more on to the skewers, will you? Your hands are still dirty from the others,' my husband says.

I get to my feet, collect everyone's skewers and thread more meat on them.

'I think you've had enough. Fetch the stick for me instead,' my husband says to the dog and throws a stick into the darkness. The dog brings it to me, maybe because my hands are still covered in marinade. I pat his head with a meaty hand.

'Come here,' my husband calls. He obeys. 'Give me the stick,' he says. The dog doesn't do as he's told. 'Drop! Drop it now.' The dog still doesn't obey. Worse still, he spits out the stick and bites my husband's hand, on which five million erythrocytes, eight thousand leukocytes and thirty-five thousand thrombocytes appear. In no time at all their number doubles. My husband tells me to bring him some toilet paper – the number of erythrocytes just keeps triplicating. I send my daughter off to fetch the toilet paper. My husband is getting angry.

'We're out of toilet paper,' my daughter shouts from the house.

'Isn't there anything else to wipe the blood off with?' I shout back. My daughter disappears back into the house.

'Does it really hurt?' I ask. He turns away and mutters something. 'To tell you the truth, it serves you right,' I say. 'You can't treat dogs like that, especially not ours.'

'He bit my hand!'

'I found something. Here you go.' My daughter flings something at my husband.

'What's that?'

'A sanitary towel. They soak up every last drop of blood!'

'Ugh!' He throws the pad into the fire. It shrivels and stretches, whirls on the burning log. My son watches the small puddle of plastic and chews on his meat.

'You disgusting animal, I'll teach you where your bloody place is!' The father of my children wipes his bleeding palm down his trousers and goes over to the dog. I know that everything will be fine now. The dog will bite him again. I really, really want that to happen. Dog! Do-og! Dooo-gg! I long to release a howl of sympathy. I keep quiet.

My husband brings his face up to the dog's and asks, 'What did you do that for?' The dog, of course, doesn't respond. My husband takes the dog by the collar and shoves him to the ground. I and possibly the children, too, can hear how his windpipe has been compressed, preventing the passage of air. My husband drags the dog further away from us, saying, 'I'll show you who's the boss around here.' He takes a swing; the dog growls. He hits; the dog bites. The sounds tangle together into a heavy ball that rolls through us then away into the silence of the night. My son has stopped chewing; my daughter comes to stand behind me. They watch, seeing how to hit, how to defend yourself. Two birds with one stone. And then a third. I can't take any more. I run to my husband and start pulling at his jumper.

'That's enough. Stop it! Stop it!' I shout. The dog is panting, wheezing heavily, then slinks off behind the house without looking back.

'Keep out of it!' My husband is breathing noisily, yelling at me. No, he is breathing and yelling at me noisily.

'Will you beat me up as well if I don't bring you a stick?' I ask.

'Yes, go on then,' he laughs.

I turn towards the children, our clever children living in comfort, getting by in comfort. They smile, since it's quite funny for your dad to ask your mum, who is mad, to bring him a stick. I smile, too. I look at the grass, dark and dirty in the firelight. I squat down, pushing back on to my heels, hands on the ground, look my husband in the eye and crouch further down.

'Throw. I'll fetch it for you.' After twisting his index finger to the side of his head, indicating that I'm insane, he throws. The same thick piece of wood, perforated by the dog's teeth, flies away into the dark. I crawl into the dark. They look into the dark.

It's dark.

Somehow I locate the club with my fingertips, lean forward and pick it up between my teeth, then meander back towards the firelight on all fours. On my knees I crawl over to my husband's feet. I never realized how down here, on a level with a man's boots, everything looks so different – everyone higher up so dominant and unassailable, making you want to wag your tail to ingratiate yourself. I swing my bottom from side to side then drop the stick at my husband's feet. The children are roaring with laughter, my son pointing his mobile phone at me. He is taking a photograph.

'You really are mad,' my husband says quietly out of our children's earshot, and with a hand under one armpit he drags me up roughly. I stand, pick up my beer bottle and take myself off into the darkness. The dog, crawling out from under the house, follows me. I sit down in the grass and cry. The dog puts his nose in my lap; my tears fall on his fur. He is used to being damp.

I go back to the fire. The children are teasing and elbowing each other. My husband stands up and goes into the house. He likes playing Russian billiards on his own; that way no one laughs when he messes up – apart from the Russian who invented the game maybe.

'Mum, did they make you better?' my daughter asks but doesn't come any closer.

'No.'

'Are you still mad then?'

'Absolutely.'

The children are no longer smiling.

'And what are we going to do now?' they persist.

'Nothing, silly. We'll just carry on exactly like before. It's fun.' My son takes a swing and throws his father's beer bottle into the neighbour's garden. 'My roommates told me that you found a large bird with a green cape and that you froze it in the life-preserving chamber. Is that true?'

My son goes completely still and doesn't say a word, whereas my daughter, pale-faced, runs into the house. Shortly afterwards my husband appears in the doorway. He isn't angry. No. How could anyone be angry with someone who, twenty minutes earlier, fetched a stick for them between their teeth?

'I would just like to have a look at her if I may.'

They finished constructing their life-preserving deep-freeze while I was in hospital. I have no idea where the keys are hidden.

'Let's get some sleep.' My husband comes over and hugs me. Then he starts pushing me towards having sex. He always hugs me when we haven't made love in a long time.

'There is no bird. Do you understand that? None. The evening you were taken to hospital, you had promised us roast green crow in red-wine sauce, do you remember that? You promised, but you never made it, although that was no surprise as you never keep your promises.'

'Of course I remember. I'm not stupid.'

'Well, maybe that was your last recollection of home, and they tend to be the strongest . . .'

'So there's no green crow?'

'No.'

My husband leads me indoors. Lays me on the bed and rolls on top of me.

'Oh God, that feels good. Oh God!' he groans, and, leaving his limp hand on my semen-splashed belly, he falls asleep.

INHERITANCE

As always, morning crawls out from the darkness. I lie on the bed, my eyes wide open, looking at the skylight down which streams of condensation from our breath run and our moans slowly glide. Words, especially those invoking God, contain a particularly large amount of water, such a great quantity that it's impossible to see through the window. The house smells of neroli oil, said to soothe the mind and energize the spirit.

I get up quietly. My husband is asleep, his legs spread-eagled, a blanket rucked up between them. A new gold chain holding a small key has appeared around his neck, as if encircling a green oak tree. The key is on the chain night and day, guarding it, thwarting anyone from drawing close to imperceptible wonders – lop-eared creatures and frozen mermaids, the Green Crow's doorless, windowless shack. I'm well aware that if I were to rip the key from my husband's strong neck the fairy tale would come to an end.

I tiptoe to my son's room. He wears an identical fairy-tale chain with a magic key. His neck is not as green and strong – maybe, if I hug and kiss him, I could undo the catch on the chain with its key, bending his neck as if bowed by the wind. I lean over him, putting my hands around his neck.

'No, Mum, no, there's no Green Crow in there,' he says. I

suddenly pity my child, unable to sleep for ever more as he has to guard his key.

'But if you really want it that badly . . .' He gets to his feet, stark naked. His dick really is much bigger than his father's. 'Come.'

We walk through the house and down into the basement. It is like being in a different house. A house of eternity underground.

A white door takes the key into its innards, and coldness enfolds me. The door closes behind us.

'If you don't believe me, you can look in every compartment.' My son turns to me, smiles and spreads his hands as if he were a demi-god.

White cupboards with drawers line both sides of the room, like a morgue. Only there's no unpleasant odour, no sense of fear.

I go past white drawers affixed with plaques on which names and years are inscribed. On one of them I think I read 'Osama Bin Laden 2011–2100', but maybe that's just my imagination. He's been in the news too much. Far too much.

'You can open them and have a look. No need to be afraid, Mum.' My son nudges me towards the white cupboard. He unlocks the drawers, one after another.

'You see? They are all humans. No crow in here. Just iced-up rich people, frozen solid, and their money.'

White snowmen appear and disappear back into the drawers' mouths. Indeed, they really are all people, complete with feet and noses. No beaks or wings to be seen. Some drawers are empty. There is just one left. At the very end.

'Only Dad has the key to that one,' my son says, shrugging.

A hot wave runs through me.

'Please, darling, please. Do something for your mother, if only this once.' I start crying and drop to my knees. My son stands naked before me. His member has shrunk, becoming tiny from the cold.

'I can't . . . not even if I wanted to.'

'But, please!' I cry out, my voice filling the frozen corners of the chamber, crawling through the white keyholes.

'Look, it's locked.' My son pulls on the handle, and the drawer opens smoothly.

We both stare at the secret within, slowly revealing itself.

There is no human form inside.

'See, I told you.' My son flicks the black shopping bag, wrinkled from the cold. The leg of a bird protrudes from the opening. 'Oh, I know what happened. Remember the night we took you to the madhouse, that night you came with a green crow to roast? Remember?'

I nod, lost for words.

'It must be the green crow you promised to cook that Sunday after church . . .'

I want to say that it was the biggest turkey in the shop, the queen of the green crows, but my feet are already carrying me away towards the door.

My husband is still asleep. The room is warm. His breath drips down the glass of the window. I sit down and count backwards from twenty-one. It's an old sailors' trick – helps calm the nerves when storms rage and the main mast is broken.

Twenty-one, twenty . . . twelve . . . six . . . three . . . one.

I pick up my phone. A moment later it rings loudly.

'Hello,' I say.

'Yes,' I say, again in English.

'Really? Oh my God!' Now I'm screaming, falling to my knees.

'What's the matter?' My husband sits up.

'Of course, of course. Yes. Please wait. I'll come for the dollars.'

'What?' My husband has moved over near me. 'What's happened?'

The word 'dollar' has magic powers, exerting the same effect as 'love' and 'forgiveness' over the Christmas holidays. Some words are known and understood the world over: *money, fuck, United States of America, Osama bin Laden, children, sex, death.*

'I've just inherited twenty million dollars.' I relax my facial muscles, my face falling into the widest smile my features will allow.

'What?' He jumps to his feet. It looks like he's getting an erection.

'Yes. I have to be at the solicitor's office in town in an hour's time.'

'Let's go straight away!' He is pulling his trousers on. Over naked flesh.

'No, no. They think I'm not married. And, in fact, I'm not . . . If I'm married I'm not eligible for the inheritance. My American uncle has laid down certain conditions, you see.'

'But I can still take you there?'

'Better not. Let's not risk it, not with so much money at stake . . .'

'Well, yes. Fine . . . Call me, and I'll come and pick you up.' He falls back on to the bed with a huge grin on his face.

I get dressed quickly and run downstairs. As I cross the garden the door swings open.

'Muuuum!' the twins roar.

'What is it?' I turn and look both children in the eyes. In the boy's right, the girl's left. They are chock-full of those words recognized the world over.

'Don't ever sleep with each other,' I say and go through the gate.

A small quiet street with colourful, glamorous houses; a shop on the corner selling wine; a blackbird's nest in a tall black alder tree. And me, a pink backpack over my shoulders. A woman in her prime. A morning that has crawled out from the darkness – that's what this is.

Cool air runs down the rusty sides of the bus. It escorts me through the city to the familiar road that, straight and inflexible, takes us to our country cottage and brings country houses to all the others.

I raise my hand and pull my stomach in.

'Where to, madam?'

We drive in silence. The man behind the wheel is at least ten years younger than me. He isn't afraid of older women discharged moments earlier from the madhouse.

'Where are we going? Aren't you afraid of hitchhiking?' he asks.

'I'm only afraid of the dark.'

'When I was small I was afraid of the dark, too. But not any more.'

'What are you afraid of?'

'Of being lonely.'

We are spilling our hearts out, bursting like the contents of like overstuffed bags. I tell him how I lied to my family about inheriting twenty million dollars. We laugh. He says my husband will be devastated until his dying day, thinking his wife disappeared with twenty million dollars.

'You mustn't joke about your family like that,' he says, wiping away tears of laughter. I wipe tears away, too, not yet sure what sort they are.

'You don't happen to know where the green-crow colony is, do you?'

'Are you an ornithologist?'

'No, just a bird enthusiast.'

The young man types 'green crow' into his sat-nav. 'Nope, hasn't found anything.'

'Try with capital letters.'

'Oh, yes! Five kilometres. We'll come to a large clearing surrounded by rare-breed saplings. I remember that place. My mum told me there'd been a massive fire there thirty-six years ago. The papers were full of it . . .'

'Thank you.'

'I'd like to give you a CD of my favourite songs as a farewell gift. So you'll never forget the lift I gave you . . .'

'Oh no, really! Thanks, but I listen only to Annie Lennox.'

'Well, goodbye then.'

Across the road a dry tree with my twenty-million-dollar inheritance gapes back at me.

'I will never forget today,' I shout at the receding car as, lights winking, it vanishes into the distance.

THE END

I pick up and carry the heavy branches of the fir tree.

There are almost no trees in my forest because it burned down. Just four of them are left standing. They continue growing even after death, like dry stubble on a dead body. There is life in the old trees' seeds, tenacious and juicy; they slumber under verdant shrubs of heather hair.

The ground has been thickly covered in ashes, barren, but the earth has a memory, and the memory says, 'I will never burn down, for I am the earth where everything grows and everything dies.'

I find everything I need in the forest across the road: fir-tree branches; birch-tree bark, which I use to make baskets for collecting berries; twigs for the fire; and a night violet to fill my house with fragrance. Beasts can come to me for warmth. Bears, lynxes, deer, elks, foxes and hares.

There is no forester in my forest, no foul-tempered witch; there are only trees and animals, blueberries and mushrooms. There are no red ants, no rabid beasts, no trails on which to get lost.

I gather up and carry the thick fronds, prop them up against a dried pine tree right at the centre of the forest. There, at the very top of the pine tree, someone has built a house for the family of green crows.

When stars start twinkling above my head and I can see the Milky Way, my house is ready, too.

I curl up on the fragrant pine fronds and close my eyes.

The Crow and I, we are standing at the crossroads of the Milky Way. She nudges me gently.

'Only in the absence of gravity do you truly know who you are,' she says.

OTHER TITLES IN THE
PETER OWEN WORLD SERIES
SEASON 4: BALTICS

KAI AARELEID
Burning Cities

Translated from the Estonian by Adam Cullen

978-0-7206-2029-0 / 320pp / £9.99

Kai Aareleid's lyrical novel *Burning Cities* is set in the southern Estonian city of Tartu. Destroyed during the war by the German and Soviet armies then slowly rebuilt, the city is home to many secrets, and little Tiina knows them all – even if she does not quite understand their import. The adult world is one of cryptic conversations and unspoken dread. From the death of Stalin to the inexorable collapse of her parents' marriage, Tiina experiences both domestic and great events from the periphery, ultimately finding herself powerless to prevent the defining tragedy in her own life.

The smells, colours and atmosphere of a given time and place always remain in a person's memory, and Aareleid, through Tiina's story, reminds us that revisiting old memories, while often painful, is essential. The past leaves an indelible imprint on the future, and Aareleid vividly shows how childhood recollections and the world of one's early life can follow a person for ever – and how every secret must be shared, if only once.

SIGITAS PARULSKIS
Darkness and Company

Translated from the Lithuanian by Karla Gruodis

978-0-7206-2033-7 / 288pp / £9.99

June 1941: Nazi Germany has invaded Lithuania and the Soviets have been forced out, and Vincentas, a photographer, has made a pact with the devil in the guise of a refined SS officer. He has agreed to take photographs – to 'make art' – of the mass killings of Jews in exchange for his own safety and the survival of his Jewish lover Judita.

Accompanying a squad of local executioners to the villages and forests that were the main sites of the Holocaust in Lithuania, Vincentas descends into a paralysing moral abyss: he is a powerless witness both to the horror of the events and to how the killers square with themselves – or don't – the consequences of their actions. But his camera cannot protect him, and, as Judita warns, the war 'will tear off all our masks'.

Through the metaphor of photography Parulskis confronts the darkest chapter in his country's history and tries to understand 'what happened to this peaceful, hard-working nation' during the Nazi occupation and how this led to the murder of 95 per cent of its Jewish population. Weaving together historical detail, heart-breaking poetic description, biblical references and elements of magical realism, *Darkness and Company* is ground-breaking, being the first major novel by a contemporary Lithuanian novelist to examine the Holocaust in his homeland.